THE FALLEN
OF LITE AND DARKE
M L Ruscsak

The Fallen

A Lite and Darke Novel

Author: M. L. Ruscsak

Edited: Chyenne Lyons

Cover Design: M.L.Ruscsak

This book is a work of fiction. Names, characters, places and incidents are products of the author's imagination and are not to be construed as real. Any resemblance to actual events, locales, organizations, or persons living or dead, is entirely coincidental.

COPYRIGHT

Except for the original story material written by the author, all songs, song titles, and lyrics mentioned in the novel The New Reign are the exclusive property of the respective artists, songwriters, and copyright holders

Trient Press

3375 S Rainbow Blvd

#81710, SMB 13135

Las Vegas,NV 89180

Ordering Information:

Quantity sales. Special discounts are available on quantity purchases by corporations, associations, and others. For details, contact the publisher at the address above.

Orders by U.S. trade bookstores and wholesalers. Please contact Trient Press: Tel: (775) 996-3844; or visit www.trientpress.com.

Printed in the United States of America

Publisher's Cataloging-in-Publication data
Ruscsak, M.L.

A title of a book :The Fallen

ISBN Hard Cover:9781953975270

Paperback: 9781953975287

E-book: 9781953975294

Dear reader,

Thank you for your interest in the Of Lite and Darke series and your continued support. As promised *some* of the plot holes from the first book The New Reign will be filled in by the end of this installment. However, you may find more questions than the answers you seek.

The spelling, and other intentional misgivings have been cut down to a minimum as many of you my dear readers have asked. I am happy to oblige as best as I can while staying true to the story.

So, without further ado, sit back, settle in and as always happy reading.

- M. L. Ruscsak

For more information about the series, including where to find the series in other languages please visit WWW.TrientPress.com

The Fallen

M.L.Ruscsak

For my mother who has watched me spread my wings, preparing to fly. In addition, for pap who pushed me to great heights.

And always for my daughter who is learning to soar.

7

The Fallen

M.L.Ruscsak

Map of the realm

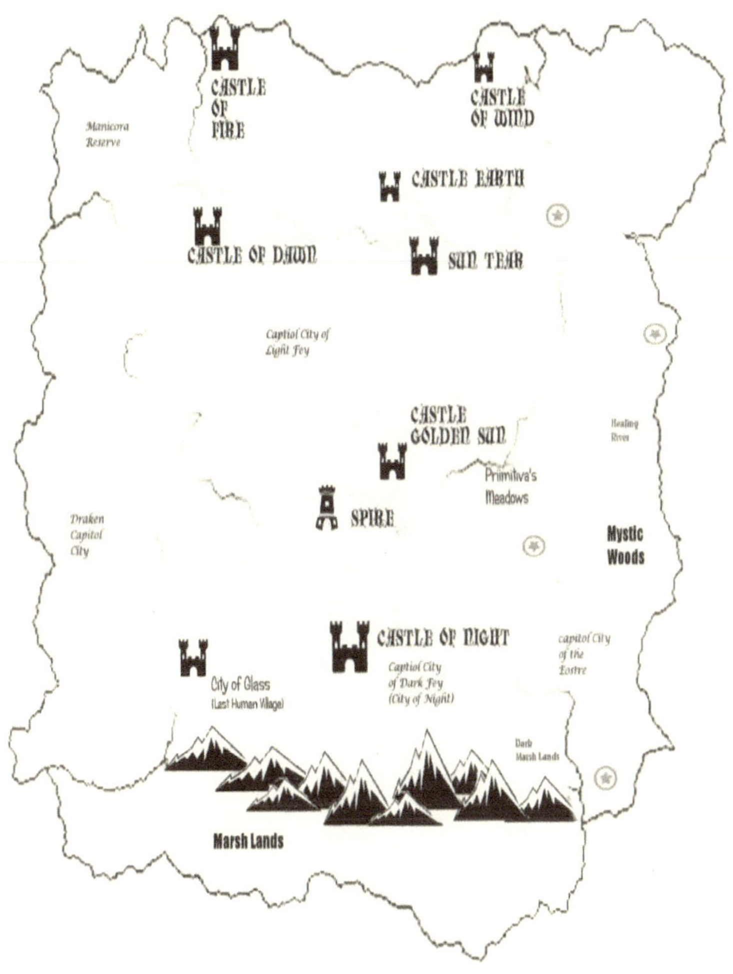

Royal Families of the Star cities

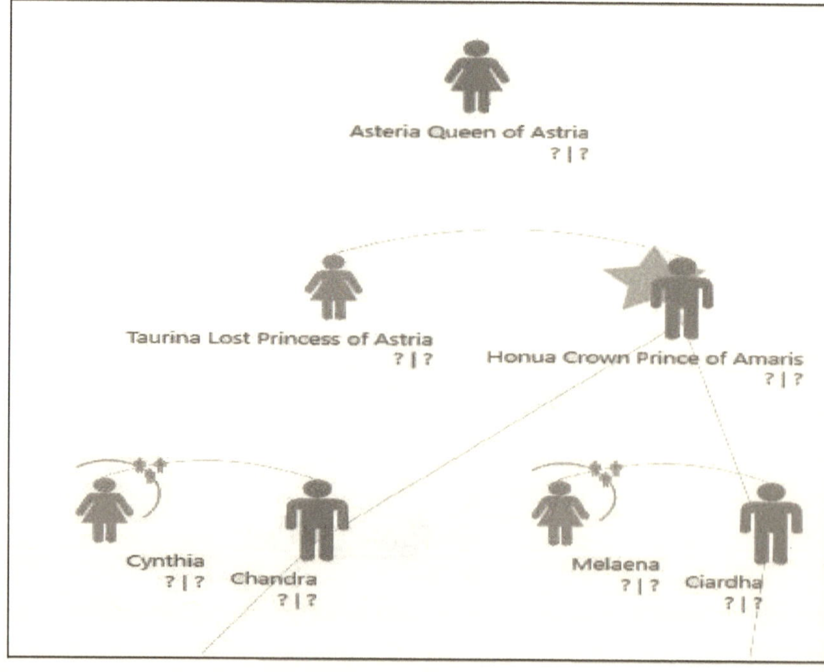

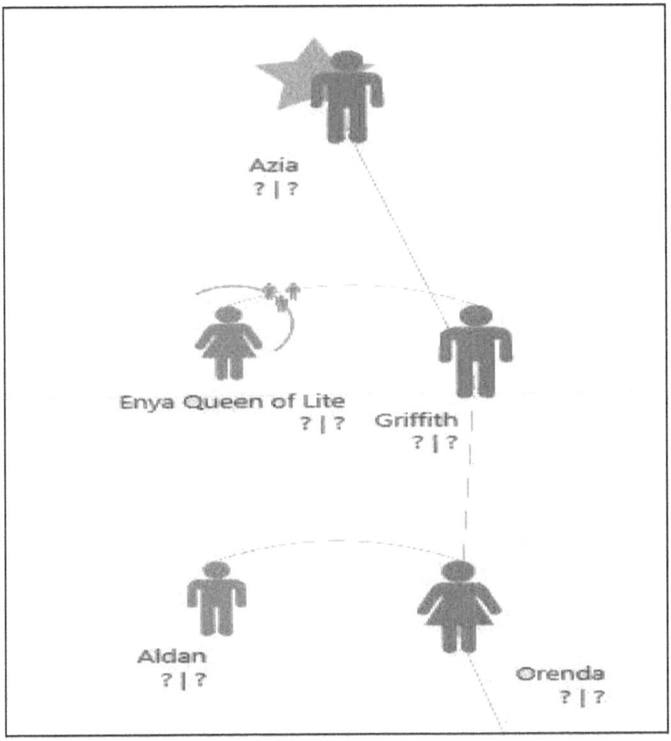

Azia
? | ?

Enya Queen of Lite
? | ?

Griffith |
? | ?

Aldan
? | ?

Orenda
? | ?

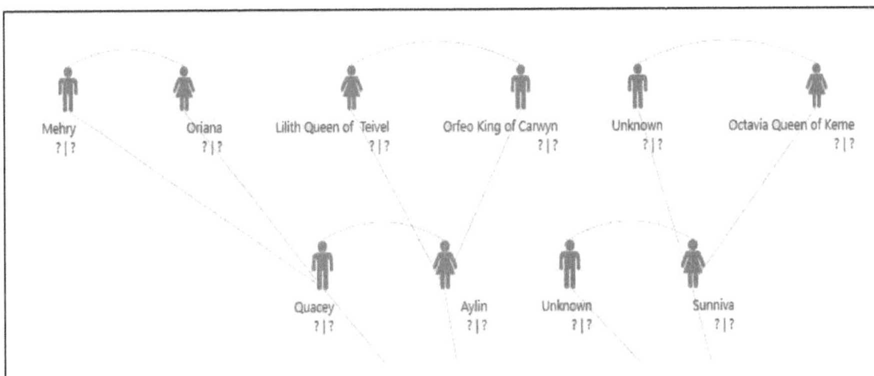

The Fallen

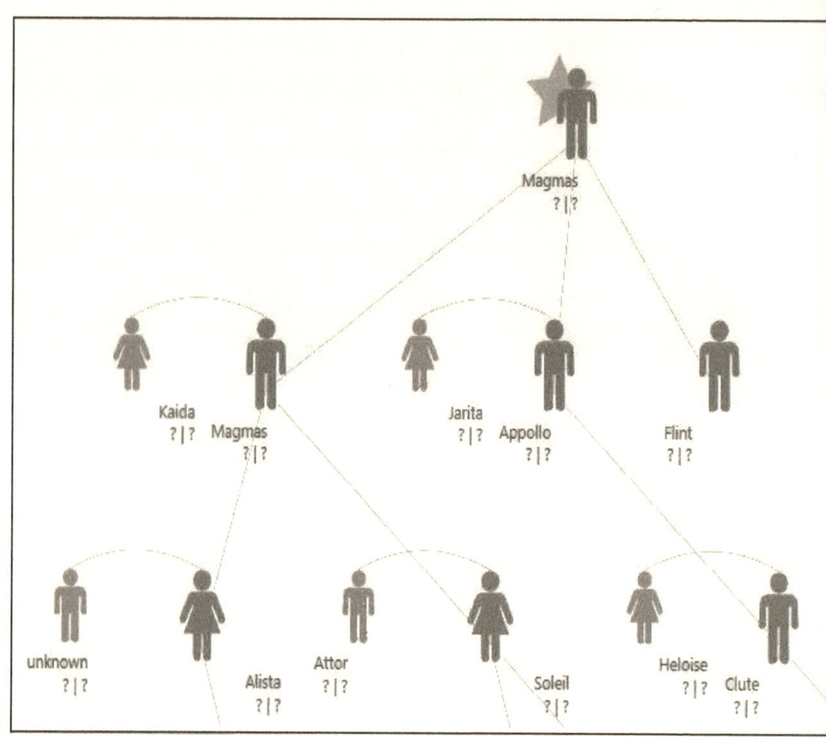

Magmas
? | ?
Kaida
? | ?
Magmas
? | ?
Jarita
? | ?
Appollo
? | ?
Flint
? | ?
unknown
? | ?
Alista
? | ?
Attor
? | ?
Soleil
? | ?
Heloise
? | ?
Clute
? | ?

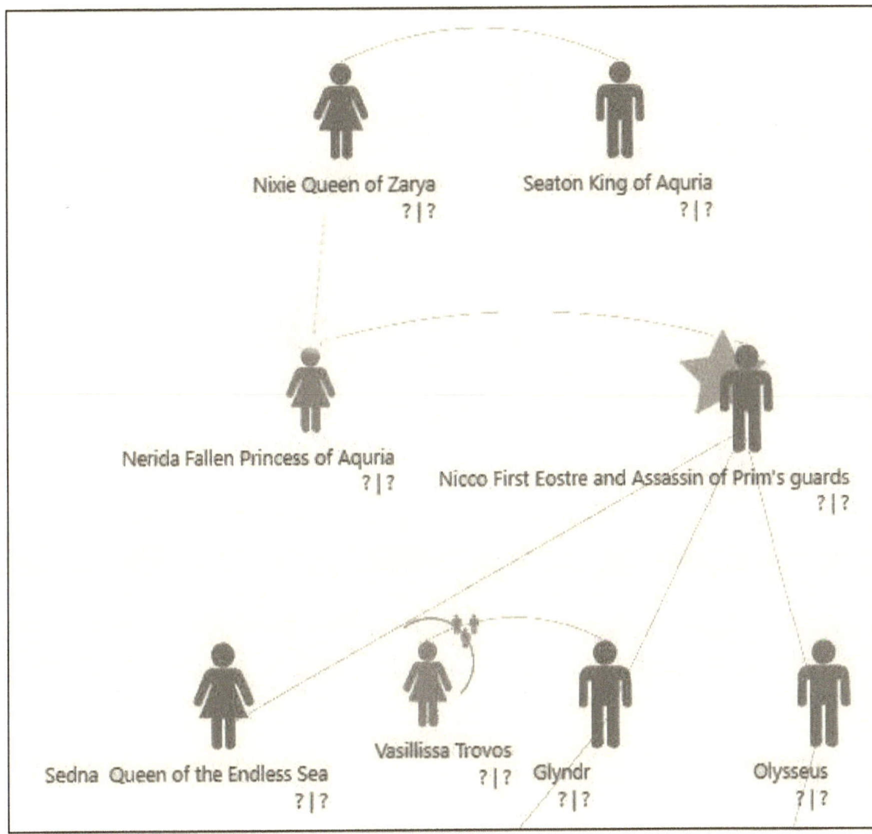

Nixie Queen of Zarya
? | ?
Seaton King of Aquria
? | ?
Nerida Fallen Princess of Aquria
? | ?
Nicco First Eostre and Assassin of Prim's guards
? | ?
Sedna Queen of the Endless Sea
? | ?
Vasillissa Trovos
? | ?
Glyndr
? | ?
Olysseus
? | ?

The Fallen

Orin
? | ?

Despina Queen of Lunaista
? | ?

None
? | ?

Alec
? | ?

Primitiva
? | ?

Magnar
? | ?

Avyanna
? | ?

Ari
? | ?

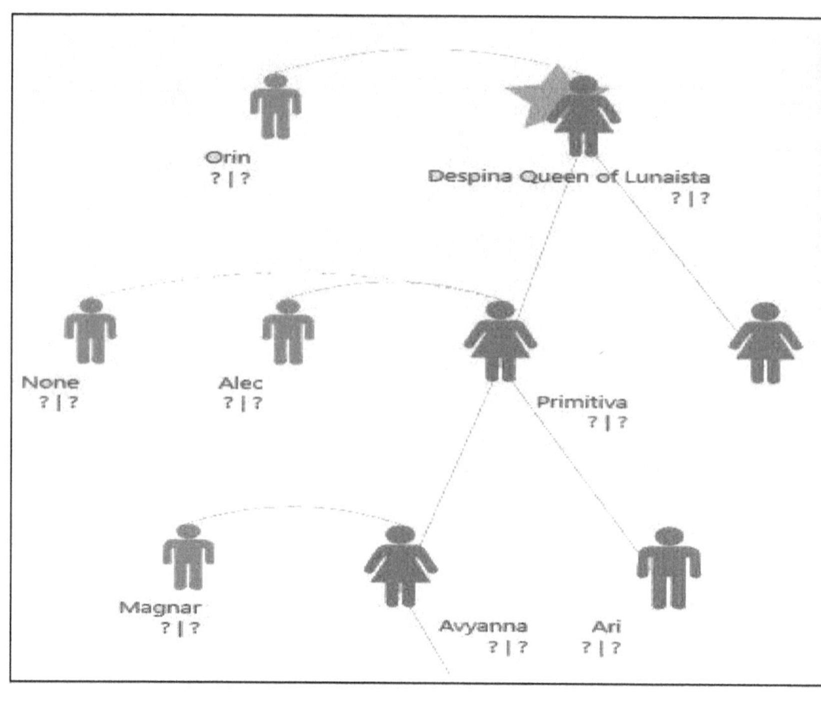

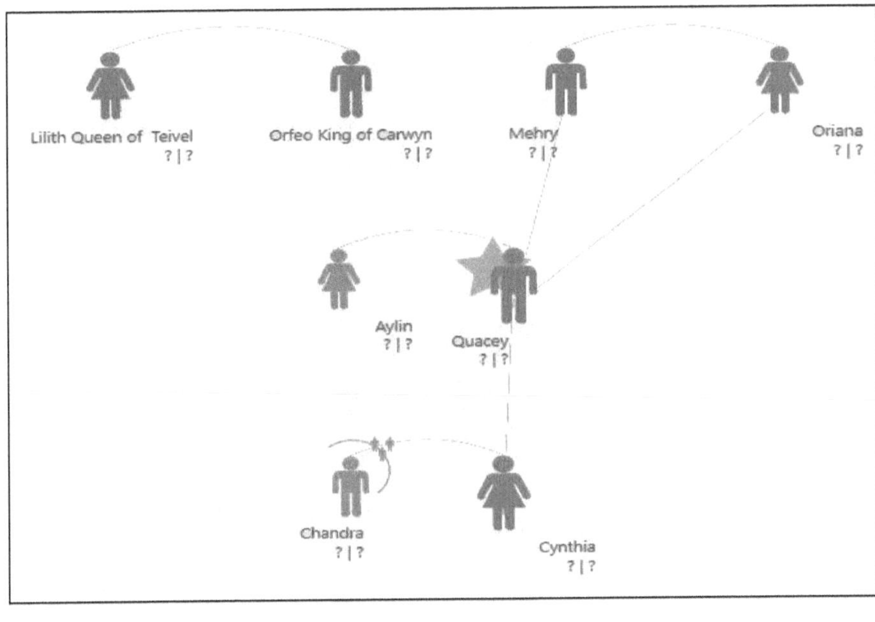

Lilith Queen of Teivel
? | ?
Orfeo King of Carwyn
? | ?
Mehry
? | ?
Oriana
? | ?
Aylin
? | ?
Quacey
? | ?
Chandra
? | ?
Cynthia
? | ?

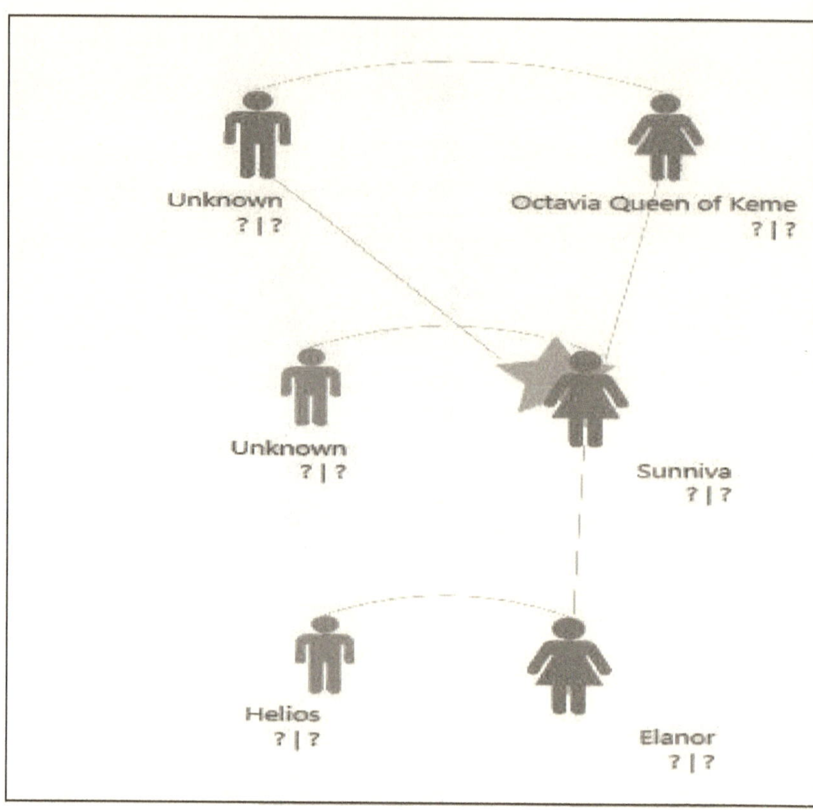

Key: Each box is a new royal line. Some you may recognize. Others will not be discussed. However, each is very important in their own way. The stars mean nothing at this point, however the half circle means there is more to their bloodlines. Only what is shown is important to this installment.

Part 1:

Part 2:

Part 3

Epilogue

About the Author

Excerpt

3,000 YEARS BEFORE THE GREAT WAR.

"Those who have the power to create are an abomination that needs to be wiped out before they come into power. They will be the undoing of the Fey."

-Royal doctrine for the ruler of Pallas

The Fallen

CHAPTER 1:

PRIMITIVA

Frustrated beyond all reasoning, she picked up her crystal brush and plopped down at her vanity. As her brush passed through her fiery red hair she counted. "One. Two." Gritting her teeth, she pulled the brush through her hair as she slowly hissed, "Three." Taking a deep breath, she opened her dark soulless eyes. Her parents were talking about her… *again*. Debating if they should make her a tribute to the city of stars or marry her off to one of the other royal star families. Slamming her crystal hairbrush down on her vanity, she shattered both. Upset and pissed off she pushed away from her now destroyed vanity no longer caring if her hair was perfectly smooth or a fiery mess. No longer cared enough to shed the tears that she had so many times before

She no longer cared about much of anything.

Holding back the tears, she held in all of her strong emotions. Her hurt. *"If you're going to kill your children why ever have more than one?"* She growled to herself. Her parents were not only not in the room, but were deep within the depth of the palace. But not deep enough where she could not hear them when she so chose. See them whenever she pleased. There was nowhere in all the Star Cities that she couldn't reach... couldn't see.

Not that any ever believed her. Not that any dared to.

Another breath, then she turned to her door. Not much of a door when you could see through it... you could see through everything except a single room in the palace. And that room was off limits to everyone except the queen herself. Frustrated, she turned away from her door. Nothing was private on this miserable star. Nothing.

"Don't even think about knocking, dear sister." She snapped, letting her thundering voice rattle the shards of crystal that now lay on her floor.

As the glass door opened, her sister smiled even though her sister turned from her, "Primitiva? You are more agitated than usual. Why?"

Damn her sister. The Crown Princess Starlis. Glaring at her sister, she dared not say what was on her lips. Instead took in her sister's rare beauty. Golden rays tumbled down her back, shimmering in the light of the room. Silver speckles dancing on her skin. But it was her eyes, the eyes of the galaxy that saw everything. "I will not marry a man who wishes only to have my power for his own."

"Ah. So, our parents are at it again? Trying to keep you from the tribute and yet you refuse."

As she turned her fire red hair wrapped around her revealing her wings. Wings that she was warned several times to never let be seen. "The only reason I am still here is because of Avyanna."

Starlis rushed over to her nearly placing her hand over Primitiva's mouth. Whispering, she said, "Shhhh. You know better than to speak her name."

Pushing her sister away and nearly allowing her to tumble, Primitiva hissed, "She is *my* daughter and I will speak her name whenever it pleases me."

Regaining her balance and closing the distance between them Starlis whispered, "You will get her killed. Now hush. I cannot protect her if you do not protect yourself."

Her sister was right, but only partly so. "You're right. I cannot protect her while I am still in Lunaista."

Then she turned sharply. She needed only, but a moment to decide what to do next. Only a moment to figure out how to bring about the change that the Star Cities needed.

A sigh of relief, then, "Finally, you are seeing reason."

Another moment to decide, "Which is why I am leaving."

Closing her eyes Starlis tried again to reason with her impulsive younger sister yet again, "You cannot just leave. There is nowhere in the Star Cities that you could go and not be found. Not that you could get to any other Star City." She let her eyes slowly open as she took a deep breath and tried to remind her sister, "Only messengers can go between the Star Cities and they have special training and abilities to do so."

As the second child, her powers... her abilities had been left untrained... even so, there was no one more powerful... no one... not even her dear sister. And certainly not that fool Azia who ruled Pallas. Slowly the room filled in a black mist. Not uncommon since she did this whenever she wished for privacy. Not that their parents allowed her, but then again, even they were powerless to stop her. Even Azia lacked the power required to stop her.

Turning back to her sister, she made sure she didn't turn away from her gaze… made sure her sister's eyes met hers. Seeing the fear in Starlis' face, she smiled a cruel and bitter smile. Hooking invisible hooks into her sister's mind, she spoke, *do not worry dear sister you will not remember much of this I do promise.*

What are you doing? How? This… this is…

Forbidden? Yes, I know. But then again, I have never been one for rules. Now hush and you will know what it is you must do.

I… The hooks drove deeper intertwining with the very fabric of Starlis' mind. Defeated, her body sagged. *What must I do?*

When asked, you will tell our parents I tried to flee and was swept away in the Void. I in a sense died just as those who were foolish enough to try have done since the beginning of time.

Starlis was mortified of what her sister was proposing. *Your powers will never feed the Star City. Our family will have no tribute.*

Actually, it will have two. Since our parents are so keen on the idea of keeping the tradition, they can offer themselves. Mother's power will pass to you as queen… but father's? Well, he can feed the catacombs of Pallas.

I suppose. I doubt the Azia will check to see who has been offered as tribute.

Primitiva smiled, *I know he will not. Now, my daughter. You will raise her as your own. She will be your child.*

But…

Your only child. Your powers are weak compared to hers and she is only but days old. None outside our parents know I gave birth. And none will think twice about you having a child with no interest in love.

Because my sister can create life out of nothing. Yes, that is plausible.

So glad you agree since you won't remember much in a few minutes. Now… She stepped back and called in a single tribute box. Silver but the inlays were not that of melting magma, but of shimmering crystal. *This will be passed down in our bloodlines for three generations. That is three thousand years where I am going. This box will only open to the first male child born who is the first-born. From now on… for the next three generations, the father of the child will be the tribute. No excuses. This instruction will be passed down to the children of the crown.*

I understand.

Calling the mist back to her, she smiled, "No sister, you do not. You do not have the gift of foresight. But that is ok for I do." Wrapping her arms around her sister, she gave her one last hug. "Close your eyes, my dear and I will be gone by the time you open them."

The Fallen

CHAPTER 2:

STARLIS

Entering her mother's throne room Starlis held her head high as she approached. Her eyes never leaving the face of her mother… of the queen. Stopping at the foot of the dais, Starlis met her mother's glare. Saw her father quietly stand just a hair behind the throne, his Midnight black hair disheveled as always. Her mother a stark contrast to his dark aura except where it truly mattered. Her temper was nothing to be trifled with.

"Mother?"

"Should you be studying. You have much to learn before I will allow you to ascend this throne."

Her mother's voice sharp like glass. A voice she would be glad never to hear again. Taking in all of the features of her mother's face, she made sure she would never forget this moment. Never forget the pale tight skin that had no signs of shimmers or sparkles beneath its surface. Remembered the hollowed eyes, silver with only a few specks of gold. And made sure to remember the dress that barely covered anything at all. So sheer, it veiled nothing. The loathing of her mother had never felt this deep before. Then again, until now she had always had her sister here to have enough hate for the both of them. "Primitiva is gone."

Queen Despina wailed in horror at what her dear daughter was telling her, "Gone? What do you mean gone?"

Starlis raised her hands in a surrendering gesture she had never… ever… seen her mother distraught over anything. Then again, not much happen in Lunaista. Nothing ever happened on any of the Star Cities. Keeping her voice quiet and respectful, she kept her true emotions out of her voice as she said, "She's just gone. She… I think she decided to jump into the Void. I know she was worried about feeding the catacombs and she would not marry any of the other Star City princes." She paused, considering what to say and what was better left unsaid before adding, "She has never followed the rules you know this. And you know she would never consent to be a mother to a child that she had to give birth to rather than create out of the air itself."

Her mother collapsed back on her crystal throne, "Do you understand what she just did… She ruined the family… ruined you."

She had always seen her mother as a cruel heartless queen. Seeing her like this… it had to be an act. It had to be. "Mother, please listen to me, please. The rules are not as complicated as you think. It states before the next ruler is crowned a tribute from the royal family must be sacrificed. It does not say which family member."

"Your father is the only other one!" Despina screamed yet again.

She rolled her eyes at her mother who was acting more like an insolent child than a Queen. "Since you do nothing to stop this silly tradition, then you are as much at fault for his death as Primitiva." Turning away from her mother, she took a step, "Now if you excuse me, I must prepare to be queen. I doubt you will want to dwell… we don't want Primitiva's dishonor to be spoken about *before* the coronation." What would be said later would be of little consequence to anyone. Least of all to her.

The Fallen

CHAPTER 3:

PRIMITIVA

Primitiva took a step to the edge of the messenger's gate and peered into the darkness. Messengers could see the lights of the other Star Cities. They knew where each one was located by some kind of locator spell. Anyone else who dared to try never survived. Couldn't survive since the spells that the messengers used were forbidden to teach any who didn't have the gift of speed.

Any with that gift were made into messengers. No exceptions. Not even if they were royal Fey. Not even if they were strong enough to rule.

That was fine. She wasn't going to another Star City she was going somewhere where no one had powers. No one would dare bother to look for her. She was going to the speck of blue light that was so far away, not even the best messengers would dare to travel.

What was there? She couldn't guess since no one had ever had the guts to travel there. Or if they did, none had made it back.

One last look at the only home she had ever known. No, this place was not her home, perhaps it never was. Perhaps it was simply the place that had given her life. Finding her resolve, she took a deep breath and spread her black dragon like wings just before diving into the darkness. Pulling her wings closed, she dove faster. Falling. Whirling past the outskirts of other cities. She could see them now that she was passing them. Every single one the same. A bright light and nothing more. What a wondrous feeling this was. Falling, whirling around… flying. Actually flying. Why hadn't she done this long before now?

Then a ball of blue and green. Brighter than any of the other Star Cities growing bigger as she drew closer. She crossed her arms in an attempt to shield her face as she entered the atmosphere. Snapping her wings open she tried to slow her descent. Finding it almost useless since she had been forbidden to use her wings at all since being a small child.

Not knowing what else to try so not to plummet into the ground that she could now see coming up way too fast… she closed her eyes and tried to create something anything that had wings… Something big enough to fly and protect her. Then just below her, a white cloud changed becoming solid. Sharp scales, then a body much longer than she needed. She didn't need scales, at least she hoped she didn't need a creature with scales to survive here, but it would do. A large head as big as her whole body. Legs then finally two large wings nearly three sizes bigger than its body.

A moment more and she tumbled onto its back with a grunt. Catching her breath, she patted its back. "Thank you for saving me."

The creature snorted a cloud of hot air before saying, "You are my queen. Why would I not."?

36

CHAPTER 4:

MAGMAS

Magmas peered into his red globe watching the ongoing of not his own Star City but that of Lunaista. He was going to marry the little princess. Not the crown princess… no that was forbidden… but the younger one. The one whose powers he could feel even here. He couldn't watch what was going on in the palace itself… no one could… but he could watch everything outside.

He could watch the mothers play with their children, teaching them how to use their gifts to build whatever they desired. Watched as the fathers taught their boys how to fight. Not that the skill was used, but it was busy work. Just something to do.

Something to fill the time between the time you are born and the time that you died.

A dark shape filled his globe, "Ah, now where are you going my little pet?"

She wasn't glancing over her shoulder. Not stopping to speak to anyone. No, she was going somewhere… Ah, the messenger stop.

Nothing to worry about… nothing…

Then she threw her simmering cape to the side revealing her wings. She paused for but a breath, then dove into the Void.

"NOOOO!" His hands slammed down on his table made of cooled magma. An impression from his fist now melted into it. "So, you would rather die in the Void then rule beside me? We shall see what the king of all kings says about your betrayal." Storming to his locked door of red flames, he yelled for a message coach to be brought.

Usually, a coach would only carry the tribute boxes to the other Star Cities then take the final one and the royal to Pallas. But this was too important. To despicable not, to bring to the attention of Azia the King of the city of stars.

Sitting back in the crystal coach Magmas scowled. Worthless messenger. Everyone hoped they could be chosen to be a messenger… it showed how little they knew. Messengers were little more than slaves for the crown. They were required to pull the coaches when at their fullest could weigh as much as twenty men. If they complained they were punished. Sometimes to the point that the offending slave would need to be killed.

After all, what good was a messenger if he couldn't pull the coaches. What good were they if they could no longer reach the other cities?

However, the one pulling this coach… he had been lobbying for a position in Pallas for years now. Hoping to be chosen for a life of ease rather than continuing to work for the crown.

Worthless being. If he didn't need this messenger, he would kill this one here and now.

But only messengers possessed the skills needed to travel between the stars. Only they knew the routes to the other landing points. And only they could survive the Void.

Well, survive it outside of the crystal coaches. So, for today this little beast was saved. Tomorrow, however, was not promised.

Pallas. The mother of all stars. Solid ground, lush with colors. The buildings made of crystals, gems and other materials that sparkled in the light. The people who lived here were said to be the most powerful. The most gifted.

And why shouldn't they be? They received the best of the tributes. They received the power before any other Star City. And they never needed to produce a tribute themselves. Of course, those who lived on Pallas also controlled when the other Star Cities were allowed to tap into the tribute boxes that were received.

Despicable creatures. Was it any wonder why the royals hated to come here? It didn't matter how powerful you were in your own Star City… you weren't half as powerful as the lowest citizen of Pallas.

Standing before the palace, he made sure his temper was in check as he approached a guard. "I need to speak to the Azai. It's of grave importance."

The guard glared down at him from the top step. His voice as cold as it was dark as he growled, "The Azia sees no one."

Backing down was not an option. Not today. Not when this was important not only for him, but for all of the Fey. "He will see me. Tell him King Magmas is requesting an audience."

"What is the problem here?" A deep midnight voice called down from the castle doors.

Glancing up, he saw the plush robes and golden crown. Immediately he went down on one knee, "Your majesty, I come bearing grave news."

Azia laughed as he turned from the grand stairs, "Ah, Magmas. Spying on the other royals again? Come I do so enjoy your tails."

Bounding up the flight of stone stairs, he rushed to catch up with the king. "I come bearing news from Lunaista."

"I see. And what is it that you know I wonder? That they crowned a new queen today? Or perhaps you are referring to the consort being made the tribute rather than the young one?"

Magmas gasped and nearly stumbled. Azia wasn't a seer so how had he known? It shouldn't have been possible. Yet… "You knew?"

Azia quickly turned to face him and hissed, "I know all Magmas. And I would have never allowed your union to that royal Fey. She was meant for the catacombs." Something dark passed within his eyes before he let out a curt laugh, "Ah well, I will allow her to feed the Void. Her death is of little consequence."

Narrowing his eyes Magmas could hear the words that had been left unsaid. Could hear the lies hidden carefully behind the laugh. He couldn't ask the questions or let on that he knew there was more than what was being said, but he could find the answers. And he would do so on his own.

The Fallen

CHAPTER 5:

PRIMITIVA

Catching her breath, she finally was able to look around at her new surroundings. The clouds felt wet on her skin, yet didn't completely drench her either. The sky nearly black now. But it was the stars that took her breath away. She could see the Star Cities. Could see each one with nothing more than a passing glance. "I never knew there were so many."

"My queen?" The creature snorted with a burst of warm air.

"Oh, forgive me. Do you see the orbs of light in the sky?"

"I see them." His wings pumped lazily as he circled the ground below looking for a spot to land.

"Those are Star Cities. My people… well, people with my blood… live there. It is where I was born."

"Hmm. Is it important?"

Snuggling down into his scales she thought for a long minute, "No I suppose not. Lest not any longer."

"I will land. There are some two-legged creatures near here. Not a problem for you. But I can eat them if you need."

"No, I will manage, but I would like to keep you near if that is alright?"

"You are my queen. I will stay as long as you desire." Finally finding a small clearing admits some densely clustered trees he continued, "Do I have a name?"

Oh… she hadn't thought of that." Of course, you should have a name. A strong name for such a wonderful protector. Let me see…" Sliding off of his back, she took in the shining white scales. His long black talons. Finally, she stopped in front of his large head and gazed into his eyes. Reaching her hand carefully to his face, she smiled, "I will call you Shesha the king of the dragons."

"There are more like me?"

"Not yet, but please give me time. There will be you have my word."

"Then I am honored." His nostrils flared picking up a scent. "Someone is coming."

Primitiva nodded once, "Then I must hide you." A whiff of violet smoke and he was just big enough to wrap around her arm. "There, I think you should be able to choose your size. But I will wait till we are alone." Carefully, she sat on the hard ground, allowing time for just one more change… being shrouded in darkness, her wings vanished beneath her cape… a hood now attached to it. A golden brooch clasped the material closed… And her dress… As she did not know what one would wear in this strange land… she decided on a soft mossy green material. Vines of black climbing from the hem to her waist. Lastly, her feet needed coverings to protect from what laid upon the ground. Deep brown with gold buckles holding them snugly in place.

Taking a deep breath, she waited until she heard something snap then a deep, robust voice, "Who goes there?"

Slowly she got to her feet, making sure Shesha was still safely on her arm resting from his long flight. "Oh, I am truly sorry for disturbing you. I only wished to rest before continuing on my journey." Not that she was truly sorry at all… but she didn't want to tip her hand. Least not yet.

Slowly a tall, thin man came out of the shadows of the wood. "This is the king's land. State your business."

Her head tilted slightly to the side not yet able to make out his features other than his frame. "The king? Oh yes, I should meet with him. Will you take me?"

He stumbled back a step, "You want to meet the king?"

Tentatively, she pulled the hood down from her cap revealing her fire red hair and glistening eyes that in the darkness now seemed to glow. "As I am not from this kingdom it is only wise that I seek an audience. Is it not?" What he would say would determine his loyalty to his king, but also, would tell her a great deal about him as well.

"Yes, I can see you are not from around here since I know all of the Gentry Ladies in these parts." The man paused, "There is a cabin nearby we will stay there until daybreak. Then we shall see if you still wish to see the king."

She didn't protest when he grabbed her elbow… after all, she could escape if she so chose to… Didn't complain about the walk… especially now that she could see through the shadows and see all that she needed… however, her companion didn't seem to be able to see anything other than the large trees that sprouted from nowhere. "Perhaps I should lead. You seem to be tripping over more of the forest than I."

He was going to protest, but even pulling her along she had yet to step on a twig beneath her feet while he now only snapped them, but was tripping over a great deal of them and some very large roots at that. "If you think you can find a cabin. Then, by all means, lead the way."

Pausing briefly as she sniffed the air. She had never smelled smoke before, but she knew almost instantly what it was and where it was coming from. "You left a fire burning."

"It's late night and on the brink of the cooler months… why would a fire not be burning?" Then again she didn't seem to mind the chill in the air either.

She didn't answer, "We are going the wrong direction if you truly intend to take me to the cabin. Is back…" She turned then pointed, "… That way. But you knew that so why are we going this way?"

For a breath, he stood in stunned silence, then let out several words she could safely assume were both vulgar and probably should not be said in front of polite company. When he finally remembered she was still standing there and looking all too amused, he hissed, "We were going this way because I refuse to take you to the palace. Or at least one in this country."

"So you intend to go against your own king and take me somewhere else?"

"I intended to take you to the border and hope you wandered into someone who would take you to their king or queen or whatever they have that rule over the people."

"And go against your king." She pointed out once more.

"The piece of filth that sits on the throne is not my king. My king was killed more than a decade ago by the imposter." He swore once more as he turned from her.

"Then you have my apologies. Maybe there is something I can do to help?"

He gave another snort, "Unless you have armies waiting in the forest I doubt anything you do would help."

"True. But please tell me about this king. There may be a solution that you have not yet thought of."

The young gentleman paused listing to the quiet rustling of the wind blowing through the trees. Listening for the first sign there was another intruder close by. Satisfied they were truly alone, he cautiously said, "We are in the king's woods. He has patrols that search for poachers here."

"And the cabin that you spoke of? Is that not in the king's woods as well?"

"Actually, it's in the part of the woods that belong to my family. Just outside of what the false king declared as his own."

So you know more about this place than you let on. Interesting. She took a deep breath, then slowly let it out.

All of her life she had wanted an adventure… wanted something that she could make her own. Not take but she would need an army should anyone seek to find her. "Then we shall go there and speak freely." She turned toward where the smoke was coming from, "Come with me, huntsmen I do not think I like tramping through the forest."

The cabin was small, to say the least. A single cot was pushed up to the side, the fireplace took up the far wall, and the only table had but one chair. Both looking as though they had been made from whatever pieces of branches that had been discarded by its tree.

Looking around, she finally took a step inside yet didn't face the huntsmen just yet. "I have never been in a place such as this." And in truth, she hadn't. Everything she had known as walls had been mostly see-through or made of light.

"It's a hunting cabin. Good for a night or two. Not a place that any Gentry, Lady has ever stepped foot in… or at least not one that I am aware of."

Taking a careful seat on the only chair, she reached her hand up and let Shesha climb out on the table. His wings now carefully hidden.

"What is that?"

Since his eyes were twice the size that they had been, she assumed he had never seen a creature such as this. "This is my darling Shesha. He does not bite. Have you never saw one of his kind before?"

"Green ones sure they make…" He paused, not wanting to offend her, "… Never a silver one."

She shrugged, unconcerned, "Perhaps we should properly introduce ourselves now that we can see one another." Now she could truly see him not just his shape but his feature. Black hair that reminded her of the sky above Lunaista. A strong jaw and handsome face. His build more muscular than what she had ever seen, but pleasantly so. "I am called Primitiva."

He looked stunned yet suspicious, "That is an interesting name."

"Yes, my parents had a sense of humor. It means the first, yet my sister is the eldest."

"Then why…" He shook his head, "I'm sorry I just… normally I hold my tongue better." Closing his eyes, he started again, "You may call me Alexander. I was named after some great grandfather, according to my mother."

"It is a pleasure to meet you, now please tell me about the current king and how he not only became into power but stays in it."

"I'm sure it's not a story for a lady such as yourself to hear."

"Darling bloodshed does not bother me. Nor does much of anything else. Now please…" Her galaxy blue eyes locked on his as she commanded, "… tell me."

A deep breath and he started, "The false king was a prince of a neighboring country here for a visit. Since he was sixth in line for the throne, no one really cared that he came. Once he saw the city and the woman who lived there, he started making plans to live there permanently. The king said he could make him an advisor or something.

Within a day, he had mustered up an army… one created from our men. Of course, he had to pay them a small fortune to turn on their countrymen but they did it. While the men fought among themselves the prince snuck into the palace and killed the king while he slept."

"Didn't the king know about the army?"

Alexander shook his head, "His military advisors were in on the coup. They told the king it was just some of the men arguing amongst themselves. Nothing to worry about. Anyways, after the king was dead the prince gave the queen a choice, marry him and make him king by marriage or die.

She had just seen her husband die… We found her body days later. Not much of her was recognizable. The princess, who was the only heir was taken prisoner until the last of those loyal to the king were either killed or surrendered. My father surrendered so my mother and I would be saved. He died on the gallows despite being told he wouldn't be harmed.

After the uprising, the women who lived in the city were given to the men who fought in the uprising. Sold like cattle. Those who fought back were killed. Some fled. I don't know what happen to them, but I pray they found safety somewhere."

Primitiva raised her hand to stop him, "You were able to keep your land?"

He snorted, "I had to work in the palace for five years. My mother was allowed to keep the property as long as I behaved. We both hid my sister to keep her from the horrors of the city. In truth, I wish that the city burned with all those inside."

"Even the innocent?"

"What innocent? Children are ripped from the mothers sent away to be raised in what are called farms. Girls learn to cook, clean, mend and see to the needs of men. While boys are taught trades and how to fight. No, there are no innocent in the city. The women who live there would rather die than live another minute. And the men… I knew a great deal of them, but they have changed. And not for the better."

Sitting back in her seat she stroked Shesha's spiny back. "Very well, I will help you. But first, does this king have any allies that would avenge him? Or any heirs that may be a problem?"

"No heirs. By some miracle, he hasn't been able to produce any in ten years. The stars are very kind in preventing that atrocity. But his brother's kingdom… it lies to the south… they have a mighty army. He would tear the country apart to avenge his brother. He assumes his second born will inherit this country when the time is right."

"Very well. We will need to invite the other to the palace once we arrive. It will not be too hard. Now how far is it from here?"

"Walking it would take two days. I'm sorry I have no horse to carry us."

"Horse?"

Still, in a trance, he went over to the fireplace and pointed to the mantle… there was a small carving just above the stone. "Horse."

"Oh, Yes, that would make better time. Perhaps we shall ride mine. I believe it followed us here."

He blinked twice as her spell ended. Horse? She had a horse? He couldn't remember seeing one, but she had to be telling the truth. "If we leave now, we could be there by dark tomorrow. The king never turns away a beautiful lady."

The Fallen

CHAPTER 6:

ALEXANDER

Stepping out of the cabin Alexander froze. There just a few yards away was a large silver-white horse lazily grazing on a large bramble bush and not wearing anything that could be considered a saddle. "How?"

"She is well trained." Gliding past him, she stepped over to the creature. "Hello, my dear may we ride you?"

The horse lifted her head, then let out a snort of hot air. Her coal black eyes eyeing the man near the cabin. Saying nothing, she bowed so that her queen could climb onto her back.

"Are you coming or do you need something to sit on?"

Several curses left his lips before stepping over to the horse. Finally, he climbed up, setting her in front of him. One hand around her thin waist the other one gripping a handful of the long silver mane. "We'll be there late tomorrow at best."

Petting her newest creation, she smiled, "Oh, I think Seren can get us faster than that. Can't you my dear?"

Another snort of hot air and she took off at a ground eating pace and being only partly guided by the one who was holding her mane.

Holding Primitive close and silently praying not to fall off this demon they now rode, he tried to keep his voice steady as he said, "I have never seen a horse that could travel at full gallop for this long." Nor had he ever been on one that didn't bounce him around while he rode.

"As I said she is very well trained. And I do wish to speak to this king post haste."

"You haven't yet said how you can help."

It was true, she hadn't but she figured it was best for him to see for himself rather than taking the chance of him not believing her. "I promise it will be very entertaining. Now, what else must I know about him?"

"He has two brothers. The others died some time ago. The two living each have their own castle but only one rules his own country. It lies to the north and is currently called Nazar. Years before it was called something else but I do not know what for it is now forbidden to speak of brighter times."

"Wonderful. Nazar mean something yes?"

"Something like to ward off evil. It's ironic since the man who rules it is twice as cruel as this king. It is said every woman in the country is brought before him on the date of their eighteenth year. The ones he deems pretty are then enslaved to him until he sells them to the highest bidder. Those who own those poor girls may do anything to them that they please. From what I hear few live long enough to see their children grow past infancy."

"Wonderful. I shall meet with the brothers as well. I would like to do all my housekeeping at one time if at all possible."

"You plan on…"

"Killing the rulers of two countries? Hardly. But I think I will give them a new role and master to follow. But we shall see. I came here to live a simple life, however I was born for greatness perhaps now I have found it."

After riding all day and the just now setting the castle came into view. Not very impressive compared to the palace of crystal that she had grown up in. Actually, it was rather hideous, mud gray stones covered in moss. Only six stories tall and each from the outside looking exactly the same. "Is this it? I imagined something more impressive."

His mouth dropped, "This is the tallest in this country. The other two… the ones that are rarely used… they barely stand three stories. Granted the moss only started to climb in the last few years."

"There is nothing impressive about a stone building with little character. It is fine for now. It will be something easy for me to fix. But perhaps not right away. But we shall see"

"Fix? You're going to… How are you going to reshape stones? By the god's woman, not even a craftsman would be able to reshape nor replace those stones."

"Are you always so excitable? I have not met many men who can't take things in stride. It is very perplexing."

It did him no use to argue with her. None. She was going to do whatever she wanted. Pity. She was rather lovely and strong-willed. If she wasn't so damn suicidal, he would love to have her by his side as his wife. Might as well push that thought from his head… by morning, she would either be dead or wish that she was.

Helping her dismount he watched her raise her head defiantly marched right up to the castle door. Two sentries crossed their long-bladed staffs then one snarled, "Who goes there?"

"I am here to see the king. Take me to him at once."

Alexander rolled his eyes at this rate she wouldn't be alive long enough to see the king. Climbing down off the horse he took two steps toward her then watched as both men dropped their staffs and bowed to her like she was royalty. "Uh…"

"Come Alexander. The king awaits." Then she pushed the tall wooden door open and strode inside with the confidence of someone who belonged there.

Catching up to her, he took notice at all of the guards who bowed as she strode by. "Is there something I should know?"

"Hmm. Probably, but not yet."

As she walked down the long hallway, her feverish paced slowed to a measured crawl. Still, he could not fathom how she knew where was heading nor any reason for the palace guards to bow before her. Then again, glancing back they seemed just as confused… yet none seemed to move from their post. "What are you? A witch? Sorceress? What?"

Now she paused. "I know not of what you speak. What are theses witches and Sorceress'?"

He shook his head. "Never mind. But it's clear you can bewitch any that lay eyes on you." When she didn't respond nor move he hurried to add, "By your rare beauty. None here have the looks of you."

"Oh. No, I suppose they wouldn't." She still gazed ahead, "Ah, the heart of the castle. The king holds court through those doors… yes?"

"He does."

"Good." Going up to the doors that held no sentry, they crashed into the wall behind them. "I demand to see the king." She hissed, her voice echoing off the walls. Only one guard had been posted inside and he met her gaze.

Dropping his staff, he ran out a door that had been hidden behind the dais.

"He may bring reinforcements."

"He will bring the king." Her head tilted to the side. "No-one here seems foolish enough to question their orders. Odd. No matter things will be settled soon enough."

He was about to speak, but the king dressed only in his long dressing gown and red robe stormed in before he could.

In a deep growl, the king yelled, "What in the name of darkness is the meaning of this intrusion?"

Primitiva took a single step toward him and lowered her hood from her cape. Her fire red hair tumbling around her shoulders and cascading down her back. "I came to discuss a matter with you. Would you wish to wait till the morrow?"

The King licked his lips. "Exquisite. Where did you find such a rare creature?"

Taking a bow Alexander quietly answered, "In the woods. Near the beach castle."

"Ah, caught trying to hide from me, my little minx? Well, that's nothing a good tanning won't fix."

Clasping her hands together, she smiled before she snarled, "There will be no tanning. Least not mine." In one quick motion, she unfastened her long cape as it fell to the floor the door that leads to both the main hall and the one the kind had come down slammed with a fury that no wind could match. Seeing the fear in his eyes, her dark wings snapped out.

"What are you?" Not the king, but Alexander said with a gasp.

"Vengeance. In the time, it took me to gain entrance to this room, I have learned all that I need to about this place. You worship gods that live in the stars. You have asked for guidance and power. You claim to be the divine ruler because the gods favor you." She took a step over to the king who still hadn't moved… nor could he now unless she willed it. "You are not a divine ruler. The gods you worship do not favor you. I do not favor you. You are weak, insignificant and mean nothing to me." She turned to her escort seeing the fear in his eyes. "Do you understand what I am now? Or should I demonstrate my power?"

Quickly he dropped to one knee, "Goddess I meant no disrespect. Had I had known…"

"You amuse me. Your life is spared." Turning back to her captive, she continued, "Bring me at least five men who you trust. And your sister."

"My… sis-sister?" He gulped. For years, he had been hiding her now…

"You have until dawn. You are dismissed." The door to the main hall barely cracked open. She didn't look to see if he had left just trusted that he had. "Now what to do with you. Ah, yes. You will invite your family here. Both brothers and your father. You will not tell them about me only that you have a matter to discuss that cannot be written into words. Go now and write your summons. You will remain in your room till I have need of you.

CHAPTER 7:

ALEXANDER

"Dawn I have till dawn to find those worthy of… and bring my sister here? How? Alexander muttered to himself as he raced back down the hall. Thankfully, the demon horse… demon? … Oh, by the god this wasn't just a horse this was her horse. A horse of a god. He had a choice… try to find what she required by himself or hope the horse had some kind of special ability that would aid in his quest.

Cautiously he approached the creature that looked at him more like he was dinner than a prospective friend. That in itself was troubling. Seeing something that was not grass dripping with blood and falling from the horse's mouth. Oh yes, he was in trouble. "My gentle mare would you aid me in my quest that your owner has tasked me with?" He had no idea if it would understand but it was worth a chance.

Seren stood there munching on what she held in her mouth for a minute longer before swallowing. "I will help this one time. And only for my queen."

He stumbled back in alarm. It talked. She talked. In sentences. No. No. He couldn't have actually heard… A deep breath and he gave a weak smile. "Thank you."

"What is the task?"

Oh. Yes. Right. Another breath to calm himself then as calmly as he could, he began to speak as he once again moved closer, "I am to find five men who are worthy to meet the queen. I - I think I know who but they will be hard to find. Then I need to retrieve my sister for the queen."

"It is unlikely that we will succeed in the given time. You will send word to the men."

Of course, that made so much more sense. Now if he knew how to find them or get a message to them. Ah, bloody hell. He turned and saw an armed guard heading toward him. The look on his face did not bode well for a friendly chat. "Sir?"

"Don't sir me. I have been ordered that I now take orders from the likes of you."

Oh good. She did understand he couldn't just teleport all over the damn countryside to get her, the requested audience. "Do you have parchment and a quill?"

"Do I look like a damn scribe?"

She sent him here to follow his orders as uncomfortable as he was giving them. "There are five men who once worked with me in this castle. Find them before and have them here before dawn. Not a minute after or it will be your hide, not mine that explains why you are late." Turning he quickly climbed onto Seren's back, "Come, my dear, we have far to travel and little time to do so."

They were out of the city long before Seren spoke, "Would it not have been easier to eat him?"

By the gods, he wasn't imaging blood dripping from her mouth, "If he does not find who I seek I will ask your queen if you may eat him."

"The other was crunchy. Is your entire race, so unpleasant tasting?"

"I'm sorry I wouldn't know."

"Very well, I will not turn away food… no matter how unpleasant."

Thinking about everything he considered food… all the things that had a pleasant taste versus all the things he ate so he wouldn't starve he patted her neck. "I will see if I can find you another choice for food. One that has more meat, though the bones may still be crunchy."

"Very well." She took another step, then bucked back still keeping Alexander on her back. Two long feather-like wings sprouted from her sides. Before he could say another word she took out in a full gallop, then leaped into the air pumping her glorious wings till she reached the clouds.

"You can fly!"

"My queen is gracious. She gives gifts as she sees fit."

Gifts? The wings were a gift to a creature who looked like a horse yet ate flesh? Perhaps he should tell the queen… the goddess… that horses eat grass and hay. Then again, would it make a difference?"

They landed outside a small cottage that was hidden by a grove of trees and vines. Not a place one would look for a person to live, but this was the only house his sister had ever known. Quickly he pushed to nearly rotted door open. There on a small pallet of straw his younger sister lay sleeping. A thin blanket made of woven vines covering her.

Carefully, he knelt down at her back and reached out his hand, "Mary? You need to wake now."

"Alec?"

It was her pet name for him. A name she had started calling him before she could fully say his name. "Yes, dear sister. You must come with me and please do not ask many questions for answers I have none."

Slowly she sat up. In the dark, she could not see his face. "Is it mama? Is she ill?"

Relief swelled in him, "No. As far as I know, she is well. Still in the villa keeping the appearance of a grieving wife and mother." Would the goddess need to see her too, he wondered? No, best not to bring anything up until he had to.

"Where are we going? Did the bastard king find out where I am?"

"No, But I need you to meet someone. I swear you will be safe, but you must trust me."

That sounded ominous to her, but what could she do. "I have little choice if I am to survive." She took a single step outside and saw the silver horse standing calmly waiting for his master, "Oh you have a horse. That is terrific. Does that mean you have the money to…"? She hated saying the words, "… buy my contract, and save me before I must be offered to the pig king?"

"Mary please hold your tongue. Say nothing else until we arrive. Please. And Know what I do now isn't what it appears to be. You have my word."

It was nearly dawn when they entered the capital city. Thankfully, Mary had fallen asleep in his arms. Fear was a living thing right now. Fear that his dear sister would never forgive him. Fear that he was handing her to a fate worse than if the king had found her. Fear that she wouldn't be found worthy of the goddess and killed. So many things were running through his head and each one worse than the next.

At least he didn't have to explain a talking horse or one that could fly for that matter. Then again, he could have very well imagined the whole conversation. Of course, after all, he had seen since his father's death, it was still possible to be going completely mad. And if he were truly mad the appearance of the goddess could just be a trap to catch his sister.

Slowly Seren came up upon the palace steps only now several guards were milling about. The one he had words with last night was at the top of the steps looking down with hard accusing eyes. "Mary?"

Slowly, her hazel eyes opened. Then she saw where she was... "You... Why? Tell me why."

"Shh. Hush, dear sister. Please do not make this harder."

Closing her eyes, she blinked back the tears. "At least you brought me yourself." She sniffled, "If I am going to be given to the crown I will make my resolve now." Then she slid down from the mounts back. "At least I know where this fine lady came from." She patted Seren neck then kissed her cheek. "I wish you a long life my lovely mare. Thank you, such a gentle ride, so I could sleep one night in peace."

Alexander shook his head. His heart aching from the pain that he was now inflicting on his sister. Tenderly he took her arm, perhaps for the last time, "I'll walk you in."

Turning sharply, she faced him as she spat out, "Of course. You'll need to collect your bounty, my lord."

The words stung past insult. He just hoped one day she might forgive him. One day she might understand why. One day… providing the goddess was real.

Coming up the steps, he held her arm as he spoke to the captain of the guards, "Did you find them?"

"They are just outside the doors to the throne room."

Neither of them spoke again until the men who had been requested came into view. All looking more than a little rumpled. But it was the definite fear in their eyes that told him he made a good choice he hoped. "Ean? You look well."

His bright blue eyes barely were able to hide the fear of being back inside of the castle. "Why are we here. We did our ten years of service. We were let go… allowed to live free. So why are we here?"

Placing his hand on Ean's shoulder, he took a breath, "Because I didn't think you would want to miss the show. I promise no matter what you are thinking right now you are wrong. Please come with me."

One of the others grabbed his arm hard enough to bruise. His dark green eyes blazing with fury, "I swear if this is a trick you will be dead before anyone has a chance to stop me."

Alexander nodded. He knew this man, though right now his name escaped him. But the memory of what he had done to survive in these halls had not. He had killed the guards under the guise of night. Strangling them in their sleep, leaving no witnesses. He had poisoned a room of women… the king's concubines… to save them the beatings and the vile things that the king had called pleasure. But more than that he knew this man kept his word. "I promise this is not a trick."

CHAPTER 8:

PRIMITIVA

Slowly he pushed the tall, heavy double doors open, revealing Primitiva sitting not on the gold painted thrown, but one not entirely made of any kind of shiny clear stones. Thousands of them now making a single chair. Dropping to one knee Alexander whispered, "I brought those who were requested."

She let out a small yawn, "So I see." Getting to her feet, she raised her voice, "Come let me see you."

Cautiously the men filed in and dropped to their knees as they saw their once friend do. Mary stayed in the back, but curtsied as best she could.

Since they we not coming to her, she took the handful of steps and stood before them. Tentatively, she combed her fingers through the dirt covered hair of the first who was furthest away from Alexander, "What is your name?"

At the sound of her voice, he glanced up. "Nicco." Then he saw her wings that he had foolishly mistaken as a cape just moments ago. His hunter green eyes widened, "You're not human." Nicco gasped out in surprise… or perhaps in fear.

"Human? I am much too important to merely one thing. However, what would you like to be I wonder?"

Nicco shook his head then quickly glanced down the row. None of the others were moving not even to breathe. "I don't understand."

"If you could be anything what would it be?"

"I-" he gulped air. "I would like to have the power to kill those who take joy in the torment of others." The words stunned him into silence since he had not meant to tell them.

Her eyes glistened with amusement, "Is that all?"

"Yes, goddess?"

She nodded, then stepped away, his head dropping back to look at the floor just like the others. Stepping over to the next she decided his hair was the color of the stars. Silver but dull. Not like those who lived in her home. Well, she could fix that soon enough. "What is your name."

He shivered beneath her touch. "Ean."

Since he didn't look up at her as she knelt down before him. Her long, thin finger held just under his chin. "There now, I can see your eyes." And she could. Sky blue and full of fear. "You have no reason to fear me?"

"It's not you I'm afraid of."

"You speak of the king, correct? The vile piece of flesh that has no use breathing the air that fills his lungs?"

A small smile formed on his bloody chapped lips, "Put like that he does not sound too…" The rest trailed off as he could not find the word to describe what he wanted to say.

Again her eyes lit up with amusement, "Would you like to repay him for the way that he treated you?"

For a moment, Ean didn't breath, "If it were possible. But I don't see how. After being here and paying for my father's crimes…" His head drooped once more, "I am unable to more than stand and breath. I am no threat to anyone."

"I see." Her voice which had been breezy turned cold and bitter before she took a single breath to calm herself once more. "And what were the crimes your father committed that he could not pay for himself?"

"He died defending the king before this one. I was told that alone was treason. My punishment for living was being whipped with a tack that was set on fire. After I healed, I was too- forced to work here taking care of the concubines. If they were not ready for the king I was beaten in their place. After ten years I tossed out into the streets." He looked at her once more. I have no skill to be more than a burden."

She kissed the crown of his head, "You have more skill than you think. I will find something that will suit you.

Standing up her enchantment retook him as she spoke to the others one at a time before stopping before Alexander. Slowly he glanced up at her not understand what else she would require from him.

"You found those with loyal hearts. I will reward them and they will be my guards. History will record them as the fallen none shall ever know it was me who descended upon this place."

Alexander shook his head in confusion, "I don't understand?"

"I know you don't which is why I shall show you." As she turned back to her throne she finished her spell. "Gentlemen, please rise." She didn't need to turn to face than to hear the rustling of their clothes as they stood. She didn't need to turn to know the girl who she hasn't spoken too still stayed on her knees. "You have shown me the depths of your souls. For your honesty, I shall reward you. You will be the first to benefit from my kindness. But know this for as long as you breathe if you try to turn against me, you will know pain for a thousand years. Do you wish to see my kindness if not you may leave knowing I will never grant this gift again."

A choice. Trust this creature or flee. The six of them exchanged looks with one another before Ean stood as tall as he could make himself. "I'm tired of living in fear. If the angel that stands before us is willing to have me… I'm her's to have in any way she sees fit."

Primitiva tilted her head, "Angel? Is that what you think I am?"

Ean turned to face her, "I know nothing else that had mystical powers and wings. Well, I do, but you do not seem malevolent. For if you were we would all be dead before now."

"My darling, I am no angel. I am Fey. I am all knowing and all powerful. I am a god, even among my people. No, my dear, I am no angel, but I am not malevolent either. Nor do I wish to be."

"I will still call you my angel. The one that fell from the sky and saved us all."

Not understanding what she was feeling she only nodded in agreement before taking her seat. "Each of you has different desires and skills. Each of you has had similar experiences yet they differ just enough to be unique. Because of that, each gift I bestow will be an example of what I can do should I choose and also encapsulate your uniqueness. Who among you shall be first?"

Seeing the concern in each of their faces Nicco stepped forward, "I will show my brothers that they nothing to fear."

"Very well, step forward and receive your gift."

One last glance over his shoulder, then he stood at the base of the dais, "What should I call you?"

"From this day forth you shall know me as Primitiva; your queen and absolute ruler without question. Do you accept?"

He had been conned like this as a child… they all have… yet there were no guards here with whips or tacks to beat them until they submitted. It was just her. The Fey… the goddess. "I accept."

A fine black mist clung to his muddied boot and slowly climbed his legs. Slowly encasing his chest and arms. Lastly, his head. He stood blinking at her breathing in the mist unsure of what was going to happen next. Then she spoke her voice as clear as thunder.

"You have protected those who you could. You used poison when no other means were available. For this, I grant you the gifts of strength and poison. The gift of speed and the ability to go unnoticed. Being able to transform into the mist that now surrounds you. You will be the first of your kind. The first King of the Eostre. Your skin will be impenetrable by any means from either those who live these lands now and those from my realm. Do you accept?" Or at least those from her realm that she knew about. It was still possible that some held weapons or ability that were still unknown to her.

His eyes locked with hers as his breathing became rapid. "Yes."

"Very well. I bestow you your gift."

In a breath, the mist tore into his flesh, yet it didn't hurt despite the blood running to the red floor. At least not till his bones snapped. Then he tried to scream, finding he had no voice. Then he could no longer see beyond the mist. No longer understood anything. Just accepted this as death.

Sitting once again on the dias she watched, knowing the others in this room could not see anything that she didn't wish for them too. They didn't see their friend being ripped into tiny pieces. Torn apart cell by cell. Didn't see his red lifeblood pooling onto the stone floor. No, they couldn't even hear his screams. She was giving him a life where he would be her greatest protector. Her champion yet it was heart wrenching to watch him struggle with the pain.

But it would be over soon. Another minute and his screaming cease. A breath more than she could see his skin sparkling as her power was being infused into him. Another heartbeat, then two and his pale skin turned almost a honeyed tan and his clothing replaced with a black pair of dress pants and wine red shirt and black overcoat. Finally, a ring of gold was left on his right forefinger as the mist subsided. "Much better I think." Then she smiled as his hair was no longer covered in filth, but permanently the color of the deep earth. "What do you think?"

Nicco studied his hands. Not a crack nor callus. His tongue feeling several rows of teeth. He could almost feel where the poison would come from if he should bite down. "Thank you, my queen, for this gift. I am your loyal servant." Slowly he knelt before her the memory of the pain still apparent in his movement.

"Rise. And take your position as the defender of all who I now rule over."

Carefully, he climbed the three steps and stood behind her, his hunter-green eyes skimming over the others.

Watching Nicco transform from a dirt covered former slave to what now stood before them Ean slid forward. "My Queen?"

"Are you ready to join your brother?" Not brother by blood, but brother through the bond that they all now shared.

"I am if you will allow it."

"Very well." This time, she stood and circled him. "The fire could not take you as a child. Nor could it completely break you. From now on the flames will be yours to command. Both natural and mystical. But I don't think that will be enough. You are observant and see things most pretend not to. I grant you the gift of foresight. You will need to nurture this gift as it does not come easily to master." She made another small circlet around him. She didn't want to cause him pain, even if only for a minute... even if the memory would fade long before he left this room... yet... Red mist surrounded him, "Do you accept?"

"Yes, my queen. With all that I am, I accept."

"Very well from this day forth you will be known as a Draken. Aside from Eostre, none shall be more powerful than you. None shall ever be able to harm your flesh. You will be a master huntsman able to smell even the lightest of scents. I grant this to you my Ean the first King of the Draken kind."

The red mist overtook him without a second thought. Turning into him with a savageness that it hadn't with Nicco. Overtaking him before he could even begin to scream. Too quickly his fingers began to extend and become plump long black nails that belonged to a large bird attached themselves. Scales covered every inch if flesh. Pointed spines ran down his back each as poisonous as the next. Fangs that any canine would be proud of filled his mouth and two long horns that were completely bovine protruded from his skull. Unlike Nicco he had not a stitch of clothing to hide the fact that he was male. "My queen."

Gone was his soft hair replaced by a golden fur going from his first spine to the top of his head. Gone was his soft scared voice and replaced with a deeply cultivated one that would scare even the sound of fighters. One day she would need to see if he could produce fire or simple control it. "Arise, and take your position as my tracker… my huntsman."

Shyly he stood all too conscious of what he was no longer wearing.

"Do not be shy. You may be the first but I assure you, you will not the only one. None of your kind will have use for simple coverings. They would only impede your movements…"

Keeping his eyes low Ean shyly asked, "Perhaps a cloth just to cover the parts I do not wish seen?"

She let out a breath of air, "Fine. If you must see for yourself I will not stop you." A moment later he was covered with a bit of cloth… just enough to cover his parts he did not wish seen.

The others were easier. One became her Fey of the dark. Black hair that was the color of the night sky. His wings translucent yet strong. And his ability to many to say, but they would be used to be the balance between the others. Unable to harm them, but still able to create terrifying creatures all his own. Creatures that nightmares were created from and just as real as he was.

Another, a minor Fey for he didn't want to be noticed. He wanted to serve her in any way she deemed fit, but he didn't want some great power or mutation of the flesh. Understanding she granted him with the gift of knowledge. He would be her scribe and historian. His sole job recording history as it has already happened and what unfolded for as long as he lived. His only other gift was the ability to grant others his gift. He was the last to be transformed.

The last before Alexander. The man who would be her consort.

The Fallen

CHAPTER 9:

STARLIS

Starlis stared out of her bedroom window watching the people of Lunaista mulling about as they did every day. But today there was something more in the air. Anticipation mixed with fear and sorrow. Drawing her sheer curtains closed, she turned from the window. She had always thought, having windows in a wall when you could see through the walls was just plain ridiculous… and in truth she still did. But being queen, she was finding so much more that has been just plain ludicrous that the windows didn't matter much to her.

Closing her eyes, she took a deep breath to steady herself.

Today she was going to do the most important thing she would ever do as queen. Or so her mother had once said. Today she would begin the Culling, the ritual where she would choose a male to be her consort. As queen, she could choose anyone that she wanted.

Anyone who could last through the Culling as well as the trials that would proceed. It wouldn't matter if they had given their heart to another. It didn't matter if they were already fathers or if they had no desire to be with a female. She could choose them and in a sense force them to do whatever gave her the most pleasure.

Her stomach turned at the thought. How could she force someone to be with her if they didn't want her? Her mother had, and it was no secret that their father despised her as a woman, but served her because he was bound to her. If he had refused it would have been a great shame on his family, both his parents and his sister who because of the union had been able to marry a man who was more powerful than she had been. Something that was normally frowned upon.

After all, everyone knew it was the females of Lunaista who wielded the true powers.

Another breath and she thought back to what her mother had told her about the Culling. Pacifically the rules and traditions. All men born within two hundred years, both before her birth and afterward were required to appear before her. They would stand in rows of ten, both because it was easier to keep track of them and also their family could see where their loved one was at any given time. After the opening speech was given the men would be required to disrobe. Not uncommon since Fey men rarely wore much in the way of clothing anyways. Really most just wore a covering over their male parts for modesty more than anything else.

She would then look at each of the men. Not so much as an appearance since she could change anything she didn't like about them once she narrowed it down to who would enter the trials. But feel their strength and the depth of their abilities. A queen needed a consort that was strong both physically and emotionally. As well as having a strong ability to make strong children.

"My queen?"

Opening her eyes, she smiled at her new maid. She didn't remember her name but since Primitiva was no longer part of the palace the girl wanted to work here. "Yes?"

"The men are gathered."

"Very well. I shall be but a moment." Watching the young girl vanish from view she turned back to her window. Those who were not a part of the Culling were all wearing full coverings, so very little of their flesh was shown. Even the women were in their finest dresses. This too was tradition and observed very carefully.

Standing on the balcony overlooking the main square Starlis let her eyes take in the rows of men all dressed exactly the same. Long white robes with gold trim. Their right hand holding the clasp at their neck while their left hung at their sides. How many of them really wanted to be here? How many already had given their hearts to another? How many lives were going to be torn apart today?

First tradition. Then she could give her directions.

Holding her head up high she let her golden hair tumbled down her back. "Citizens of Lunaista let us begin the Culling." The crowds clapped happily even though she was picking up on the sadness of so many. "As tradition states, I will choose a consort from those who stand before me today. Gentlemen, thank you for volunteering I am pleased to see so many eager to bring honor to your families."

It was a lie and everyone knew it. These men did not volunteer to be here… they had little choice. They could stand here and hope something about them made her look else were for a mate, or they could refuse and bring shame to their families. The shame that would last until the next Culling. The shame that would be carried to every member who was related by blood. The children would not be permitted to play or be near other children. The adults would be forced from their homes to live in the undesired area of the star. A place that was cold and saw only darkness. No everyone here would rather face the trials, then force their family to carry the burden of shame for centuries.

"Of those who stand before me if you have already chosen a mate and given them your heart you are dismissed from the Culling without shame. Please leave the lines."

A wave of relief hit her fast as several of the men hurried over to their loved ones. For a moment, she watched as a couple tore out their hearts from their chest and gave it to their mate. Then she watched as their mate's hearts were deeply embedded in their own chest. They would always belong together. Two bodies, but one soul. When one died so too would the other. They would feed the catacombs together.

"Those of you who are left, please reform the lines."

The rustling of cloth was the only sound as the men took new positions. Nearly half of the men had been freed from this Culling. Now for the hard part. The final speech before she began to search for those who may finish the trials. "Before you disrobe know this. Until the trials are finished and I have found the one who is to be my consort, you are forbidden to speak unless directed to do so by me. Those who are dismissed from this moment will still be held to the rules of the Culling until the end. Even if I dismiss you I can recall you at any time that I see fit. Do you accept?"

"Yes, your grace." A chorus of voices said nearly in unison. From where she stood, she could not hear one that sounded sincere.

Spreading her translucent goldened wings she glided down from the balcony. "Then I affirm that this Culling has officially begun. Please disrobe."

Carefully, she stepped up to the first not really paying attention to his physical body… After all, this wasn't about the body but the power they could wield. The emotional strength that they possessed. And their willingness to follow orders regardless of what those orders may be. Gazing into his eyes, she felt his power. Strong and waiting to be used. Softly she spoke, "Kneel."

Without hesitation, he took a knee and bowed his head.

Making her way through the first row she found one more that appealed to her and ordered him to kneel. Then she glanced down the endless rows. Even after dismissing more than half of the men there were still close to a thousand of them waiting to be either affirmed or dismissed. Their families all hoping they would be chosen. Others hoping they would be cast aside. If she continued this way it would take days to look at each one. Days and she wanted this over as soon as she could.

Taking to the sky, she flew up as far as she dared. Flew up just far enough to be able to see the lines of the men standing still facing forward… none daring to gaze up to see what she was doing. Not even those who were standing aside to watch were daring to gaze upon her. She was the queen and she could whatever she wished. She could strike them all down if she pleased. Turn them into creatures of her own imagination. She could do anything and none would dare question her.

If her dear sister were here as queen, she would have no trouble testing those who would serve her. She would have no trouble seeing if they were worthy by inflicting pain both mental and physical. No, Primitiva would draw this out for day's even months until she found a male that she could tolerate. Perhaps one that would add to her own powers and strengths.

She was not her sister. And she had no desire to drag this out longer than she needed to.

Still focusing on the men, she took a deep breath, then called on her powers to show her the strongest of those there. Called on her strength to find those who could feed the catacombs when they were offered as tribute. Golden flecks of dust fell from the sky turning to light as they touch the skin of those who could wield great power. The light then encasing them. A golden glow radiating just a breath above their skin.

Drawing upon another of her powers she spoke, knowing every word that she spoke would be heard in the head of every Fey that dwelled on Lunaista, "Hear me, those of you that now bare my mark remain where you are. All others return to your homes. There is nothing left to see here."

She waited until all her citizens hastily made way to their homes. Waited until the men who didn't bear her mark were escorted by the sentries, that belonged to the crown, to some place that they would be housed until a consort had been found. Gliding back down to her spot in front of the man she turned sharply to face the castle. "Get your robes on, I have no desire to see your flesh now. Then follow me. Tonight you dine with your family. In the morn, we will begin the trials."

The dining hall was filled with several scores of round tables all set for several guests. Another silly tradition if you asked her… but it was the social event of the century and one every family looked forward to. It was the last night they would see their son. Their brother or whatever these men were to their family… Well, the last time before the trials. It was hardly a secret that once a man entered, he was never the same. Though the reason for the change was a closely guarded secret. One that no one save that of the queen was permitted to discuss.

Knowing the men were still behind her, she spoke as clearly as she could, "Sit where you choose. Members of your family will join you soon. For this one event, you are permitted to speak, but only to those who are of blood relation. Talking among yourselves is prohibited." This too she understood. The ones that wanted to be here could make deals with the ones that didn't so that they looked better during the trials. Not that it ever worked, but still, why give them the illusion of controlling the outcome when in truth they didn't.

Taking her place on the royal platform so she could see all those who were dining she took her place. Under normal circumstances, her mother would be here as the dowager queen. As would her father. Under normal circumstances, this would be their last night with her in Lunaista before leaving to live out the rest of their days on Pallas. But these were not normal circumstances. Since they hadn't sacrificed her sister to be a tribute… not that she would have been anyways… her father had been offered up. And her mother instead of facing the Azai like she would have done had she married Primitiva off to the highest bidder… She had offered herself as a second tribute.

So instead of having her mother's company she sat by herself bracing for the flood of raw emotions that was about to come through the doors. Proud parents. Worried sibling. Mothers worried that their sons would do something to dishonor the family. Fathers who, although looking calm were frightfully unnerved at being in the palace. Several remembering the last time and not liking that their sons were going to be subjected to the same cruelty.

All of this she felt. Heard within her own mind. Each voice… each thought as loud as it had been spoken to her.

She gave a moment for the relatives to be seated before speaking, "Welcome to the feast. Please speak quietly among yourselves as you enjoy the best that the palace has to offer. After tonight's meal I will ask one person from your family, please help the chosen ready themselves for the morrow. The guards will instruct you after the rest of your family has left." A shiver went through her. One of the fathers she couldn't tell whose… was having a harder time being here than the rest. What had her mother done to the men that after a century the mental wound was still so fresh?

Not a question she could get an answer to. Nor one that she wanted if she could.

Only partly paying attention to her own meal, she listened to the voices. "Do what she asks without question." "Do whatever it takes to be chosen." "There is no shame in not finishing." "Do not let your family down." "Pain is all relative learn to ignore it."

The last one shocked her. Even more that it was a father who had said it, when all about the Culling was forbidden to be discussed. She could have him punished for the remark… but she wouldn't. But it did give her an idea of the trial of emotional pain.

Slowly the families started to thin out as they finished their meals. Finally, it was only the hundred or so men and one family member left behind. For most, it was their mother… most but not all. In one case, it was a younger sister. An odd choice but acceptable. And in the other a father. The ones whose thoughts were filled with worry and understanding of what was about to take place.

"Guards, please show the men to where they will be staying tonight. And instruct their family member on what is to be done."

Her instructions had been simple, unlike the list that her mother had suggested. She had simply told the guards that she wanted the men properly bathed. Their nails trimmed, hair shaved… It would be better than them looking un-kept during the trials… then they were to be tucked into bed. It was a stark contrast to the list her mother had left for her as suggestions.

It had included. Scrubbing them free of the first layer of flesh. Removing the nails. Using a collar so even if they wanted to, they could not speak. There was more but they had been too vile to even read let alone remember. She knew that her mother was fond of cruelty, but that was too much for her to take in… mostly because it made her wonder things that she didn't want to know about the on goings between her parents.

Was her father punished when he disagreed with her mother? Did she keep her pet… her lover that everyone was forbidden to speak to… just so she could practice her cruelty? Or did she care even a little about either man?

When she entered the interior courtyard, the men were already in position. Yesterday they had been full of nervousness… now after a decent night's sleep and full bellies, they all seemed ready to begin… they all had a false sense that whatever they were about to face was not going to be too hard. Just hard enough to weed out the weak. Just hard enough so a consort could be found and possible an alternate.

She wished this could be as easy as they were hoping but the laws dictated otherwise.

"Gentlemen, please kneel as I explain the trials and give my final instructions before we begin." They all looked confused but did as she had asked. Squaring her shoulders, she began, "The trials are not set by me but the Azai. I have no control over what you are about to face, but I will try to make this as quick as I can. For any reason, you cannot complete the task given to you, know that it does not mean shame for your families. I see no reason to punish you or them for something none of us can control."

She took another breath, "The trials will test several things the order is up to me. I have decided on the easiest first, then working to the hardest. You will be tested on combat skills with the use of weapons. I will allow a day for you to adjust to your surroundings. You will then be paired randomly. You will be allowed to lose one battle each. The second you will be removed from the trials. Know this, half of you will be leaving within two days."

They couldn't speak, but they understood something she didn't say. They could stop the match and forfeit or possibly die. It was their choice. One of few.

"Next, you will be tested on your ability. After that loyalty to the crown. This will be an emotionally tasking test as well as a grueling physical one as well. If you have any doubt about completing these tasks, please stand now and you will be dismissed without punishment."

None of them stood. It would seem they all wanted this chance. Not for themselves for the consort had little say in anything, but it would give their families more rights. And that was something they all wanted.

"Very well. Let us begin." She turned to face an arched doorway, then closed her eyes. As she did the ground began to shift and stairs lead down into the furthest depth of star. This was the one place that held no natural light. The one place that wasn't see through. And the only place where the trials could be held without prying eyes.

Not turning to the men she understood their unease. Fey were never enclosed somewhere that they couldn't see the outside world. They were rarely anyplace that didn't have some kind of natural light. And they were never allowed to be below the ground. Or at least that was how for those who lived on this star.

Calling over her shoulder, she very calmly spoke, "Follow me."

The room was large enough to accommodate the whole populous of Lunisista. Or so she could assume.

There were several rooms... cells for the men to rest. Each would be assigned one tonight. Then, as the bulk of the were thinned out they would be clustered closer together. Lighting a torch she allowed the glow to fill the room. Allowed for the men to see the weapons that they could use.

Swords, both single edged and double edge. Some longer than their arms some short for closer contact. Maces hung on the wall. Whips coiled on tables. Throwing knives and several other things that she had no idea what they were or how they could be used. But she would bet the men did. After all, men were trained from the time that they could stand on how to fight.

Not a useful skill since there had been no fighting for well over a hundred generations. But still, something they were taught, regardless if they needed to or not. Taught because it was really the only way to show physical strength.

"You will have today become acquainted with your surroundings. The weapons are off limits until you are chosen to show your skill." She turned slightly to the guards who were moving slowly around the room wands of lightning held in their hands just in case one of the men tried anything foolish. "Guards please show the men their rooms."As she turned to leave, she hesitated, "For this trial, a covering will be given for your modesty."

She was back upstairs before the men were placed into their tiny cells.

Not really paying much attention to much of anything she turned a corner and bumped into the man who had been her mother's pet... her lover as it were. "Wrage?" He flinched at the sound of his name... not his true name but the only one he had been allowed to be called since the culling. When he didn't speak she continued, "I'm sorry I wasn't paying attention to where I was going."

He nodded once and took a step back. Not uncommon since he rarely spoke. Then he took a deep breath, 'You are gracious my queen."

She had almost asked him about where he was going, but refrained from doing so. Instead, she gazed into his Sunkissed eyes. He seemed more relaxed than he had ever been before. "Please walk with me."

"My queen?"

She could see the fear in his eyes so she tried to reassure him, "You are the only person I can ask about my mother's Culling."

For a moment, he froze, not even daring to breathe, "What would you like me to tell you?"

She knew he would rather face being beaten till he passed out rather than speak about this, but he would because as queen it was her right to have any question answered. "Start with the physical test. What did my mother do."?

"During the physical test half of the men died. We fought to the death. One match each. If any cried out during the test the match was called. The victor would have to slowly kill his opponent. If the victor refused, he joined his match in death. The bodies were taken to the catacombs. The next day we fought with our abilities thankfully not to the death but close to it. Again, we were not allowed to forfeit. We fought or we were fed the catacombs. If we fed the catacombs because of forfeit so too would our families."

She had known her mother was cruel, but this? "Go on."

"From the beginning, your mother made it clear she was taking two men. One would be her consort and the other as a pet. It was her right to do so… we had no say in it."

Placing her small hand on his arm, she softly said, "I understand."

"After we were down to a dozen or so men she pulled us aside and into a private room. We had to demonstrate our worth in the bedroom. Those who pleased her were then paired up and…" He swallowed hard, "… are you sure you want to hear this?"

He was the only one that she had ever asked about the Culling and hearing the emotions clogging his throat, she was sure that she didn't want to hear more… Sill, she had to have something to compare what she was doing to what had been done in the past. "Yes."

Closing his eyes, he nodded, then hugged himself, "We were taken two at a time to see how were would work together. None of us ever wanted to be with her… and certainly, none of us wanted to be with a male." Another paused and he opened his eyes seeing more pity then understanding in them. Still, he continued, " After those who didn't perform as she wanted were sold to other Star Cities. I don't know what happen to them."

"So you and my father…"

"Knew each other very well. Personally, we didn't care one way or another before the Culling. But after if one of us spoke out against her the other was beaten in his place. It was just another barb to our own dislike for one another. But we made sure your mother enjoyed her bedroom games."

"You're glad that she's gone."

"I'm glad I didn't have to go with her to Pallas. Nor with her to be another tribute which I would have if she had married your sister off."

"If you would like to leave the palace I understand."

Now he shook his head, "My family has thought me dead for many years. It would only shame them to know how I had survived."

"If you prefer I can have you taken to another Star City and even paired with a lady of good standing? Perhaps one that would bear you a child?"

"I thank you.. But.. I… if it pleases you your consort may want someone to help him settle in."

"One more thing… the test of loyalty what was it?"

"Kill a member of your family. Not just any family member but the one that had helped prepare you for the trials. The deaths had to last hours and be beyond cruel."

Now she understood why the one father had stayed. He hadn't wanted his son to bear the burden of killing his mother.

CHAPTER 10:

ALEXANDER

Quietly he followed his queen… through the empty halls of the castle. Each step… each breath, feeling like tiny knives beneath his skin. Yet the feeling slowly lessened. Soon he hoped it would be less than a memory. Trying to think back to the events of the last few days he was finding it more difficult. Each was becoming hazy.

Then he focused on those of his new brothers… and his sister. It was no use. All he could remember was that he had known each his entire life. Yet something felt was missing. Some piece of himself that he was searching for… Something but now it didn't seem important.

Then a heavy wooden door open to her touch and a dozen of half-dressed females were laying on large floor pillows and now looking not at her… but at him. He thought he heard a scream, but the women were not moving. They were all still as his queen bestowed them with her gift.

Harpies, Long black hair and beautiful faces. Lean bodies. Wings hiding their arms. Arms that now held clawed hands with deadly talons. Others transforming into sirens. Their hair blonde or red. Breathtaking faces. Their voices able to convince anyone to dive into a pool of water where they would drown. Of course their bodies… why wouldn't someone follow them into the water? They were the embodiment of every man's dreams.

Then the room filled with others… the goddess called them fairies or elves. The fairies had wings where the elves did not. Each unique and all now solely belonging to the goddess… to his queen.

"My queen?" Finally finding his voice after the last of the females were transformed.

Clapping her hands cheerfully Primitiva asked, "Are my darlings, not wonderful?"

"I am pleased that you are pleased." And in truth, he was he just could understand why. "Something is troubling me?"

Slowly she stood before him and placed her hand upon his cheek. "You are fighting my gift. You will only draw out the pain. Embrace it and the world as you know it will be whatever I make it."

He couldn't embrace it, not yet. Not with the king still living. Not with his family on their way from their own kingdoms. "There is much that still needs to be addressed. Please forgive me, I do not wish to…"

Her finger pressed against his lips. "It is not the time to deal with those who have harmed you. Rest assured they will be handled soon… "She snapped her head to the far wall… "… As I was saying soon. Come now my Alec, it is time to meet the former king. Have your brothers join us."

"Of course, my queen. I shall be but a moment."

Quickly he made his way to where they had left the others. As he opened the door, he watched his sister play with a vine that she was creating. "The queen requires us to join her. The former Royal family has just arrived."

Slowly Mary glanced up, "Should I remain here?"

"She only requested our brothers."

Nicco glided off of the platform, "We should not keep the Queen waiting."

As Nicco glided by, he grabbed his arm, then looked deep into those soulless eyes, "What game are you playing Nicco?"

"Game? Me? Why would I try? The queen knows every move we make before we make it. However, I am starving and this room has no food that can see."

Slowly he let go of the arm, "I'll be watching you."

A slow, sly smile curved Nicco's lips, "And what would you do to stop me? The queen granted me a greater gift than yours… obviously, she wanted me as her weapon and you for a good tumble in the bed." With that, he transformed into a fine mist and disappeared from the room."

Mary rolled her eyes, but still offered her advice,"You shouldn't try him… his lust for fresh blood drives him more than any other. I doubt he would spare you even if the queen does forbid it."

Taking a breath Alexander nodded, "I don't trust him…" yet was left unsaid hanging in the air like an unspoken feeling of foreboding, "… I have no reason not to."

Karnack, the queen's scribe, stepped forward patting Alec on his shoulder, "Of course, you do. Out of us here Nicco is probably the only other one who will compete for the queen's affection."

"Perhaps I should ask her to find him a bride."

Ean smiled, then slowly stepped forward, "That would be a wonderful Idea."

The Fallen

CHAPTER 11:

PRIMITIVA

Metal clanged as armed guards entered the castle. An angry voice barked orders from inside the heart of the castle. And men argued. All the while Primitiva smiled as she listened. These men had little in the way of wits and much in the way of temper.

Lazily she flipped through the pages of a book that she had found during her exploration of this castle. The castle itself would need to be remade, but what she had found inside… written words… books Alec had called them… those she would keep. Many of them like this one gave her ideas on what to turn people into. Those who would be her high-born citizens and those who would serve those who belonged to the crown. Of course, some would remain human. She just simply couldn't transform every living person into a beautiful fallen creature…

Well, she could, but why would she?

Feeling her first creations drawing near she smiled. It would figure Nicco would be the first to arrive. Once he reformed into a solid mass he took a knee, "My queen?"

Her fingers run through his black hair, "You are a trouble maker. I see it in your soul."

"Would you have me be something else?"

She shook her head, "After today we will find something suitable for you to do with all your time. But for today… You will not do anything without my approval. Is that understood?"

"Yes, my queen."

"Good. Now stand the others are arriving."

She waited for only a heartbeat before after they came into view before addressing them, "You will remain here until I summon you." She paused letting her gaze settle on Nicco, "Quitely."

"Yes, my queen." They all said in unison.

Pushing the doors to where the former royal family had gathered Primitiva Glided into the room. In an instant, all of the arguings ceased and one of the other kings growled, "Guards cease her."

"Oh come now, do you really wish to play mindless games?"

Quickly the armed guards surrounded her their silver swords held tightly in their hands. "Kneel wrench."

"Kneel? Yes, That sounds like a fabulous idea." With a flick of her hand, all of the guards knelt before her. She gave the others a moment to realize what she was before stepping over the men who no blocked her path. The brother of thing that she had seen last night took a step back in horror. Thinking he was trying to escape the room filled with thunder. Bolts of lighting, blocking every exit. "Now, perhaps I should ruxplain why you are all here."

"You, what are you?"

"Some call me goddess and others Queen. You may call me your grace. I do like the sound of that."

In a breath, he pulled his sword from its hilt and charged at her. Unfazed, she yawned, then he froze, unable to move more than breath and blink. "I think I have had enough of mere humans trying to pull a sword on me." A snap of her fingers and all the swords that were held turned into a puddle of melted silver cooling on the hard stone floor. "There, much better."

Slowly the black mist filled the room and with it the lungs of the human men who had been frozen by her. A few coughed as the mist clogged their throats, others tried not to breathe at all. Useless because there was no way for them to escape the mist. One by one each subcommand to her power and helplessly submitted to her orders.

"Now, Those of you who claim to be rulers you will go and address your subjects. All that was yours, you will give to me. You will tell them… " She paused needing to have something plausible to tell the citizens so they would not fear her but also do as she told them. Turning, she let the heavy doors once again open, "My darlings, please enter I am in need of your counsel."

Their eyes barely scanned the room before they kneeled, "How may we be of service, Goddess?"

"You know the human race… What should be told to them so they will follow my orders and not try to harm me?" Not that any of them could but why shed their blood if she didn't need to?

As the scribe, Karnack slowly approached as he said, "I may have a suggestion, my queen."

"Ah yes, please enlighten me?"

"Since you are a goddess, perhaps you should play into it. You fell from the sky to deliver them from these worthless creatures who have controlled them for far too long?"

"Ah yes, that does sound about right." Turning back to her captives, "You will tell those who live within your realms that a goddess has come to your realm. She is displeased with how her children have been treated and is here to take back what had been created so many millennia back. Then will introduce me as the goddess Primitiva."

A day later King Gregor stepped foot onto his balcony of burnt stone. "People of Westernesse stand before me, your king."

Slowly the city square started to fill with people. No-one making so much as a single murmur of speculation about whatever the announcement could be. None daring to look directly at the king but at the castle walls that stood before them.

"As king, it is my sole job to see to the comfort and discipline of you, my children. But is would seem one thinks that I do not take pride in my responsibility and has come to take back what is rightfully theirs."

The crowd gasped. How would be so foolish to challenge the king?

"After speaking to this person, it would appear that they are right and I have no recourse but to give them my throne and this kingdom. Please welcome the Goddess

Primitiva." He didn't step aside, but looked into the sky to the silver dragon that was lazily gliding down to the castle walls.

As it landed just above the balcony on the castle walls she glided gown the few feet to where the now former king stood. "Citizens of… what did you call this place again?"

"Westernesse, Goddess."

"Westernesse? What a horrible name for a city. As of this moment, this city will be called Night. This shall be the largest city in is now my realm."

Slowly the citizens began to kneel understanding the woman who stood before them now was more menacing than the king that they had been just dispatched before their eyes.

"To show you my powers let us being with this creature who called himself a king." She turned to face him, letting him see a cruel smile form on her lips. "You are an abomination of flesh and I do not grant you a gift. Instead, I grant you a life of a monster so hideous that you are only to be kept in the mines working until the day you no longer draw breath. Leave the mines and you become food for my darlings. "

Not waiting for him to reply a brown and green mist overtook him. The sound of bones snapping echoed throughout the city square as his screams turned to the growling snapping of jaws. When the mist subsided He stood nearly twice her height. His skin, thick with slim now the color of pond muck. Only four teeth remaining in his mouth and those overgrown and pointed. Only his eyes were left untouched.

"Any who diss obey me will be turned into a troll and enslaved in the mines searching for treasures. The rest of you know this those who serve me well will be rewarded with kindness and possibly a life much better than most. Those who wish not to become one of my favorites… do so at your own discretion. I will not waste my gifts on those who don't deserve them."

CHAPTER 12:

STARLIS

Sitting in the dining hall Starlis took a deep breath, today they would begin the first trial. Today she would dismiss half of the men to their families. Looking over her notes that she had started last night she almost missed that someone was watching her. Not the maid who should be clearing her morning dishes, but an older man.

Lifting her head just enough to really see who was watching her, then quickly she got to her feet. "My lord forgives me, I was not informed that you were here."

Slowly he took a step into the room, "I did not wish for you to know. Lest until I was able to get a good feel of this Star City." When he was standing at the head of her table, he growled, "I do not like what I see here. I expected more from your mother given her choices during the trials. I see now I should have kept a closer watch on her."

"I don't understand my lord?"

"Perhaps it would be best to show you. Since you have never been to the other cities, it is possible you don't know what is wrong with this one."

"Thank you, your grace." She paused, "May I bring my daughter?"

"Daughter? I hardly think a child born from mist qualifies as a daughter, however, seeing she has more natural ability than you, my dear, I will allow for her to rein when it is time. Where or not you will be still ruling Lunaista… Well, that is to be seen."

He would remove her… Why she hadn't done anything wrong. At least to her knowledge she hadn't. Swallowing hard she tried to smile, "Any guidance you can offer would be appreciated."

Narrowing his lava red eyes Azai hissed, "You chose those who will attend the trial." Not a question but confirmation.

"I have. Those who will undergo the trials are waiting for me below ground."

"Good. Intrust the guards to feed them. The silence will do them good." Then he turned leaving her once again alone.

The coach that was waiting was much bigger than anything she had ever seen before. So big in fact, that it needed three messengers to pull it rather than the single messenger that every other tribute coach that was currently in circulation had needed. "Your coach is very grand."

"And why should it not be? Am I not the most powerful Fey in all of the Star Cities?"

"Yes, my lord, I only meant to compliment your taste in travel."

Slowly he leaned forward, "Because your mother did not raise you properly I will allow you some time to learn what it means to be a royal Fey. Your first lesson is this; say what you mean and mean what you say. I will not tolerate this lackadaisical attitude that your mother allowed. It is distasteful. It is also why when I leave Lunaista I will be taking the child with me. Lest she will be well trained before taking over such a pitiful Star City."

The coach landed with a gentleness that she couldn't have imagined yet, just sitting there her simple golden dress was already becoming wet with perspiration. "May I ask what Star City, this is?"

"Soraista. It is the closest Star City to Pallas. But not the hottest."

After he exited the coach, she collected herself before following. He was the Azia… it stood to reason he would be grumpy. Then again, he could be testing her. Convincing herself that this was just a silly test she took a single step outside the coach and froze. There were men working… building something… with their hands and brute strength. Others… guards hovering just above the workers a lighting staff in one hand and a long whip in the other. Not moving her eyes watched as the men moved quickly placing some kind of gray blocks into place. Then the sound of a whip hissing through the air made her turn to the sound just as it hit the bare back of a worker who had not been moving fast enough.

What a horrible place. Horrible indeed.

Not that she would say that but think it… yes, her thoughts were her own.

Hurrying she caught up with Azia who was holding Avyanna like she was his very own.

The palace of Soraista was not what she had expected. Where her own palace was nearly completely see through this one was made of the same gray stone blocks and a river of red liquid oozing down the south wall and into a river that surrounding the palace.

"Be careful my dear your skin is not immune to the touch of the lava."

Lava? Oh, the red liquid. Saying nothing, she just nodded and followed him inside.

The queen was on her throne A dress of white that barely covered anything at all. Her tan belly completely bare and her wings… as red as the flames and was being carefully rubbed by what she assumed was her consort. Slowly the queen opened her eyes, "Ah, My lord, I was wondering when you were going to come indulge in the hot springs. They are extra hot right now."

"Good. You consort can tend to me while I soak. In the mean time tell Queen Starlis about the trials. I recall them adequate for what you had to work with. And find her a proper gift."

"Very well. Aden, show the Azia to the hot spring. And have one of my pets report to the Undercity."

Not speaking a word he bowed slightly before following the Azia to the deeper part of the palace.

It wasn't until they were alone the queen stood up and stretched, "Well, we might as well get this over and done with so I can get on with my day." She paused, "Since we are both queens you may call me Sera."

With a slight nod of her head, Starlis smiled as she forced out, "A pleasure."

"Doubtful, but we shall see." Stepping to the main corridor, she called back, "Do you like your pet meat or more boney?"

For a moment she hesitated, "I don't understand?"

"Skinny or muscular?"

"Muscular I guess? I have never really thought about it before." *What does that have to do with anything?* She wondered.

"By the gods, what did your mother teach you all theses years?"

Now her smile was not forced, "Apparently not very much. And what she did teach is not appealing to the Azia."

The Undercity was just that. An entire city under the first. Except this was shrouded in darkness. "This place is massive."

"It is the same size as the city above. The unattached males dwell here. When I am ready to match them with a female then they are granted access to the above. Those who are royal blood are trained as guards. The rest as workers. They are all trained in how to best pleasure a woman." Sare turned slightly, "Now before we find a proper gift as the Azia suggested let us begin with the trials.

Sera paused briefly before starting again, "Now for mine, I started with strength and ability. Doing both at the same time, let me also see their temperament. We started off with the men in a circle each facing the others back then they were to tear the wings from the man in front of them until they came free from the flesh."

Starlis' eyes widened. The pain the men would have gone through…

"After aft that we started the combat part. Of course, they weren't allowed to kill one another. For the most part, they didn't. The ones who lost became gifts for the other royals who were ascending. At any given time there are at least fifty."

Well, that explained the trading of unworthy men. But didn't explain why, if what Sare was saying was true, why her mother only had one pet. "My mother didn't have any gifts."

"Oh, I know. Neither did she send any out. Since she killed the unworthy ones no-one was going to send her a pet."

"I never knew that."

"Your mother's Culling was legendary. It also sets the boundaries of what was tolerated and what was not. Such as killing the unworthy is not whereas making sure they can tend whatever royal may visit is."

"What do you mean whatever royal may visit?"

"We do travel my dear and it is customary for the pets of the other royal's choosing to tend to them while they visit. It's best if the pet is versed in massage, as well in other things."

Starlis nodded once already having a bad thought about what those other things maybe.

The Fallen

TWO THOUSAND YEARS BEFORE THE GREAT WAR.

"War is coming. Death and destruction left in its wake. To do nothing all will be lost. To choose a side nearly impossible. Now is not the time to end this war. Too many want power that they cannot control. The one who will wield that power not yet born. I see this but am unable to stop what is about to happen. I just pray my choices are correct."

-Private Journal of Primitiva

CHAPTER 13:

ALEC

Alec rolled to his side as he lazily opened his eyes. The room was dark and chilly, but it was the shadowy figure standing on the balcony that forced him to crawl out of bed and see why his queen was standing outside when the weather was starting to turn cold. Carefully, he came up behind her. As he folded his golden wings around her, he kissed her neck softly, "What's troubling you?"

For a moment, she didn't answer her gaze fixed on something only she could see. After several moments, she leaned back against his bare chest and shivered. "Another royal Fey has ascended."

Ah, so it was to be one of those nights. He let his eyes watch the streaks of white light crossing the sky. Humans called them shooting stars… The Fey knew the truth. They were messengers taking the tributes to the Star Cities. At least twice a year or sometimes more if the sky was clear, you could see them racing across the dark sky. This was the first time in nearly a hundred years that he had witnessed so many at one time. "Do you worry about your sister?"

Not yet facing him, she remained silent for far too long. Finally, she let out a sigh, "No. Starlis is still queen. How, I do not know… but this? It is not from my home. Still, something feels off about this ascension. There are too many messengers. This cannot be just from a single Star City unless Azia has now ordered that the royal pets be sacrificed as well. But that would make little sense. Then again, nothing about his rule has ever made sense."

"I don't understand." And he didn't. Prim rarely rambled and when she did… not even the handful of times that he could remember, she would still be clear with her words. She would still be able to say the words that she needed so that he might understand some of what she was trying to say.

She took a deep breathtaking comfort in his embrace, then slowly started to explain, "I still can see what happens within a few of the Star Cities. My home is one of them. No, whatever is going now is from one of the outer stars. From here it is too far away for me to see." That wasn't entirely true, but she had never hinted about the true depths of her abilities. And tonight, was not the night to reveal all that she was.

Most days she spoke in a form that was closer to how the humans still spoke… but her tone… the ways the words seemed forced… No this was different… almost worrisome. Almost like she knew what was going on but was hoping that she was wrong, "Would it help if you returned to your homeland?"

Could she return? It may be possible for her to fly there. Even possible to ride Shesha that far… but if she did it was more likely that she would never return and those who she had cared for all these years would be killed by Azia. "No, When I came to this place I made a choice. If I return now everything here would die."

He held her tighter not so much to comfort her, but to assure himself that she was safe. His eyes still scanned the night sky as he decided on what to say… or do. Choosing not to ask her about her certainty of their deaths if she left, but rather asking about the other worry, he could hear in her voice he carefully asked, "What else is troubling you besides the ascension?"

"I cannot see my daughter. She should be on my home star with my sister yet she is not."

Daughter? What daughter? He almost allowed himself to tense. Almost spun her around demanding answers. Instead, he very calmly whispered, "I didn't know you had a child before coming here."

Still not turning to him she replied as her eyes still searched the stars. "I wanted to know what it felt like to be a mother… so I created a child born from the mist. She is stronger than my sister could ever dream of but only half as powerful as myself. I dared not give her my full strength least someone tried to use her against her family." Taking a deep breath, she continued, "I fear that already may be the case. Or at the very least Azia has taken an interest in her."

He felt betrayed… hurt. How could she have kept this from him? How for nearly a thousand years, could she not tell him that she had a daughter? Not that he could do much about it… but still, she could have told him. "This is why you have never wanted a child… because you already have one?"

Now she turned to him. The hurt in his voice too much for her not to explain, "I did not tell you because it is of little importance. I do not want a child because if I gave you one both Nicco and Ean would too want a child of my blood. Those two are…" She paused, trying to find meaningful words that would describe those she called her first. "… They want what I give you freely. Some things I allow them to indulge in but I do not think I could tell them no if I gave you a child and not them."

Of course, she was right. It was hard enough for him to know when she took the others to her bed. Even if by the title he was only her consort… they still held a piece of her heart. "You could tell them no. You are the queen if you tell them no they will listen." It sounded foolish to hear the words out loud but he may not be given another chance to say them. Then again, he could try to discuss it with the others. It may be easier to get Prim to agree if the others backed him on this single request.

Softly she stroked his cheek, "I will consider …" Hearing something explode in the sky, she quickly turned from him before she could finish her thoughts. "Tell Nicco to meet me in the woods. Now!" Then she dove from the balcony and into the night.

What had she seen? No, he would find out soon enough. Tell Nicco? Fine since he had permission, he could use his thoughts to find him. Not something, that he liked to do, but it was the quickest way to find him. Not to mention the easiest. *Nicco?*

A vision of white sand and waves crashing against large pale rocks came to him following a woman… thin body tan in color stepping up from the waves, moonlight caressing her velvet skin. As she stood, he could see not a stitch of clothing on her body. No wings or anything that said she was a Fey or even another kind of creature that their queen had created… lovely all the same. Nicco's voice came not a breath later and was filled with an annoyance that only he could convey through mind-speech. An annoyance that was boarding pissed off and nearing the verge of becoming deadly. *Problem?*

You are requested in the woods.

More annoyance came back to him, but the anger had left. *There is more than enough Eostre there to tend to the river. Now leave me. I wish to have time with my wife without you watching.*

Wife? Did the goddess know about… of course, she did? She probably created this creature herself just for Nicco's enjoyment. It didn't matter. Al least not right this minute. What did matter, on the other hand was getting Nicco to do what the queen requested. *You are required in the woods. The queen commands it.*

A pause that lasted only a single heartbeat, then… *I will see you their brother. And my wife is mine, she was created for me and not to be shared among our brothers.*

I have no desire to share her. I only hope it, she keeps you from our queen's bed. He didn't receive an answer, nor did he expect one, after all, if the goddess wanted Nicco in her bed the choice was hers alone.

Giving himself another minute to dress and another to make sure his lightning staff and sword were adequate for whatever he may need, Alec launched himself off the high tower of the castle of Night. With all the haste that he could manage he flew toward the Mystic Woods and hopefully whatever this was, it wasn't anything related to the tributes or the Star Cities.

No, hopefully, it wasn't another god deciding to come here to take their queen away.

The Fallen

CHAPTER 14:

MAGMAS

Avyanna sat at Azia's feet within the confines of his largest coach fanning herself with boredom. Laying her head on his knee, she batted her long dark eyelashes as she pouted, "Why must we visit this worthless Star City? The princes are hardly worth seeing. And its king is hardly one of your favorites." She pouted her blood red lips waiting for an answer.

Azia sat back and smiled, "My dear think of this as a lesson. I want to see *your* worth as a royal Fey. These princes are all beneath you and none have my favor as you already know. I want to see how you would handle the trial of accession. Do to them as you wish."

Her eyes lit up with balls of black fire flickering in the distance, "Anything? Are you certain?"

His long bony fingers held her chin. "As you will ascend shortly to your rightful place this will make good practice for you… Use the princes as you will those who enter the trials. Test them. Only one will rule this pitiful place in a few years. And we want to make sure the right one ascends… do we not? Of course, it is possible that not will ascend. It would be unfortunate, but Magmas could always sire another."

"Oh, very well." She closed her fan with nothing more than a flick of the wrist. "I will test them. I do hope you will not think less of them after they scream for mercy?"

"My dear, if you collar them, they will not scream at all."

She pressed her thin lips together, "No, they wouldn't, but if they cannot scream how will I know which is truly the strongest?"

Sitting back, he let out a cruel laugh. "I suppose you wouldn't. Come, child, we will see Magmas and tell him about what will take place. I am sure he will agree this is the best for Pallas. And his own pitiful Star City."

Magmas sat on his throne grinding his teeth. This was not how things were to take place. His firstborn would become his heir. His other two? One would be sacrificed sure, but the other… The other he had hoped to send to that speck of blue that Primitiva had found so many years ago. He had been preparing Apollo for the journey. Preparing Flint to become the sacrifice. Now?

Slowly he rose from his seat. There was only one way to handle this mess… only one-way for all of his children to survive. "It is a shame I hadn't thought of this myself. However, since this will be at least two of my children's last days on this star or any other I have a request."

"Magmas, do you really think I wouldn't allow you time with your offspring before this trial?"

"My lord, you're gracious, but my request is also this. As the two weakest will feed the Void, they should take all of their troublesome belongings with them. I really don't need their trinkets left behind."

For a long moment, Azia just stood there weighing his options before finally saying, "I do not think the Void will care if they come with objects or just their flesh. I will allow it."

With a single nod, Magmas bit back the anger he was feeling before choking out the words that he had to say, "Thank you, my lord. I will prepare the children for their trial. Please enjoy my pets while you wait." He didn't wait for a dismissal just strode from the room, making sure his temper and thoughts were carefully kept in check.

He did not speak when he entered his children's shared room just gestured for them to follow and do so without making a sound. Leading them to the most private room where none could listen he finally spoke. "Lord Azia had lost his mind."

"Father?" Apollo asked, worried by his father's tone.

Turning from his children, he spat out his anger too hot to choose his words more carefully, "Lord Azia has decided the three of you will be tried to see who will become my heir. I cannot stop what is about to happen. Nor will *any* of you." Separately, they could not change this since they didn't have the power… but together? It might have been possible to stop Avyanna. They would all be dead before reaching Azia.

Flint's small voice shuddered as he asked, "And the ones who lose what will become of them?"

That made him shudder. He couldn't tell them what was to take place, but only what he hoped would, "Pack your belongings. Once away from Osiris, head for the blue star. Dive do not allow yourself to float. You must find Primitiva."

Apollo turned away from the little group. He had been preparing for this for more years than not. Still, that was no way of telling if he would be successful. And certainly, no way for either of his brothers to join him… "Are you certain she is there?"

Stuffing his hand into a small brownish gray box he pulled out a red gem he placed it into his son's hands. "I've seen her. She is there and even now; her powers grow to frightening capabilities. They will be needed for what is coming. I am not a seer, but I know enough to be certain that war is coming and she will be needed to end it."

A collective gasp of the young voices, then in disbelief that all said nearly in unison, "The Azia is going to declare war on her star? Prim's Star?"

Magmas nodded, "We must warn her that Azia is going to force Avyanna to ascend any day now. If Starlis stands in his way he will destroy Lunaista. Either way Prim cannot count on her sister to help her. But there are others who do not like this path Azia is walking. I think I can rally them behind me. With her help even, remove him from power. But only with her help."

Flint looked down at his feet. Finding out he would either die today and feed the Void or live and become king made him hopeful. Knowing the cruelty Avyanna possessed made him ask, "And Avyanna? What will become of her?"

"If this works… *If* I take over Pallas… She will obey me." Not something, he wanted, but there was no other that he could trust to bring the change that the Star Cities needed if they all hoped to survive.

Scared Apollo turned from his father trying to find another solution. Any solution that didn't end in pain or death. "If we fled now…"

"No. We need to play this out. I already know the ending, but Azia must be satisfied. And above all else, he must not know what is going to take place." Before leaving the room, Magmas closed his fire red eyes, "Today I am grateful that despite all his power he is not a seer nor can read thoughts. Let's hope Avyanna cannot either."

They were not scared nor nervous when they were led into the depths of Osiris. Led to the hall or trials. No, they all knew what was going to happen. There would be pain, there would be blood. And there would vile things that would be done to them. No one would see them until this was over. None would hear their screams. And no one that could stop this would.

Taking a deep breath Apollo stopped seeing Avyanna standing alone in the center of the great room.

Her wings, black with ribbons of burning embers outlining them. Her fire red hair tied on top of her head forming a crown. A cruel smile on her otherwise beautiful face.

The last thing he remembered was the tearing of his flesh as his night blue wings were torn from his body. By who or what he never knew.

CHAPTER 15:

APOLLO

Apollo choked back his tears. If not for needing to be the one in the Void, he could have won the trials. He knew that, but Flint didn't have the strength for this last effort for life and his eldest brother didn't have any signs of life at all. This had nothing to do with what was best for their Star City but rather what was best for all of the Fey. Taking another step, he almost collapsed from the pain. He could barely stand, let alone walk to the platform. His brother had been shoved off not even aware that he was being pushed into the Void. Neither had their wings. Neither could dive as their father suggested. No, they had a little less than minutes to live unless…

A single glance over his shoulder… his father stood there looking fierce as always. Only a hint of sadness in his eyes. Flint? He was barely able to stand… but he was standing. Blood still dripping from where his wings had been. More running down his bruised legs and pooling on the ground.

Nothing to say he allowed his body to fall backward into the Void. When he could no longer see the landing platform he recalled the one spell his father had drilled into all of their heads… drilled them until the pain no longer mattered.

His wings quickly formed to his back-searing pain that only made staying awake that much harder. Another breath and he could see his father's namesake floating limp, not far from him. His pack preventing him from falling at the speed required.

Pumping his wings, he grabbed the pack, then drove through the darkness. Dove past the whirling lights of other stars. Kept diving until his lungs burned in his chest. Just before darkness took him, he saw a glimpse of the blue star. His final thought was that he had seen it and almost made it.

CHAPTER 16:

PRIMITIVA

Flying as fast as she could, she darted toward the ball of white light that was plummeting fast toward the ground. She barely glanced over to her side, seeing Shesha coming up behind her. Quickly she yelled, "Get the furthest one I have the other!"

His silver body moved quicker than she had ever seen before she just hoped whatever this was would be able to leave her star when this was over. Grabbing the limp body that was pulling her toward the ground below she knew that wouldn't be the case.

Struggling, she pulled up trying to slow his descent. She had almost gained control when Shesha was below her another limp body caught in his mouth. Landing on his back, she pulled the limp body close to seeing his midnight blue blood seeping onto her hands. A royal Fey. Quickly she snapped, "Do not eat that."

It wasn't until they landed that he spoke, "Of course I would never eat one of your people."

Primitiva glared at him for just a second as her eyes narrowed into tiny slits. She knew him better than that. Not only would he have eaten it without a thought he would play with his food before he enjoyed his meal. Not that she would say that. Least not yet.

A quick glance and she saw several Eostre were already coming out of their grass made homes to see the commotion. Still, she didn't see... Then just at the edge of her natural vision, she saw him quickly fastening his shirt and looking annoyed that he had been disturbed from whatever he had been doing. White sand still speaking his hair. Later she would apologize for disturbing his time with his young bride... right now she had more important things to take care of. "Nicco... Take them to the healing river. Quickly"

He didn't wait to debate just motioned for a few of his guards to help the injured off of the great beast's back. "Would you like their packs?"

They had come better prepared than she had... but how would they have known? That was a question that was more than worrisome. "Place the packs in the draining house. I will deal with them later." *If at all.*

Nicco bowed slightly, then went with the men to the river. The women could deal with the packs and anything else for the moment. That would leave Alec to deal with the queen… After he arrived.

Looking back up at the night sky, she cursed, "What in the name of the gods is going on up there? Have they all lost their minds?"

Donovan landed not a moment later. His dark soulless eyes already scanning the area, "My queen?"

She didn't turn to him, but growled with frustration, "I want every available warrior made ready. I do not know what is going on up there, but I do not like it. And I will be damned if I do not prepare my subjects to defend themselves."

Taking a step back, he bowed slightly. As he straightened, he very took in her temper and the fact that she hadn't yet turned to greet him… Hadn't yet turned to speak to the captain of her dark Fey or her elite warriors. "Of course. Should I have Freya prepare the elite squads as well?"

"Yes, and tell the Drakens to watch for any unwelcome guest. They can eat any who cross their borders."

This time, when he took a step back it wasn't out of caution but out of survival. A single ember of burning magma landed too near his feet. Something had pressed his queen into a rage. No whatever was going to happen wasn't just going to meet her citizens in battle, they were going to meet the goddess head on. "As you wish." *And may whatever they prayed to have mercy on them because this goddess… this Fey queen… would not.*

Both bodies were taken to the draining house after being bathed in the healing river. Not a place many would choose to come, but a place where abilities that had been learned rather than born with would be taken away. At least while the person remained in the house. And sometimes for days after. No, this place was punishment for those who used their abilities against another. Well, at least part of the punishment.

The rest would depend on what else the person had either done or had been planning on doing. Having their abilities taken away was the least of their worries after that. No that was only the first part of the punishment what would come next would ensure the crime never happen again. But these two were not here for punishment. No, they were here to heal until she figured out what to do with them.

Two pallets of weaved grass hovered above the floor just below her waist. The two boys… children… that she had rescued were each placed on one. A thick wall of mist formed between the two until she decided if either a threat to her or her people were.

Carefully she brought a three-legged stool over to sit near who she thought was the eldest of the two boys. No way for her to really tell, not till one was awake… but this one had midnight blue wings and was nearly a head taller. His injuries were also not as severe. Then again, he might have tried to heal himself before diving into the Void. Depending on where he had come from it was a possibility.

Tentatively, she moved a stray lock of coal black hair from his adolescent face. As she did his weak and tired eyes gazed back you at her. "Easy now. I am not here to harm you" She sounded comforting... didn't she?

His eyes slightly closed as he winced, his lungs still raw from the trial and from the fall. "My brother... is he? Did he make it?"

Brother? Ah, so they did come together and not from two separate Star Cities. One less thing for her to worry about. "He is resting. It will be some time before he well enough to wake."

It was several moments before he once again looked at her, "Are you Primitiva?

Arching her back, she let out a low hiss and pulled her dragon like wings around herself, "And why would you ask me that?"

He swallowed hard now understanding the danger in those few words, "My father, King Magmas, sent me. We are no threat to you. You have my word."

Magmas? The fool she would have been forced to marry if she had stayed on Lunaista. "Your father is a fool to send you here. More so if anyone ever finds you."

"Possibly." He started to cough before he could say much of anything else.

Holding out a cup made from bark she snapped, "Here this will soothe your throat."

After draining the glass, he tried to smile, "My name is Apollo. My brother is Magmas the second. He was to be heir to Osiris."

"Yet he was tossed into the Void? Not even worthy enough to feed the catacombs of your own Star City? That makes no sense." And what didn't make sense had to be a lie…

… Yet.

"Lord Azia decided he would choose my father's replacement. We had no say in the matter. He held a trial to test our mantal. Scream and we failed. Cry and we failed. Beg for mercy and fail. Those were the only rules. Avyanna made sure we would all fail. After our wings were removed I don't remember what happen after. My youngest brother, Flint, was the only one who didn't fail the trials. I could have passed but neither he nor our eldest brother had the strength to try to make it here. Nor did either have the strength to reform their wings so soon after having them removed."

Getting up from her chair she paced. Each thought that she had, growing increasingly darker. Azia had become frightfully cruel. Avyanna was helping him instead of learning from her aunt as she had hoped. *What had happened since she left?* Not that she could go back and find out… however, perhaps Magmas had figured out how to communicate secretly. The thought that the boy could be lying crossed her mind as did so many other things. "How did your father know I was here?"

Closing his eyes once more Apollo softly answered in hopes nothing had happened between packing his bag and being brought here. "In my bag. A red stone. Wasn't told how it worked, only that he saw you."?

Taking the bag that now laid against the wall, she used mist to empty the contents on the floor. A few coverings. Some books. Then… The red stone… the Seer's eye as it was once called… rolled on the stone floor before resting near her foot. "This shouldn't have been able to find me."

"True, but my father has had both for some time. Apart it can only see within the Star Cities. Together? He found you."

For a moment, she gazed at him. His eyes… now open once again… were defiant yet apprehensive. He was there for a reason and she needed to find out what that reason was. Gliding over to the bed, she took a seat near his feet. Her long dragon-like wings pulled tight to her sides looking more like a cape than that of wings. Still, he didn't move.

Didn't speak. He didn't even flinch.

She couldn't find a lie within his words, but any powerful Fey could force a memory to be changed… force one to remember only what they wanted them to. Force them to say only what they knew as truth. But she was not just a powerful Fey, she was so much more. She was a seer, a truth seeker. She was a creator. The most coveted and most elite kind of Fey; even among the royal Fey. She was the one who could create power, life or anything that she wished. She was the only living one of her kind. And more than that she was the most powerful creator in more than a hundred generations. She would learn the truth one way or another.

Slowly she let a vine of soft blue light creep up his leg. She could learn a lot from this vine of mist. She could tell where his injuries were. What had healed and what still needed to mend. Later she would have to really see what was hidden beneath the flesh and what still needed her talents. But that was later, right now…

The vine crept further up his body wrapping his torso. His arms now trapped at his side. Still, he made no attempt to move. The way his heart was racing was her only sign of the fear that he was now facing. Once the mist reached his throat and ears, his breathing became rapid. She didn't want to harm him yet in order to protect her people she would without a second thought.

Quickly the mist overtook him plummeting deep within his skull. Entering into every fiber of his mind. Into every memory. From here she could tear apart his mind. Rebuild it as she saw fit. Make him forget about his home and those who lived there. She had the power to create a life for him here. Perhaps later she would but right now she would only look to find out what he truly knew.

The memories were there. Right in the order she knew they would be. The first had been changed. It was clearly a rush to change it since she didn't have even the hint of trouble deciphering what was true. He was the first-born son just as she had guessed. However, because his mother had been a pet rather than the consort Apollo couldn't be the heir. However, what was puzzling was that Magmas had forced the truth suppressed.

Why would he have this child shortly after birth, claimed by his consort and changes not only his status but conceal his age as well? Then again, perhaps Magmas had considered being made a tribute a better fate than being sent to Pallas. Living there as either a servant or a slave. Or worse, being sent to another Star City to live as a mute pet living by the whims of whoever ruled. Yes, perhaps this had been a show of his kindness after all.

Going back through his memories that had been the only one that had been forced upon him. What he had told her had been the truth.

Carefully, she withdrew the mist and allowed for him to sleep. If he woke now he would know only pain until his mind repaired itself. She would spare him that torment. It was one that only a few of her people ever knew and only if they deserved it. This child did not. He had already survived more than he should have given his age.

Pulling a forest green cover over him she kissed the crown of his head. Such a motherly gesture. Too bad he was not awake to understand what it was that she was offering him.

Alec was waiting just outside the main hall when she stepped out of the room where the boys were recovering. She stopped him from speaking with nothing more than a look. In her most authoritative tone she spoke, "Please have all of the first gather at the castle of Fire. You and Nicco will escort my guest there."

"And the warriors?"

"They are to remain ready for anything. I will explain further at the castle." She almost turned away, then hesitated, "I want the boys to wake before being moved. Do not harm them. They have already been through enough."

He nodded once. "As you wish, my queen."

Somehow, she doubted that. Then again, he was very jealous of anyone who might share her affection. Not that he would ever say anything to her… not when she did anything that she wished and he was just her loyal servant, not her life mate. Not the one who would share her heart, but the one that she trusted to create this world with her. Trusted enough to be her ears when she was not around.

The Fallen

CHAPTER 17:

APOLLO

Lazily Apollo's head rolled to the side. His head was throbbing, but it was the sensation of his skin being both cold and wet that made him open his eyes. When Primitiva had been here he had been warm. Not as warm as he had been if he had truly been home, but warm enough not to notice the cold.

But now? A shiver ran through him.

Cautiously he pulled the soft covering tight around himself trying hard not to think much about what his new life would be. What Primitiva would allow for it be? After all, this was no different than if he had been sent to another Star City. There too he would have to adapt to the weather. It wouldn't matter if it was hotter or colder, he would have to adapt if he were to survive. The only difference was here he still had his wings. Still was granted permission to speak. And hopefully, wouldn't be forced into doing things that he really didn't want to do.

His body hurt, but right now the cold was worse. He needed to move, and hopefully, with moving from the bed, he wouldn't do something that was forbidden. Carefully, he swung his legs over the side, then froze. There, just out of reach were a set of golden eyes watching him. They were set at the height of a small child or that of a large animal. Swallowing hard, he forced a smile, "Hello?"

The eyes shifted from one spot in the room to a few feet away before a child stepped out of the darkness. "You're going to be in trouble."

Wonderful. Either he was dealing with a child that was barely older than a toddler or a shapeshifter who was trying to act like a child. "Why will I be in trouble?"

The child ignored the question, but took a step closer and smiled, revealing several rows of sharp pointed teeth. "You don't have enough flesh. I will not eat you."

What?!?! It took every bit of strength that he had not to move away from this creature. "I appreciate that. Thank you."

"I will…"

A deep growl came from the darkness behind the boy then it snapped, "Bradwr, Get out of here. Now."

The boy disappeared without saying a word. Slowly a tall man in a black suit came out of the darkness. "I see you're awake. And no doubt trying to figure out what you are currently allowed to do."

The boy had unnerved him, but looking at this man… he could see his own death in those dark feral eyes, "Yes, sir?"

"Not sir. Nicco. You are in my home village. As it is I am the king of the Eostre. Make no mistake, if you betray my queen I will do more than just eat you."

Oh yes, he was in trouble. "I have no intentions of betraying her, nor could I, even if I wished. Fey are honor bound and I cherish my life too much to break that bond." Not to mention the life of his brother. Or that of his father who had sent him here.

"I will see. In the meantime, if you wish to roam the village you may do so. Stay away from Bradwr. Even among my people, he is troublesome. Personally, I do not see how my son deals with him."

"You're a father? You barely look older than I am." Why had he said that? He had meant only to think it not actually speak the words.

Nicco crossed his arms, "I have several children. And three wives. Cerimon is my eldest and will ascend soon. My queen had decided I need more time seeing to my duties to her as well as time with my wives."

"And Bradwr is…"

"The second son to Cerimon. His eldest was born ready to lead. The queen named him herself. It was great honor even for those who rule in her name." There was so much pride in those words. But also something that had the weight of gloating.

So not much difference between Pallas and here then. Instead of Azia ruling as the king of all Star Cities, Primitiva ruled as queen. And as a queen, she could require anything of those who served her even choosing when another would ascend. Of course, rules under a queen varied greatly compared to those of a king. And sometimes those rules had more leeway for their citizens. He just hoped this was the case. "Am I allowed to see my brother?"

Nicco looked at a space beyond the darkness before he answered. "When he wakes. His injuries were much worse than yours and the healing river can only do so much." Letting out a sigh, he rubbed his thumb over his brow, "My queen has the power to heal him… but needs time to let her temper calm. What needs to be done can wait until daybreak. Until then, you have my word, no further harm shall come to him."

"Thank you." Placing his feet on the hard ground he shivered from the cold stone floor. "May I have another covering. I have not yet adjusted to the chill here."

"Cold? My boy this is not cold. Here and near the marsh is the warmest places in all of what my queen rules. Well, aside from the deserts and the castle where you will be housed. But there are places much colder." Again he paused, "Alec is outside. Whatever you need he can fetch for you."

"Alec?"

"The queen's consort.And the resident pain in the ass." He let a consprital smile form on his lips. "No, he's fine. A little rough around the edges, but I have yet to meet a light- bearer that isn't. But he has been more broody since finding out I will be taking residence in the place once my son ascends. Must be because he thinks I want his position."

Yes, he could understand the moodiness then if the two were both interested in warming the queen's bed. Or if one *thought* that was what the other wanted. Either way, it was none of his business. Yet he felt compelled to ask, "And you don't?" *What in the name of the creator was wrong with him?* He knew better than to ask stupid questions like that. However, Nicco seemed pleased that he had.

"I have three wives and I will not give them up to lay in the queen's bed. Even if she hints that is exactly what we do behind closed doors."

He should not be having this conversation. He really shouldn't' be. So why did he feel the need to require answers? "So you…"

"Talk. There are things I cannot say in front of any including her favorites. What they think is happening and what is…" Nicco shrugged, "It matters not to me. Now if you excuse me, I would like to spend time with my bride before she returns to the waters."

Wife? Waters? What kind of strange creature was he bound to? Knowing that he could not say that, he asked instead, "Thank you, your majesty, for speaking with me. It has been enlightening."

Carefully he made his way down the long, windowless corridor, keeping his thin cover wrapped tightly around himself. The flat stone floor was cold against his bare feet and the air was becoming increasingly wet the closer that he drew to the main door. Or at least what he assumed would be the main door since he had not the tiniest bit of light to lead the way. Then just a few feet in front of him, he could not see light… but darkness. Night.

At least he knew where the door now was.

Poking his head out of the opening he tried to take a deep breath. The air was much warmer than inside. Almost tolerable. He could do without the water that seemed to hang in the air, but… he could adjust to this.

Eventually.

Standing in the middle of what he could assume was the street, he saw the light- barer. His wings of golden light pulled tight to his back. His eyes watching the sky. A lightning staff firm in his hands while a long knife hung from his belt. This wasn't a sentry this was a trained warrior looking for the first signed of trouble. Not taking another step from the building he let out a soft cough.

Alec turned his head slightly before looking once more to the sky. "You want to tell me what it is I'm seeing?"

Taking a step over to him, he very softly asked, "What..." Then his eyes saw what Alec was watching. White streams racing across the night sky. Little orbs glowing brighter then dimmer. "I -I don't know." Oh, but how he wished that did. How he wished to know something that would be useful here.

Slowly Alec took a deep breath, "No, I don't suppose you would. Even my queen has yet to figure it out completely."

"The queen... Primitiva... Is she close?"

Puzzled Alec glanced down at the boy then dismissively said, "Hmm. She's bathing in the Healing River. It calms her when she over thinks."

So many questions that he could ask. Too many questions that he knew that he shouldn't. But a safe brotherly question? Maybe... just maybe... "Is she really going to help my brother?"

Turning back to the boy Alec smiled, "She already has. In the morning, we will go to the Castle of Fire. From what I can guess that is where you will live for the foreseeable future."

Castle of Fire. His home? More like his prison. "Thank you for telling me."

The Fallen

CHAPTER 18:

PRIMITIVA

Primitiva gazed out of her solaris window watching the magma bubble up from the riverbed. She heard his light footfalls coming down the long hallway but didn't turn until he gave a hesitant cough. "Alec? Are the boys settled for the moment?"

"They are." Carefully he took a single step into the room. This was one of her private rooms and not a place that she would normally choose to have anyone for any reason. Yet he had to give her his report on the boys. "They seem younger than they did when you brought them here."

Another bubbled popped as she sighed, "As they should. Magmas used an incantation on both of them to help hide who was older. Apollo is barely fifty light cycles. His brother just a few less. From what they both remember their youngest brother has just had his tenth light cycle… but looks much older."

"Light cycle?" He sounded puzzled. And Alec was rarely puzzled. Yet she had never explained life within the Star Cities.

She narrowed her eyes. In a thousand years had been able to refrain from speaking too much about her home… now? Did she have a choice? "Each star has a different measurement for light cycles. Those closest to Pallas come into… um… adult form more quickly than those further away. It has something to do with the tributes and how the power is divided between the Star Cities. I know not how it truly works. Some things are forbidden to ask about. And my life is much too important to be killed, asking a silly question."

She heard him shift his weight from foot to foot, unsure of what to ask. Hear his deep breath just before he asked, "So the boys…"

"Since they're no longer bound to their Star City or to the power that fed the incantation their true forms are becoming apparent. In another day or two, their forced memories will fade and their true one will surface."

Alec slid closer to her, but not yet daring to be close enough to touch. "I don't recall you going through this change."

A soft smile twitched her lips, "I didn't. The moment that I could I broke the bond while still within my home. My parents were not happy. I think my father was punished because he is the one who told me how it could be done." She took a breath and turned back to her window. After several long minutes, she shuddered, "In my Star City the queen and all of the women there have all the power. Or at least are the ones allowed to use the majority of those powers. Most women control every aspect of a man's life. In my father's case with him being the consort, punishment meant pain. My mother relished in it. I remember days where my father could barely stand even if no wounds were visible. Her pets faired far worse. At one time she had three, only one was still alive when I came here. The other two? Were killed some time before. I assure you their deaths were the only measure of kindness that they ever knew."

"I don't understand." And he didn't. If someone did something that needed punished, they were brought to Prim for judgment. There had only ever been one case where a person was punished in a way that caused pain.

"No, I don't suppose you would. I try not to rule the way that is done within the Star Cities. I do not take joy in causing pain. Although if I had to I would have no problem doing so. No Fey does."

He needed to turn her thoughts before she either harmed herself or something around her. Just standing several feet away, he could feel the heat rising from her now milky white skin. Could see her hair changing at the tips to embers. "Is that why you came here to show them what is possible?"

"I came here so I would not marry Magmas. I was barely what humans refer to as a teenager. I knew not of what I wanted. And In truth, I still don't, But my heart still belongs to me and that counts for something." Another deep breath she cast aside all her thoughts about her home. There were more pressing matters that needed to be taken care of. "Please notify all of the villages both big and small… on moments notice all children must be taken to the nearest castle. They will be housed there until whatever trouble arises has been dealt with."

"You have already notified the other castles…"

"My darling, Do you think I would tell you before I had already made plans for the children? When the castles were built, I had several floors placed well below the surface. Karnack knows of these places since his work rooms are in the lowermost …um… floor seems wrong as does cellar. If this was a Star City it would be below the catacombs… as such I no word for the place."

It was good to see his goddess slowly returning to her normal behavior, "Then I will help you come up with a name for this place of safety."

"As you wish. My mind is too full of other things right now."

Alec bowed his head slightly, "Is there anything you need before I see to the preparations?"

Suddenly the red gem appeared in her hands. "No. I need quite as I find out how to make this cursed thing work in order to speak with Magmas."

Pausing Alec let his eyes lock on the gem that now rested in his queen's hand. Then very hesitantly asked, "Are you sure that is a good idea?"

"No. But he sent his boys here for a reason. I wish to find out why before I decide on what I will do with them."

It didn't take long for her to figure out how to use the seer's stone to look at the other Star Cities… but much longer, not only to find the one that belonged to Magmas but to also figure out how to use it to communicate with him. Actually, it wasn't until he was holding the mate to it that he even came into view. Trying only once she softly spoke, "Magmas?"

His eyes, which had been filled with grief, lit up with hope and relief, "I knew you would figure it out." A moment to pause then he whispered, "My boys?"

"Sleeping. Your incantation is fading. I suspect I will have to deal with adolescent questions in the marrow."

Magmas closed his dull lava red eyes. "Can… when you think it's right… tell them that Flint didn't survive." His face tightened with anger, "Azia had the gall to tell me that none of my current line has the power to rule. As far as he knows he killed all those who could have ruled my Star City."

Seeing the rage building within his eyes, Prim hissed, "Magmas. You need to calm down lest someone hears you."

"I am in the private room known only to the one that rules. Not even Azia has the power to see within these walls."

Primitiva rolled her eyes as she took a measured breath, "Very well. Your boy. The young one. He has been sent to the catacombs?"

"No. Azia doesn't want him and had forbidden him to feed the ones here. He is to be thrown into the Void. However, I have decided to place him in the ancient catacombs of the first Fey. They have not been used in years, but I..." He let the rest trail off.

For a long moment, she didn't speak. It was a simple gesture, but would he accept it? "I can retrieve his body and bring it here. I make no promises, but I can find something honorable to do with the prince of Osiris."

His through clogged with deep emotions, "I-I would... Thank you."

"If you can send what you need for me to know. And Magmas know this if you betray me, I will destroy your Star City and everything in it."

"My sweet, you are my only hope of destroying Azia… why would I ever betray you? I will write down everything you need to know not only about my boys, but the ongoings of the Star Cities. War is brewing but it is still sometime a ways."

When the image of Magmas faded, Primitiva sat back on her solaris floor. If what Mamas said was right then she had time to prepare. And possibly do something to help the Star Cities in the process. But she would have to wait until she read what Magmas chose to tell her. What he didn't would prove more valuable than what he did.

Making her ways outside to the main courtyard, she called for her darling Shesha then waited for the great dragon to appear. She smiled as he came into view. Just a streak of white on a starless night sky.

Back winging as he landed his head bowed slightly, "My queen?"

Coming up to Shesha's side, she stroked his neck lovingly. So, few were easy around her beloved dragon. Something he never seemed to mind. Today that didn't matter. Getting to where she needed to be quickly... did. "Come, I am in need of your speed."

Shesha bobbled his head in his way of showing her respect. "Of course. Shall I take you to your meadows?"

Climbing up, Primitiva sat petting his long scaly back. "Not today. Do you remember when I told you about my homeland?"

He snorted out a cloud of white smoke. "The balls of light that light the night sky?"

"Yes. We need to go there now. There is one that I seek. We must find him before he enters the outer rim of Pallas."

"Pallas?" The word said more to test how it sounded rather than asking where.

Pointing not to the glowing ball of fire that lights the daytime sky, but rather the large white orb that was currently resting in its shadow. "The great ball of light that glows even during the day."

"Very well, I shall take you there."

CHAPTER 19:

MAGMAS

Carefully Magmas lifted his son's lifeless body off of the stone platform where he had been placed so that he could be made ready to be laid with the first Fey of their little star. Holding his son close to him, he let a single tear roll down his face. Why had it come to this?

Why?

The Azia had taken to power longer than anyone could remember. In all that time he had never been this cruel. This destructive. He had never killed an entire royal line. So why now?

For a moment longer he sat there collecting not only his thoughts but his emotions. If anyone saw him this way Azia could kill him as well. And if he did, he would find Prim.

Laying his son back down on the cold stone slab Magnus forced himself to go upstairs. He hated what he was about to do, but it needed to be done. If only to protect Prim and to buy himself some much needed time.

Finding the first guard that he came across he carefully spoke. The lad that use to play with Flint and was known to trade identities with him." The guard raised an eyebrow, "Bring him to me. He is to join Flint in the catacombs. I have no use for someone who has my son's looks within my city."

The guard swallowed, "Of course, my lord. I will retrieve him at once."

Making his way to his children's room, he looked around. Empty shelves lined the walls. Nothing of his children remained within the walls. Flits belongings were already packed and being stored with his body. Prim would find something to do with them, but what she needed now…

… What he needed to do was give Primitiva was a reason to do more.

His fingers ran across the slag wall as he made his way to his private room. Every castle had a room like this. One that no seer could gaze into. A room that was solice for the royal who ruled. Most housed their most prized possessions here. He, on the other hand, housed his maps of the other Star Cities. Housed his notes about what royal Fey ruled each of the known stars. Notes on what royal Fey had an excess of children. One to rule. One to be sacrificed and the rest to be sold.

Carefully, he placed the maps into a large bag that he could attach to Flint's body. A careful spell would keep him from drifting too far away from their star until Prim found him. This had to work.

Taking a seat at his desk, he glanced over at the Seer's eye, tempted to call out to Prim once more. But he shook off the thought. Instead, he took to writing everything that he knew as truth, since she dove into the abyss.

From his visit to tell the Azai about her dishonoring her family to his objecting to Azia raising her daughter. He left nothing out. Not his feeling of betrayal when the Azai killed his wife and all of his pets. Not the rage of losing his children. Not even his plan to remove the Azai from power.

It was a risk telling her that much. A risk that she may decide to side with Azia for the sake of her daughter, but was a risk he was willing to take. After all, it would only be his life that would be affected. However, if she sided with him… or at the very least swore to house the children of the royal Fey that needed to survive in order to rule… that would be more than worth the risk.

Carefully folding the parchment he placed it in the sack with the maps… This had to work or his children had died in vain.

"The boy is waiting in the hall of tribute, my lord."

Magmas paused, seeing the grief hidden in the guard's eyes. He knew too well what that grief meant. "Your son will forever be with the prince, he served deep within the royal tomb. It is a great honor."

The guard nodded once and turned. Not surprising when he was king and he could require anything from his subjects including their deaths. He hated that his citizens blindly followed his command, but right now he was also thankful.

Slipping into the throne room, he saw the boy standing alone facing the door. Fear in his eyes. "What did your father tell you?"

"It is a great privilege to be forever linked with the prince."

If he sounded any more grateful tears would be pouring from his eyes. "I swear you will not feel a thing."

"May I speak plainly?"

As he would be dead in the next few moments Magmas nodded for the boy to speak.

"It's not the pain that fear. It's the loss of all that I will never get to do."

Going down on one knee, he smiled, "What you will be doing is far greater than anything you could have done otherwise. Now, please follow me. I do not think it wise to delay what is to come."

"Yes, sir."

Letting the lad walk in front of him, they entered a stark, dimly lit room. Not a single piece of furniture. Nor anything to offer even a glimmer of hope. The boy paused as he took his first step into the room. Then made a move as if he was going to turn around. In one quick motion, Magmas snapped his neck, saving him any pain that he might have felt otherwise.

Closing his eyes, he prayed to the gods that he had made the correct decision. Prayed that he didn't take this life without cause. But most of all he prayed that the boy had the strength that Flint had so the deception would not ever be discovered.

Carefully, he lifted the boy's body from the floor and carried it to where his own son laid. Then began the slow painful task of dressing the boy in a similar fashion. Long robes bearing the colors of royalty. A small incision on the neck and a vine of mist forced all of the blood… hunter green blood… from the boy's body. Allowing it to pool onto the floor below the body.

In the morning the body would be moved to the ancient catacombs. Laid on a shelf with the ancestors. Laid forever in slumber with the first Fey of Osiris. No one would ever know the difference. The slit on the throat would be seen as a father's act of anger that his offspring had died so shortly after being made the crown prince.

It was a reasonable explanation.

Waiting until the halls of the castle were quiet and the city was bedded down for the night, Magmas carried his son's body to the messenger's platform. He had stowed the heavy bags here earlier knowing none would care to disturb the bags nor care to glimpse inside.

Securing the packs to Flint's lifeless body, he held on for a moment longer. Held on wishing for only one minute more with his youngest. One minute for with any of his children. Before he could change his mind about sending his son's body away, he let his body fall from his arms and into the Void. He watched as his son's body floated away from the platform. Watched as the pack that held his belonging pulled slightly from his limp body.

Primitiva would find him. She had to. Not that she could do anything to help him… except give him a final resting place due to any royal Fey. His now crown prince.

Magmas closed his lava red eyes so not to allow them to fill with the tears that were held deep inside him. He could not appear weak. He couldn't. Prim's life would be lost if he did.

Then again, if anyone ever found out that Prim had taken the body or that she was somehow still alive…

Closing his eyes, he took a deep, controlled breath. He had to keep the appearances of indifference. He needed to look like he didn't care that his children… *all of them*… were gone. Even the Void couldn't touch them now. Another breath. He would need to sire another child to prove his indifference.

He just hoped that child would survive what was coming. Deep down, he didn't think that hope would be answered.

Of course, if Prim actually helped the Star Cities... War could be avoided altogether. But this was something she wouldn't do. She had no desire to rule the Fey. She didn't want more than she had created on her little blue star.

No. The only help she would offer was a place to hide the children of the royal Fey. The ones that were strong enough to rule. Yet too young to do so. And she would only do so if she star was never found. That was her only term and one that was not negotiable.

Slowly he turned away from the platform. Tonight, he would grieve the loss of his youngest. Then tomorrow he would carefully see which Star Cities grew tired of the Azia and who would follow him till their last breath.

With his long red robe trailing behind him Magmas took his first step into his palace since the Azia had left. The first since his sons were no longer there. The first step and utter silence surrounded him. He had no wife as of now. No concubine to amuse him. And no children to detract him from all that had happened in a mere few days.

How could one live like this?

His people were content to live by themselves until it was time to take a mate. And he knew lots of other royal Fey that sent their crown prince or princess away to grow on Pallas until it was time for them to rule. Yet how did they manage the silence? It was deafening.

He needed to either start his way to the other Star Cities seeing who could be trusted or start looking for a wife. Neither sounded palatable right now. The thought of becoming a father again turned his stomach. The knowledge of why he would be traveling to the other Star Cities felt far worse.

One of his maids scurried past trying to stay in the shadows… trying not to draw his attention nor his wrath. Or possible, trying not to change her position from maid to bed warmer.

As he turned away from her he made sure she understood he was not looking in her direction. Least not yet. As of today, he was not that desperate to have a common house Fey warming his bed. No even today he had standards and only a royal Fey would do. Only a royal Fey would be worthy of the title of wife.

Luckily, he knew a few Star Cities that had an abundance of royal Fey children and all ripe to be married for a sake of an alliance. And it would make no difference if the child would become a first wife, a concubine, or just a pet. No, the only thing that would matter would be if he kept the child alive.

CHAPTER 20:

PRIMITIVA

As she flew higher the air became colder and dark. Soon she could see her blue star with a clarity that she hadn't seen before. Breathtakingly lovely, but she was not here to take in the rare beauty of her little star. No, she had to find the last of Magmas' line; she had to find his youngest son. If only she knew where to look.

Sitting on Shesha's back, she stroked his long spines soothingly. Her eyes already focusing on each of the stars still thousands of miles away. Osiris was known for its violent volcanoes and lava baths. Even if she had never seen them herself, she had heard about them. So, with that much heat, the star had to be close to Pallas. That narrowed it down to about a hundred stars. Perhaps even a few more.

Patting Shesha she pointed, "That way. Head toward the bright ball of light and quickly. The pull of Pallas is much greater than any other."

He spiraled toward the requested ball. His wings pumping furiously trying to gain as much speed as he could. This was his first time in what his queen called the Void. A place where the air was barely tolerable. A place leached from all light except that of her Star Cities. A place he did not wish to return to ever again. Still, his queen requested his speed and strength for this one mission. Finding every bit of strength that he could, he pushed further into the Void.

"There. Over there." Prim pointed to a lone something floating yet not being pulled toward anything. As they drew closer she could see two large packs attached to the body. Almost upon it, she could see it was a truly lifeless body clad in the robes of a crown prince.

Flint. They had found him. Shesha stopped just close enough for Prim to pull the body to his back. "We are too late?" He asked, his voice full of mourning.

"I…" She paused combing her fingers through his blood matted hair. "… No. He is not so far gone that I can grant him a full life."

Shesha turned to head home, then heard a loud sobbing gasp from his queen, "My lady?"

"Look at them. All of them. Why…" A tear ran down her face as she gasped out, "What is Azia doing to the Fey? He will surely kill them all."

"My queen." He paused, seeing hundreds of bodies mindlessly floating between the Star Cities. Carnage even he could not fathom. "Should we help them?"

Prim scrubbed her hands over her face. A few more sniffles to calm herself, then she quickly pulled herself together. Her only thought was what was coming and the choices she would need to make. Most more difficult than this one. "We must if anything they will be highly trained warriors that will be needed for what is to come."

Slowly and cautiously she stood on her great beast's back and closed her eyes. Carefully, she felt for each of the lifeless bodies. Nearly a hundred close to Pallas alone. From where Shesha had brought her, she could feel thousands of them. Possibly more that were too far from where she was to feel.

A thin string of light no bigger than that of a spider's web attached to each of the bodies. Quickly she attached the string to Shesha's massive tail. "Go further into the Void. I wish to make sure I have all of those that I can."

The further away from the giant ball of light that they went the fewer bodies they found. "I do not see any more, my queen."

"Then the gods are in our favor. Let us return to our home."

"Where should we take them, my queen?"

That was the question, wasn't it? So many from different skills and different abilities. All of them would be needed when the war truly started. But for now, what could she do? Taking a deep shaking voice, she made her choice. The only real choice as far as she was concerned. "I will manually drain them into the healing river, it is the only place large enough that will accommodate this many at once. I will decide after they are whole once more, what I will do with them."

Shesha bobbed his head in agreement, "You are wise my queen."

Tens of thousands of bodies drifted in the river. Bouncing off of each other as the current flowed downstream. Each only partly attached to the river bed so not to float way completely. Royal Fey. Common Fey. Fey that was born little more than a slave all of them now mixing together within the warm waters, unaware of who it was they were floating next to. Unaware of their blood mixing with those of lesser rank.

Their blood floating on the top of the waters. Royal blue… Forest green… Lightning yellow… Earthy brown… Lava red… Smoke black. All of it swirling around covering every space that was not occupied by the fallen Fey.

For a long moment, Prim hovered high above the healing river watching the bodies bump into one another. Watching the rivers seep away the abilities of those who now rested within its waters. Knowing that the abilities that were now being taken away would forever feed the lands of her little star. Knowing those abilities would once again be reclaimed in the years that would follow. Knowing that once reclaimed so too would a better understanding of how to use those abilities.

Her eyes swept over the banks of the river. She needed to decide what she was going to. The Eostre were all there. Proud warriors standing keeping watch over those whom she had brought to their lands. Their eyes looking for any sign of life. Looking for any signs of trouble.

More Eostre were there creeping along the river bed and clinging to the trees. A fine black mist where no shadow should be was the only sign of them. The only sign they were seeing if they could devour the lifeless bodies.

Closing her grief filled eyes, she touched each of the fallen Fey. She never wanted this. Never wanted to rule over actual Fey. Never dreamed of living on a star with so many… all with different talents and abilities. All born for different reasons. No, she didn't want this, but what she wanted no longer mattered. They didn't deserve to die like this. To die unrecognized for their talents. Unrecognized for their power. Not they didn't deserve this.

She just hoped they would come to see her as her creations saw her and not someone to be feared. But most of all she prayed they would be the strength that she needed to keep her little star safe.

By the gods, how she prayed.

In one quick motion, the bodies sank to the riverbed. The waters already tainted and cloudy with their blood. Gone was the translucent waters replaced by the blood that had been steadily draining from their bodies. One Day the water would become clear once more…

… Hopefully…

Thin strings of bright light touched each of the Fey. Touched each of their minds… their hearts. Before reviving them, she forced a simple truth into each. They had been dishonored in death. Dishonored on their own Star City. Their bodies tossed into the Void to be swallowed up and destroyed. Their abilities and powers not worthy of feeding even the most pitiful of catacombs. Not worthy of feeding their own Star City or that of any other. She the creator of life found them and took mercy on each of them. Granting each a second chance to prove their loyalty. She granted them a second life and she could take her gift back, leaving nothing of them but a memory.

Slowly she withdrew each of her strands of light and allowed for each of the fallen to claw their way out of the water. Each gasped as their heads found air. Each coughed and gasped loudly as they found dry land. When their eyes found the sentries stand over them, none dared to move.

As the last Fey climbed from the water Prim calmly fluttered down to the bank. Nicco was keeping a place for her. Thankfully, all of the other first were still in the Castle of Fire keeping watch over her other two charges. Luckily they hadn't wanted to come here to witness this show of power. Powers that she had no way to explain.

Softly She landed just an arm's length away from Nicco, who gave a slight bow yielding to her will. "People of the Mystic Woods stand aside and allow these Fey room."

The warriors did not yield, but those who were not trained guards nor fighters took to their misty forms. It was the most consension that she was going to receive until her guards were satisfied that none wished to harm her.

Yet none of the Fey spoke. Their eyes now locked on her. All looking apprehensive and fearful. Many still breathing heavily, not yet understanding what had just happened.

"I am the goddess Primitiva. I collected you from the Void cross me and your faith will be one worse than the dishonor you have already faced."

Her eyes shifted just slightly. Motion coming close to the river's bank. A man. A Feyen man bronze skin and midnight black hair was clearly shifting closer toward her. One of the royal Fey. If she was correct, he was from one of the dark stars. The home of Dark Fey. Those who were not easily controlled. Still, he was weak compared to her.

For the moment she pretended not to notice him drawing closer to her. "For the moment you will be given anything that you need. In time as you settle into your surroundings, I will help you find your place within my home. As this star offers many different climates and habitats I'm sure you will find places that best represent who you wish to be." She paused then choose to speak directly to those of royal blood. "Those of you that are of royal blood, you will be housed in my castle of night. You will be paired with those who I see fit not of your choosing."

The Fey, who had been slowly approaching suddenly stopped and hissed, "I have never heard of a goddess. And I will not blindly listen to… "

With nothing more than a look, she began pulling air from his lungs… Pulling his blue life blood to drip from his nose. Just a heartbeat or two from what would have killed him. She released his lungs and allowed him to gasp for air. "I can be merciful or not. The choice is up to you. If you live that will be up to me. Any questions?"

His body collapsed to the ground before his lungs filled with enough air to breath without gasping. Slowly he shook his head.

"Now what is your name since you seem to be the one who is most vocal."

Still gasping for air, his dull smoky gray eyes looked up at her and for the first time noticed her wings. Not wings of a Fey… or at least not those of a known Fey.

But those of a creator. She had called herself goddess… oh, but she was so much more. He could see that now. He could see the mistake of speaking to her as he had. Swallowing hard, he closed his eyes, "Honua. I was once crown prince of Amaris. The largest dark star. I…" Again he swallowed, having never needed to explain his actions to anyone. "… I apologize for my actions I have never heard of one more powerful then Azia." *Or at least none that were still alive.*

Prim nodded once. "Nicco please have the carriages come to collect those whose blood runs blue. All others see they are taken to my meadows. There is plenty of food there for them. Once they are rested see that they are settling within the castle."

Nicco stepped closer, "Perhaps they all would like some coverings until proper ones can be made for them?"

"Very well. I must return to my private castle. I will not be disturbed."

Her private castle. The one that she had created for those who were no longer capable of life. The ones that were never truly dead. That is what she was telling him. With a tip of his head Nicco smiled, "Of course my queen. I can take care of everything here. The others can take care of the children until you return."

The Fallen

CHAPTER 21:

FLINT

The feeling of floating brought him back to his body. Something warm and soft covered him. His pain no longer filling every thought. The feeling of fingers passing through his hair. Slowly his amber colored eyes fluttered opened. Even slower his vision cleared the haze of sleep as a shape took form before him. At first, it had been mist. Then fire. The flames, hot enough to give his body the warmth that he craved. Finally, a figure. A woman. Radiant fire red hair that the volcanoes of Osiris could not do justice to. Then those eyes… those galaxy blue eyes complete with the stars… together with her narrow face "Your breathtaking." The words slipped out before he thought about saying them.

When she did not speak, he wondered if he had actually said them. After all, his mouth felt fuzzy numb as his tongue licked his dry lips. Hoarsely he asked, "Is this what death feels like?"

Slowly a shy smile formed on the woman's lips. "Hardly. But you, Flint, are not dead." Then her eyes lit up with amusement, "But you are trouble. Mostly forgiven since Magmas is also a known flirt."

He blinked unsure how this creature knew his name. Struggling to sit up, he took in more of her beauty. A thin frame and dragon wings. Wings of a creator. Her legs blending into a scaly tail. Long and coiled around her. Fins of golden fire at the end. A blink and the tail turned into legs. Whiffs of red mist creating a covering. Asking "*What are you*?" would be rude so he asked instead, "You know my sire?"

She leaned forward in her seat. "I do. Though I think my first impression of him may have been wrong." Taking a measured breath, the woman added, "I am the queen Primitiva. You may call me Prim."

Carefully he tried to sit and found his body felt more like the lava in a bath then of a body, "I don't feel well."

"No, dear, I suppose you do not. Perhaps we should start with a simple conversation before we get better acquainted."

"Yes, I suppose that would be good."

Flint swallowed hard now seeing the room that he was held in. Bones for walls. Light illuminating out of nowhere. Red blood… a river on the floor. "This place… What is it?"

"This is my private castle. Those who are no longer capable of life dwell here. Their power feeds this place. At least until their bones turn to dust."

Alarmed, he pressed himself to the head of the bed. "You said I was not dead."

"Darling, I was asked to take you someplace safe. I cannot think of a safer place than among the greatest of my creations. For every bone that you see… it is that of a gifted warrior. Their blood is the river that you see. They are dormant now, but are still capable of being should I need them." She paused for just a heartbeat, "Do you doubt what I tell you?"

Flint shook his head. His father had taught him that a creator was to be treated with the greatest respect. Never doubt them. Never ask them to prove their power. A single creator was a hundred times more dangerous than all other Fey combined. Their power… their gifts alone could do so many great things. Or so many horrible deeds. It made sense now. His father had been preparing him for this. "What will become of me?"

Prim slowly got to her feet. Feet that never touched the ground. Her hand passing lovingly over the bones that she passed. Then she turned, her wings no longer visible. The mist that had covered her turning into a shimmering midnight blue dress. Her fire red hair cascading down her back. A simple crown of silver now adorned on her head. "That is up to you. You may come and live among my creations and be with your brothers. Or you may stay here until you are ready. It makes little difference to me."

Before he could think, Flint squeaked out, "My brothers are alive?"

"Alive, yes, but not how you remember them. All enchantments that made them appear older and stronger are now gone. As they are with you. Those who come here cannot hide behind enchantments such as those."

Again, he swallowed and held his hands out before him. Small hands. A child's hands. Then at his sides… stone gray wings. His wings, they had been reformed. Carefully, he pulled them around himself. "My brother's, they have their wings?"

"They do. As do all those who have them naturally."

Swinging his legs over the side of the bed he gulped. There were several feet between the floor and the bed. A river of blood waiting to catch him. It hadn't been until then that he realized what he had been seeing. She was walking… hovering well above the ground. The floor that had looked within reach was in fact too far away. She was creating an illusion to keep him at ease. An illusion that he broke just by sitting up. There was no wall of bones… there were mountains of bones. Some still covered in flesh. There, just at the edge of his vision he could just make out shapes. Focusing on them, he could see… could make out… bodies bathing in the river. Gulping air, he tried to smile, "I would like to be with my brothers. If you would permit me."

Slowly Prim drew closer once again. "You are better mannered than your brothers. I should hope you teach them all that you know."

The Fallen

CHAPTER 22:

APOLLO

Apollo slowly opened his eyes and smiled. He was home. Everything had been just a bad dream. He was still in his father's castle. His brothers were safe. Magmas would be crowned, king. Everything…

No. Everything was not as it should.

His hands were much smaller than they should be. His arms were covered in a robe of light blue. His wings were nearly translucent instead of solid. Wings of a child… of a youth.

Closing his eyes, he tried to shut everything away. Every emotion. Every thought. Everything. He was in a better position than he would have been had his father sold him into slavery. For that matter, he was in a better position than he would have been if he would have become a pet to another queen. Taking a deep breath exhaled slowly. He was safe. He was warm. And he had at least one of his brothers with him.

It was enough. It had to be.

Carefully, he slipped out of the bed. A bed that he could not remember falling asleep in last night. A bed that now that he could see it was nothing like the plain raised platform that he was accustomed to. But rather a large rectangle shape with layers of thick coverings. Each layer a different color. Coal black on the top and a light cream for the one closest to his face.

Letting his eyes take in the room, he saw the smooth gray walls. Clear glass windows revealing a red sky. A large polished stone desk with matching bookshelf. Letting his feet touch the floor, he smiled. Warm. Lava rocks. And if there were lava rocks there had to be a pool of hot lava nearby. Something he could soak in.

Providing the lava here was the same temperature of that of his home. And providing he was allowed to swim in it.

Carefully, he padded over to the open door. A private water closet. The tub was large enough that he could lay in it with his wings open. On second though his father could lay in it with his wings opened and still have room for another person. Turning the faucet on he let the moment of disappointment flow over him. Clearwater not molting hot lava.

Something he would have to get use to.

A knock on the closed door had him shuffling back out to see who was bothering to announce their intrusion. The man he met the other night. The one made of mist "King Nicco?"

"Ah, so you remember my name."

His smile was not comforting. Not now that he could see his teeth. Razor sharp and ready to devour him." Yes, sir?"

"Do you find your room adequate?"

Was there a safe answer? "It is almost like home."

"Good then my queen shall be pleased. Now you have a choice. I can show you around your new home or I can take you to the dining hall."

His stomach answered for him, "Food would be wonderful. Thank you." He paused, "Am I dressed accordingly?"

"Since this castle was built for the Drakens, you are dressed better than they are. Except for Ean few dress at all. Then again, they rarely come here."

"Then why is it for them?" He paused, seeing the veiled amusement in Nicco's eyes. "I mean..."

Nicco chuckled with amusement, "No, it is fine. The castle was once a... forgive me, I forget mundane words... Volcano. Yes, I believe that is it. The spewing of lava and ash intrigued my queen. So, Prim had the castle built inside of it. Lava flowing at all times. This is where she comes to think. It becomes too hot for most to tolerate for any length of time. Except it would seem for those who she has brought here."

"Fey? She brought other Fey... here?"

With a shrug, Nicco answered without concern "Some." Then he paused before carefully adding, "Most are resting. Others are milling about. One is creating flowers in one of the courtyards. Another has refused to leave the lava bed."

"Lava bed?" How he longed to lazily rest in the warmth of a lava bed. To swim between the magma bubbles. Hopefully, it was something he could do fairly soon since there was at least one Fey that was already enjoying the pleasure.

"It flows around the base of the castle. I assume it is several feet deep. Personally, I lack the ambition to see if I could survive a swim. But then again, I do not temp things just to see if I should survive. I leave that for the youngsters."

"Your son?"

For a moment, Nicco paused, then sighed as he said, "No. His children. Now come we shall see if there is anything that you will enjoy eating. I am assuming my queen has some knowledge of what you may prefer to eat. Then again, she may wish to see if you find the normal fair here more appealing."

The castle was not as he expected. Solid walls made of shimmering red and amber stone. Flecks of gold embedded within the gray lava rock floor. Paintings hung depicting great battles with various monsters. Every few yards anther battle, each with a different creature. "Did any of these battles actually happen?"

Pausing, Nicco narrowed his eyes at the nearest painting. "This one." He tapped the gold frame,

"Is the battle of the Endless Sea. It happened no less than fifty years ago. See this worm-like creature here."

Apollo nodded once looking closely at the worm-like creature. A circular mouth and several rows of sharp teeth. Several what looked like part Fey and part something else that swam fighting the creature that was many times larger than they were.

"This is a Charybdis. Nasty creature. Prim had been reading about them and decided that she wanted to see one up close."

"So, she created it."

"Created? Summoned? We have never been sure. Then again, it is possible that it had already existed and came fourth after being disturbed. In any case, it started attacking the water dwellers. They, in turn, began to fight back. Several scores died trying to defeat this creature. Since then only smaller, more manageable ones can be found."

"Oh." For a moment Apollo thought about what he had been told, then shook his head, "If they are so dangerous why does the creator not just do away with them. Surely she has the power to do so."

At that Nicco smiled, "They have a delightful taste. Even if they are difficult to kill. At any rate, it is a good way to get in some proper training."

Continuing down the long corridor and seeing many more battles. Apollo asked, "So each of these happened then?"

"Some. Others are depicted from stories that the goddess found interesting. Although if you ask I'm sure that she can create anything you see here… just on a much smaller scale. She has no intention of bringing forth a creature that she cannot control. Or one that would harm her people."

"She could not control the water worm?"

"It would not listen to reason and stop attacking. She destroyed it with no more than a thought. It is the only time I have seen her kill anything. I do not wish to see her do so again."

So different from what he had been told about her. He had half expected her to have most of her people enslaved, but certainly not this. Perhaps it was a blessing that his father had found her. But it was also reasonable that now that he was here the creator lacked the ability to really do anything should Azia come here. "If she needed to protect those she rules over would she kill?"

Nicco stopped understanding the boy's worry, "I pray that we never allow her to need to. Prim has created everything that you see. She can destroy everything if she chooses. All those who serve never forget that. And we all do whatever we need so that she never needs to kill."

As the two-story marbled white doors opened Apollo paused before letting a smile fill his face. His brother… Magmas… was already seated and the long onyx table. Plates of delicacies filling the place in front of him. The light-bearer Alec seated across from him looking relaxed yet still making sure his charge ate his fill.

There was no need to say anything until he was nearly an arm's length from his brother. "Hungry or if the food just that good?"

Pausing from taking another bite of some kind of airy yet fruity pastry Magmas glanced up. "Both." He held up his fork, "Try it. I have never tasted anything like this."

No use saying, he could get his own, so he bent over and took the offered food. His eyes closed at the sweetness. Swallowing Apollo scanned the table for whatever it was that his brother had given him. There just in front of Alec was a platter filled. Using a simple spell to move thing the plate raised, then set itself in front of them. Satisfied, he took a seat carefully sampling everything provided.

Taking a seat to Apollo's right Nicco smiled, "I assume manners were not standard teaching upon your star."

Blankly both boys looked at him, but it was Magmas who answered, "Since I was told by the light-bearer that everything on the table was for us. We assumed that we needn't ask for anything."

We assumed. Meaning the two had a conversation without actually saying a word. "Even so the queen likes us to uses pleasantries such as please pass… or may I have? Especially among the younger ones." Nicco paused, then raised an eyebrow as he added, "And mind, speech should not be used unless needed."

Apollo paled, "We meant no disrespect. Mind speech among royal Fey is common practice when speaking to each other. Within the Star Cities, verbal speech is not as common unless speaking to someone who is not blood-related."

Leaning back Nicco nodded to Alec, "We will make sure Prim discusses what she will and will not tolerate. Until then…"

"We will use our voices. You have our word." The two said nearly in unison.

Alec smiled, "Ah, let them be. You know as well as I if Prim didn't want them doing something they wouldn't have the ability to do so."

"Or she was distracted that she overlooked something so obvious." Nicco snapped back.

Scratching his chin Alec shook his head, "Could be but I doubt it. She has had more than enough time to consider everything. And I know for a fact, none of the other guests are able to mind speak. Least not yet."

Narrowing his eyes Nicco leaned forward, "We will discuss it with the goddess. Or I can eat you."

"You wouldn't dare."

In a breath, Nicco faded into a shadow and crossed under the table. Alec seeing the threat, pushed away and hovered just above the table. Both of the boys stopped their meal and carefully slid away from the table wanting no part in whatever was about to happen. Then just before Nicco could take solid form the double door crashed open. The sound of deep thunder filling the room. Another door. This one made of bones and mist formed opposite of the marble doors.

In the doorway leading out to the hall, a dark Fey stood his eyes locking not on Alec but where Nicco was now seated. His face drawn tight with controlled rage.

Stepping out of a door made of bone and mist stood Prim, her face spoke of her displeasure, but her voice hid any of her anger as a small boy stepped out behind her. He poked his head from around her side and smiled, "Magmas? Apollo?"

Both boys smiled no longer caring what the adults did. "Flint." A breath later, the three were hugging.

Prim glanced at the table, "Boys please finish your meal. I doubt it will taste as good should it get cold."

All three boys look at one another before answering, "Yes mama."

"Nicco. Alec with me. Now." Prim turned and stepped through the mist, leaving no doubt that one or both would be received the sharp side of her tongue. Another crack of deep thunder and the door vanished from wherever it had come.

The Dark Fey shivered, then took a step into the room. "I trust we will not have any problems while the goddess is away?"

Magmas' eyes widened. His eyes taking in the features of the man who was now crossing the room. Midnight black hair. Dark eyes… too dark to determine the actual color. Deeply defined muscles under his black robe. This could only be one kind of Fey. One that held dark abilities. He swallowed hard. Dark Fey were dangerous and unpredictable. Calm one moment then … bodies would be torn apart littering the ground not a breath later. And that was only *if* they were playing. Only the gods knew what they would do if truly provoked for none had ever lived to tell. "No trouble from us, Sir."

"Sir, is it?" He straddled a seat near where Nicco had been seated not a moment before. "My name is Donovan. I govern all Fey with we shall say darker abilities. As well as serve as general to the queen's elite guards. However, you may call me Donny. Most of the children do… at least until they cross me."

Apollo pressed himself into his seat. "Where did the others go?"

"Considering the look in the queen's eyes? I would bet on the under castle. Those two have been hissing and snarling at each other for years. Personally, I find it entertaining. The queen on the other hand… Not so much." Slowly he stood. "Now I will leave you to your meal. Once you're finished, I'll be outside. Prim wants you to see the grounds."

The three of them waited before the door closed behind him before drawing an easy breath. "A dark Fey?" Magmas finally gasped out.

"I think we need to learn the rules here and fast."

Flint leaned back in his seat, "I don't think they're allowed to harm us. But I could be wrong."

With Magmas' shrug, Apollo asked, "Flint?"

"Father asked Prim to protect us. Keep us safe. I doubt doing that translates to killing us."

"Even so." Apollo sighed, trying to take everything in, "I for one do not wish to find out if it does or not."

Magmas glanced at both of his brother's, "Agreed. Whatever enchantment father had on us to appear nearly grown is now gone. As are most of our abilities. Plus, if any of the stories about dark Fey are even remotely true… we could all be in serious trouble."

Keeping his head down Flint gave both of his brothers a sideways glance not yet ready to voice what he knew. The dark Fey could possibly be a creation and not a true Fey. If that was true, then it was possible that he only had about half of the powers that a true dark Fey would be born into. Even so… he for one was not willing to cross that man. Or anyone here for that matter.

CHAPTER 23:

ALEC AND NICCO

"What in the name of all I have created do the two of you think you were doing!" Primitiva yelled her voice shaking loose several bones of long forgotten citizens. The echoes rolling over the vast empty landscape like deep thunder.

Both of her favorites flinched. Over the centuries they have butted heads a time or two never had they done anything to make her this mad… mad enough to make her bring them to her under kingdom where the dead still roamed. The place where her temper could run without recourse.

Carefully Nicco swallowed, "I was only trying to make the children relax. I meant no harm goddess."

For just a moment she let a vine of dark mist wrapping around Nicco's throat prohibiting his transformation or escape. "I should strip you of your gifts right now. Leave you for my children to feast on. I should…"

Alex shifted his weight deliberately shifting her attention to him, "The fault is mine goddess. I have been too occupied with the fallen Fey and misinterpreted Nicco's intention."

She let Nicco go seeing the fear in his eyes. A long, tense moment longer so that he could understand the rage that was deep within her eyes and she pointed a long, narrow finger at both of them, "This will not happen again. Is that understood?"

"Yes, goddess." Hanging their heads like two boys who had been scolded without understanding why, both Alec and Nicco said in unison.

Sharply she turned from both of them, then hissed. "You both will remain here until I decide what I will do. For this one time, you are saved from my pets." A clap of thunder louder than any storm then the doorway appeared. "You should come to the understanding right now… this silly game you play with each other ends… *now*. I will not tolerate this game any longer…"

As she stepped through the doorway they both breathed in relief. "Shit."

Nicco rubbed his throat, feeling the bruise already forming. The first bruise since he could remember. "She is more irritated than I have ever seen."

"Irritated? Irritated? Damn it Nicco don't you realize you could of cost us our lives with that damn stunt. She's not *Irritated*… she's pissed off and overwhelmed. "

Kicking the dirt that seemed to cover everything Nicco shook his head, "No something else is wrong far beyond us. And it started with the boys coming here."

"At least *that* we can agree on." Alec paused, seeing something moving far beyond the edge of his vision. "What pets does she house here?"

"You would know better than I but I think those here do not need food or air to survive."

Giving his brother, a menacing look Alec growled with frustration, "How delightful. More so now that I am stuck here with you along with them."

Turning Nicco shrugged, "Well, I'm going to find the castle it may yield some answer to help the goddess. You can do as you please."

Alec turned, "If I could kill you I would… but you may have a point this time."

"I always have a point to everything that I do. It is you that have yet to understand that."

Taking a step over a pile of fresh bones Alec hissed, "Then please enlighten me."

"You see the goddess and I enter her private room… You see that the room is sealed from all others. You assume what we do is what you do with her. Yet you do not look beneath the surface. In all of the years, you have not considered why Ean and I go into that room."

For a long time, Alex didn't speak instead choose to watch where he stepped carefully not to step on the bones of Prim's chosen. Letting Nicco's words tumble in his head, he finally hissed, "So what do you and Ean do with her?"

Nicco let out a soft laugh, "You make a poor excuse for a guard. But since you asked, we keep her informed on several things. Only Eostre can be everywhere at once. Our ability to travel… to see and hear all that is around us. Couple that with my ability as the king of my people I can see and hear all that they do. Or at least most of the time. It is very confusing to hear thousands of conversations at one time, but it is useful."

Alec paused too stunned for words. "You have never mentioned that once. Damn you, do you realize how many times that could have become useful over the centuries?"

Nicco shrugged, "I am not a guard. It is not up to me to keep our lands safe. That is what you are to be doing. However, considering the amount of true Fey that is now in our lands it is becoming more apparent for me to help you."

He could strangle Nicco. And would if the demon would stand still long enough without turning into mist. "You are infuriating."

Rolling his eyes Nicco pointed. "I think that is the castle."

All of the castles that they knew were built up into towering structures. This one was round and made of more bones. "Am I to believe that every living person who becomes no longer living is brought here?"

"That or the bones that are too hard for even me to eat. Prim said once that every tissue carries the power of the one who body it once came from. From her point of view bones *are* tissue."

"How wonderful. Remind me if I die I do not want to become a wall."

Nicco bared his teeth in an insincere smile as he joked, "Of course not. You could become a chair."

Alec narrowed his eyes and hissed, "I hate you."

It wasn't a castle, but a maze filled with rooms. Doors made of pulled flesh. Behind the doors were those who should no longer be alive. Trolls who had died from some illness. Ill-tempered and trapped behind the doors. Their drool still dripping from their jaws. Another room. A creature with large coral red eyes and a breathtakingly lovely face. Until gills came from behind her ears, hiding her hair. Her legs turning into a tail and her arms into fire. Too quickly Nicco closed the door before she could attack. "What was that?"

"You sound scared for an almighty king."

"Shut up Alec." Nicco paused. "Perhaps we should not have come here."

Seeing the great and fearless king becoming unnerved Alex gave a conspiring smile as he said, "Perhaps what we seek is deep inside."

The Fallen

CHAPTER 24:

PRIMITIVA

For her little star, it was early. For Osiris? She just hoped Magmas was close by his private room. Holding the seer's eye in the palm of her hand Prim called out. Slowly the fog of the eye cleared just enough for her to make out the empty room. Just enough to see Magmas was not there. Annoyed, she sighed as she thought of her home once. Thought of Lunaista. The image within the eye changed. People scurried from place to place. Their bodies, tight with fear. No longer did children play in the streets passing time until they were old enough to be useful. The palace was filled with more guards than it needed. Several of them showing signs of recent beatings. Deep gashes and welts. Most no longer wearing their wings.

A few might be able to recreate their wings. For most, it would never be. Not unless they had help.

What had happened to her home? Her mother had been cruel, but Starlis? Starlis despised cruelty. Hated seeing anyone in pain. She should have been able to stand against this. Too clear now that her sister was far weaker than what she had thought her sister should be.

It would be years… several light cycles before her daughter would be able to rule. From what Magmas said he didn't want her ruling anything. And with good reason.

Pulling back Prim sat the eye on a stand that she created to hold it. She needed to think about what she could offer. Needed to think about what she was willing to do. War was coming. Her choices would decide the outcome.

Frustrated, she paced. She had to do something. If she did nothing to help Azia would destroy most of the Star Cities… most of those who would one-day rule would be slaughtered. Innocent children were torn apart because they were royal Fey. Pallas would survive, but just barely. For Pallas to be destroyed would be the end of all Fey. She had seen that in her last vision. ` Only she held the key to saving not only her home… her little blue star… but most of the Fey. Most of those who lived within the great Star Cities. All she had to do was figure it out.

Letting her eyes close she let the mist seep from her body. Let the tendrils seek out those whom she had brought to her home. Slowly caresses each of their minds seeking an answer to an impossible riddle. Slowly a dark smile formed on her face.

Azia was searching for something. Searching for someone to keep him in power. He knew his time was coming to an end. His choice was to eliminate all those who could overtake his position.

Fool.

Did he not realize by killing those with true power and natural abilities, he was going to forge alliances against him? Obviously not. However, this was not her problem. Least not yet.

Then again, it did give her a reason to act. Yes, that would do nicely.

As she wielded more power than any other Fey in the history of Fey she could do this. As her little star was larger than Pallas and had more than enough room, she could hold a summit.

… No. Not here. That would put her people at risk.

With her eyes still tightly shut, she sought out a place. Ah yes. On the dark star. The star of the ancestors. A place that was sacred and was no longer used by any. Yes, that place would do nicely. The Azia would have to yield to her or risk waking the Silent Ones. Risk waking those with true power. Even he was not that reckless.

Calling the tendrils of mist back to her she allowed herself only a moment to decide her next course of action. She didn't need the seer's stone to reach Magmas. Actually, she had never needed it, but she hadn't wished for that truth to be reviled. At least not until now.

Her mind reached out across the Void to him. In a moment she knew all of his thoughts. Knew he was just buying time until he could bring his children home. Knew he feared her more than the Azia. Knew she could trust him because he did not seek the power of Pallas. Lest not any longer. No, he only sought a way to end the madness that Azia was now forcing the Star Cities to live by.

Magmas, she called out directly to his mind

Puzzlement then, *Primitiva?*

Bring all who will join you to the dark star. I will meet with them. The choice of action will be left on their shoulders. Not mine. I will not rule Pallas. Nor any Star City.

Not even a moment of hesitation to her request before he answered, *Agreed.*

The Fallen

250

CHAPTER 25:

PRIMITIVA

Shesha landed gently on the solid cold ground of what his queen referred to as the dark star. "Shall I wait here, my queen?"

Primitiva let her eyes. Focus on the empty ground of solid gray ground. The others would be here soon. Magmas had told her of more than two hundred rulers would meet with her. More were willing but feared if more of them traveled this far the Azia would find out. Still, she had agreed. "Yes, But I think you should take a smaller shape."

"As I did when you first created me?"

His deep voice was filled with amusement. She appreciated that. "Yes. If you would not mind too terribly?" Her answer was the tiny dragon coiling around her arm. Petting her little companion, she spoke more to herself than to him. "Now I need for this star to be seen yet those who land on it to be hidden." She took a few steps seeing something sticking out of the ground.

Drawing closer it appeared to be some kind of heavy door. Pulling it open she gasped in surprise. A large golden staircase led deeper into the rock. Carefully, she followed it… followed the light now streaming out of the darkness. Then at the bottom she let out a startled gasp. A large waterfall of purple mist cascaded into a pool. Flowers that she had never seen sprouting from what she assumed was grass despite it being every vibrant color other than green. Tiny creatures flying around the flowers. Looking more closely she could see that they were in fact fairies. Tiny fairies only the size of her long nails.

"Can I help you?" A deep, annoyed voice spoke from behind her.

Holding her head up high she turned to the sound and fought hard not to quiver. There standing just a few feet away was a Feyen man. His wings, matching hers in every way. His violet colored eyes filled with anger. But was his face that held her. She had seen that face only once before. It was the night before she had jumped into the Void. It was the face of the man who would create life with her daughter. Shaking the memory from her thoughts, she slowly answered him. "I am sorry for the intrusion, but I had been told none still lived on this star."

His eyes narrowed as he glared at her not caring if she was older nor if she was another creator or not. "We do not wish to be disturbed." He snapped out. Then he took a breath, seeing her unfazed by his temper. Slowly he asked, "But you are not just some Fey. You are a creator… yes?"

She bowed her head slightly, "I can create things yes. But I do not have formal training."

He turned from her and spat out, too worried about what her being here would lead to, "Is that why you came here? To expand your own training? Or perhaps to conjure up your own populous and create a new Star City."

"No, sir. I came here to hold a summit. There is a war brewing among many of the Star Cities. I wish for my own star to remain neutral for as long as possible. I have already seen the destruction that this war will bring. I see no reason for the children to suffer."

Circling her still not trusting her words he hissed, "And you came here… Why?"

"I came here it speak to those who oppose the Azia and what he is doing. I came to offer my star as a sanctuary for the children of the royal Fey. Perhaps show them another way to live. One where the populous is free to live in a way that makes them happy, but causes no harm to those around them."

For a long time his closed his eyes. Finally, when they opened, he nodded. "You speak the truth. We have known for a long time Azia was no longer fit to rule. Because of that we will allow you to use our home for this summit. The Silent Ones will not wake while you are here."

"Thank you."

Finally calming his anger, he shook his head, "No my dear, thank you for having the wisdom in finding a way for peace without the use of your gifts. You are not yet ready to wield that power."

"No. I will never be ready for that. The one that will has yet to be born."

Letting his long, narrow fingers scratch his chin a slow, calculated smile formed on his thin red lips, "Yes, I see her too." He paused now letting that smile brighten his thin face, "Would it surprise you that she will be in my blood."

Prim looked around her and gasped now seeing the danger of this Fey. "You led me here."

Not concerned about her any longer he didn't answer her question, but rather continued his original thought. "I am Magnar. You and I are the Last of our kind. Unless you count the Silent Ones."

Glancing back up the stairs she could hear the rustling of stones. "They have arrived, but I wish to speak to you further."

Magnar turned to slip down a long tunnel and away from her summit, "We will. But not now. Do what you can. And I will keep the silent one in slumber. Pray that we never come face to face with them." He paused, "Those who arrive will not see my home only solid rock. Should they come into this tunnel their lives will be forfeit."?

Shesha landed gently on the solid cold ground of what his queen referred to as the dark star. "Shall I wait here my queen?"

Primitiva let her eyes focus on the empty ground of solid gray ground. The others would be here soon. Magmas had told her of more than two hundred rulers would meet with her. More were willing but fear if more of them traveled this far the Azia would find out. Still, she had agreed. "Yes, But I think you should take a smaller shape."

"As I did when you first created me?" His deep voice was filled with amusement. She appreciated that.

"Yes. If you would not mind too terribly?" Her answer was the tiny dragon coiling around her arm. Petting her little companion, she spoke more to herself than to him. "Now I need for this star to be seen yet those who land on it to be hidden."

She took a few steps seeing something sticking out of the ground. Drawing closer it appeared to be some kind of door. Pulling it open she gasped in surprise. A large golden staircase lead deeper into the rock. Carefully, she followed it… followed the light now streaming out of the darkness. Then at the bottom she gasped. A large waterfall of purple mist cascaded into a pool. Flowers that she had never seen sprouting from what she assumed was grass despite it being every vibrant color other than green. Tiny creatures flying around the flowers. Looking more closely she could see that they were in fact fairies. Tiny fairies only the size of her long nails.

"Can I help you?" A deep, annoyed voice spoke from behind her.

Holding her head up high she turned to the sound and fought hard not to gasp. There standing just a few feet away was a Feyen man. His wings, matching hers in every way. His violet colored eyes filled with anger. But was his face that held her. She had seen that face only once before. It was the night before she had jumped into the Void. It was face of the man who would create life with her daughter. Shaking the memory from her thoughts she slowly answered him. "I am sorry for the intrusion but I had been told none still lived on this star."

His eyes narrowed he glared at her not caring if she was older nor if she was another creator or not. "We do not wish to be disturbed." He snapped out. Then he took a breath seeing her unfazed by his temper. Slowly he asked, "But you are not just some Fey. You are a creator… yes?"

She bowed her head slightly, "I can create things yes. But I do not have formal training."

He turned from her and spat out, too worried about what her being here would lead to, "Is that why you came here? To expand your own training? Or perhaps to conjure up your own populous and create a new Star City."

"No, sir. I came here to hold a summit. There is a war brewing among many of the Star Cities. I wish for my own star to remain neutral for as long as possible. I have already seen the destruction that this war will bring. I see no reason for the children to suffer."

Circling her still not trusting her words he hissed, "And you came here... Why?"

"I came here it speak to those who oppose the Azia and what he is doing. I came to offer my star as a sanctuary for the children of the royal Fey. Perhaps show them another way to live. One where the populous is free to live in a way that makes them happy, but causes no harm to those around them."

For a long time, his closed his eyes. Finally, when they opened, he nodded. "You speak the truth. We have known for a long time Azia was no longer fit to rule. Because of that, we will allow you to use our home for this summit. The Silent Ones will not wake while you are here."

"Thank you."

Finally calming his anger, he shook his head, "No my dear, thank you for having the wisdom in finding a way for peace without the use of your gifts. You are not yet ready to wield that power."

"No. I will never be ready for that. The one that will has yet to be born." Letting his long, narrow fingers scratch his chin, a slow, calculated smile formed on his thin red lips, "Yes, I see her too." He paused now letting that smile brighten his thin face, "Would it surprise you that she will be in my blood."

Prim looked around him and gasped now seeing the danger of this Fey. "You led me here."

Not concerned about her any longer he didn't answer her question, but rather continued his original thought. "I am Magnar. You and I are the Last of our kind. Unless you count the Silent Ones."

Glancing back up the stairs she could hear the rustling of stones. "They have arrived, but I wish to speak to you further."

Magnar turned to slip down a long tunnel and away from her summit, "We will. But not now. Do what you can. And I will keep the silent one in slumber. Pray that we never come face to face with them." He paused, "Those who arrive will not see my home only solid rock. Should they come into this tunnel their lives will be forfeit."?

Taking only a moment, no longer than a heartbeat or two, Primitiva calmed herself. For years she had believed that she was truly alone. That she was the only creator left. The fact that there was another… warmed her heart. True, he was younger, but he would have to be if he was to marry Avyanna. No, not marry… rule… he would rule over her. In turn, she would rule over Lunaista. When their child was old enough to rule both would feed the catacombs. And with their deaths, her vision would come full circle.

Another breath and she turned to once again to the above. The others should be arriving soon. It would be best to greet them. However,… She turned once more. With nothing more than a thought, a wall formed at the mouth of the tunnel. Whatever else happened the Silent Ones would not wake. Later she would like to gaze upon them. Take in their features. And if she dared perhaps reach out and touch one of the first Fey. But that would have to be after the summit. And after all of those who came were well on their way back to their own Star City.

Standing near the opening she waited to see several tribute coaches coming into sight. Primitiva turned slowly… looking at each of the messengers before they could reach her. Slowly she let a smile twitch her lips. Her sister was among those who had come today. She could see the emblem of Lunaista. At least she would have this time to see her sister once again.

Then she turned as more messengers came into view. Magmas had said nearly two hundred; it didn't appear that he had told her wrong. One by one the tribute coaches landed. Each then pulled to a resting place due to their ruler's ability. Dark Fey gathered near the back where Fey of Light came to the front. The others… Fey of fire opposite of those of Water. Ones of nature blending in with earth, both groups of minor abilities compared to the others. Those who controlled air and the Void setting in wherever they could. But it was the Fey that controlled death that came the closest to her.

Until now they had been nothing more than a myth. Then again so had the Silent Ones.

Keeping her voice level, she spoke to each of the Fey. Each would hear her words as though she had spoken directly to them. However, the messengers would not hear a word. "Come. We have much to discuss. There is an area below for our privacy. Betray me and you will be forfeit." Primitiva Turned and started down the steps not waiting to see if those here would follow her. She didn't need to. This was far more important than any one of them.

Slowly and hesitantly the royal Fey descended the golden stairs. The look on their faces said they had anticipated some grand tomb worthy of the Silent Ones. The ancestors of the Fey race. The disappointment very apparent in their eyes. All that remained was the stairs.

Primitiva did her best not to smile. Magnar had hidden what was really here quite well… still not enough to fool her. But then again, she suspected that he lacked the skill that she had already processed. Later there would be time to discuss things with him. Right now, she had to keep those here from fighting with one another.

No more than that… she had to keep the Fey who controlled the dead… or at least they said that they could… from finding the stone wall and entering the actual tomb.

Her eyes watched one who she assumed was a female already examining the wall. Her skin barely covering her bones. That one reminded her of one of her chosen who guarded her under kingdom.

Then her eyes caught sight of a sparkling silver dress. Slits on both sides going from the small feet to nearly the hips. Silver glitter covering just enough of the chest to say it was covering the female shape. Then the hair… no longer bright sunlit gold, but the dull sun bleached framing the face of her dear sister. Starlis. Her sister had come.

Emotions collided. Joy at seeing her sister once more. Worry that she looked ragged. Anger that she had let Azia take Avyanna. The frustration that she lacked the backbone to stand against Azia. She could not afford to acknowledge those feelings right now. Instead, she reached out to her sister's mind and simply said, *remain here after the others leave. There is much to discuss.*

Starlis looked stunned for no more than a heartbeat before a slight nod of agreement.

With the last Fey to arrive Primitiva took to the air. Took to hovering at the roof of the massive cavern. Then she smiled as Magmas descended the last step. As he did a wall closed off the stairs and any way of escape. Worried murmurs rose up. More when they recognized her wings… the one ones that marked her as a danger to all of the Feyen race.

Taking a deep breath, she closed her eyes choosing to have this discussion without looking at any of them. "By now you have realized who and what I am. Know this I require nothing from you. You may leave this place and return to your pitiful Star Cities and continue to live under the hand of Azia. Or you can seek a way to end his rule. Your choice matters not to me."

One of the dark Fey edged closer to her. Dark wings and dark eyes common within his kind. A chiseled jaw and a hint of mischief that was almost recognizable to her. Then he spoke and she knew his son was the dark Fey, who had challenged her. "Why should we trust a creator? Your kind is nearly existent."

"Trust me or not. That is your choice. I can leave here now and not think twice."

Joining her in the air Magmas towered over the others, "Enough. We are all here because we agree that Azia needs to be removed from power. Primitiva is our only hope of doing so."

"No." The anger in that one word surprised even her. "No, I am not your only hope. Each of you already has the power to end his rule. I am only here to offer something that none of you have already thought of. Except for maybe Magmas."

"My dear?"

"You are a terrible flirt Magmas; now please join the others I wish to be done here quickly." Nodded with the respect he fluttered down to stand with the others. Starlis grabbing his hand in earnest as he did. "As a seer, I know many in this room will die in the coming war. Your people will be torn apart. But so too will those who stand with Azia. No course of action will stop this." Angry murmurs came from several of the dark Fey. Darker thoughts from those who are said to control the dead. Fear from the lighter Fey, the ones who abilities were of little use. "As such, I am willing to house your children on my own Star City. Providing it remains neutral. I will not choose a side in a war when I see little need for a war, to begin with."

"You have the power to end this before it even starts."

"Why won't you help us?"

"I told you she doesn't have the power that it is said their kind has." More shouts rose up. Anger from all sides. Distress. Worry. Grief. More emotions than she could possibly know.

"ENOUGH!!!" her voice roared through the caverns shaking loose stone from the ceiling. Unraveling part of Magnar's work. Revealing only part of the underground waterfall. "Enough. Now..." Her voice becoming a low growl that scared even her first. "… I will not help because this as of now is not my time. And to show myself too soon would destroy all Fey. Not just those who *might* die in the coming war."

An eerie hush fell over the crowd as they looked upon a Fey that knew the depth of her power. And knew that she needed more time to prepare. Then a light-bearer, a woman who was barely clad in enough fabric to say that was covered in anything softly spoke her voice quite yet strained as she asked, "How would you collect our children?"

Taking a breath to calm herself Primitiva started again. "Azia has already given presidencies for this… and it has the extra benefit of keeping all of you in power a bit longer." Letting the puzzled questions, fill the air, she continued, "You will send all of your children or any others whom you need to hide, into the Void. I will then collect them and take them to my star. As I have already done this once before I am confident in being able to do so many more times."

"Wouldn't the Azia wonder why…"

Magmas shook his head, "I know for a fact he has already done this for more than a dozen Star Cities.

Eliminating all of the children who could rule. Killing the consorts, concubines, and pets for the royal who rules. Forcing them to start over. Doing so yourself will save him time. If anything, he would be pleased and may even think you are following his example."

Another voice, this one airy and light, "How soon?"

"As I am already here... I will stay for one light cycle of this star. Have those you send to the Void carry anything you think that will need. Magmas can share his spell that he used for his boys. It proved most useful."

A dark Fey stepped forward, his eyes lit with dark fire, "If we are doing this what assurance do you have that our children will survive?"

With a bored yawn, Primitiva closed her eyes. As she did the Fey who had questioned, she fell to the ground. His body still as his midnight blue blood seeped from his body. Wounds that none could see. For a long time, no one moved. Then only did so when the blood threatened to touch them. "Does anyone here question that I could kill you? Question that you are only alive because I, so will it?"

One of the Fey who looked little more than skeletons with skin tried to use their abilities to revive the fallen Fey. Then two more joined frantically trying to help. Finally stumbled back. All three gasping from fear.

"What say you Fey of the dead? Is he beyond your grasp?"

The three Fey exchanged worried looks with one another, then fell to their knees, bowing as that would only do for her. Submitting completely to her and her will. Carefully and hesitantly one spoke, "He is beyond even our grasps."

Listening to the worried murmurs and the fear in those who were now pressing themselves against the walls of the cavern, Primitiva fluttered down to where the dark Fey lay lifeless on the ground. She didn't care if his dark blood stained her glittering sky-blue dress. Didn't care if it covered her shoeless feet. For a moment she did nothing more than to stare at his body. Already had she shifted through his mind and found out everything that she needed to know about him. She knew the star in which he ruled. Knew his children were not born to his wife, but from others. None worthy of ruling. Yet he cared deeply for each of them.

She turned away from him as he started to curl his fingers, trying to grasp for anything. Turn just as his body took just the barest of breaths. Keeping herself from giving even the hint of a smile she spoke her voice filled with annoyance, "Very well he may live."

When she turned back to him, his eyes were just barely open, yet he hadn't even tried to get to his feet. Hadn't tested his strength. "Oh, come now Orfeo, surely you have more strength than a day-old babe."

Carefully, he forced himself to get to his feet. Fear lit his dark green eyes. Dark Fire lying just behind them. "You know my name." Not a question, but an accusation.

"I know much about the king of Itzal. The star that lies deep within the shadows. One of only two hundred that gives off no light. I know you have the most potential among the dark Fey. And that you only came here today because you have yet to choose if you will remain loyal to Azia or will fight to end his rule." Now she let a cruel smile twitch on her lips, "You have already seen that I can not only take life but give it. If you wish for your children to live, then prepare them… and do so now. If not, they can remain with you." She took another breath, letting her wall crumble to the ground revealing the golden steps. "Now leave me."

As the last Fey left the cavern Primitiva reformed the wall, trapping both her sister and Magmas inside with her. As her feet touched the ground the last of the illusion spell broke once again revealing the actual beauty of the tomb.

Starlis gasped, "You created this?"

"Don't be drafted, dear sister. This was created long before we were even born. Another creator only hid its beauty from those who had come. Both he and I agreed that those who came should not be trusted more than what they offer."

Magmas closed his eyes, "What are you saying?"

"I'm saying that you Magmas need to rule Pallas, when this is over."

With a snort, he shook his head, "There is Fey here that have more power than I."

"True, but they will be corrupted by the power of Pallas. You will not."

For a long time, Magmas didn't speak. Then his eyes locked onto Starlis, "What do you think?"

"I think… My sister has never been wrong… Except in thinking that I could raise her child."

"No, you could have raised her, but you lacked the backbone to do so. But we are not here to discuss that. We will discuss what will happen after I take the children back to my star."

Starlis lowered her gaze, "I have no child and your daughter will not just jump into the Void because I so will it."

"No, she won't which is why you will do what has not been done in more than one hundred generations. It is still the law and as the queen you can choose to live with it or not. The answer to what is to be done lies within the private sanctum." Turning away from both her sister and Magmas she sighed, "Now before you leave to make preparations… does Azia have any children?"

"He has a son. Still very young." Magmas paused, then asked, "Why do you ask?"

"I want him with me."

Letting out several curses Magmas hissed, "You… damn, you any that get near that child will die."

"Not exactly." Starlis closed her eyes, "He is currently visiting my Star City. Azia gave him it to rule for the next light cycle."

Turning to her sister, she created a small bottle and slipped it into her hand. "Give him this to drink. Any who sees it will think it nothing more than nectar. Actually, any that drinks it besides the boy will taste only that."

"What will it do to the boy?"

"My darling sister… do not ask questions that you do not wish to have the answers to

CHAPTER 26:

STARLIS

With the tribute coach landing safely on the platform of her own Star City Starlis shivered. First, she would do what needed to be done with the hateful little demon spawn that was Griffith. Hopefully, he liked nectar. Then again, she didn't know a Fey that could refuse it either.

Letting the messenger open the door for her, Starlis took a single step her eyes scanning the once filled streets. Just years ago, when she was yet a small child she played happily on these streets. Fathers taught their sons warcraft. She remembered watching them teach the boys to do battle with dull blades. Mothers sang as they created glorious works of art. As they made meals for their families.

Long gone were those days. Now adult men were either guard for the crowns pleasure or slaves. Either way, their abilities were no longer theirs. Their children were ripped from their arms the moment the child could feed and bathe themselves. Mothers no longer sang with joy, they were now forced into silence. Their powers now seeping away every day into the very star that they lived.

If Primitiva was right, she, the queen of Lunaista, could stop this madness and return her home back to its former glory. She had the power to end this. She had to end this. No, she would end this.

She could no longer afford not to.

As she made her way to the palace, she heard the snap of another whip as it hit flesh. She heard the wails of a mother as her child was torn from her arms. The screams of a child having their wings ripped from their backs.

Her feet moved with earnest now. This ended now.

As she entered the heart of her castle she checked her stride. She needed to play the part of the subdued queen. She needed to appear indifferent. No matter what was on the other side of the now cloudy crystal door… she had to see this through.

Opening the door just enough to slip into the room unnoticed she breathed out a sigh of relief. Griffith was meagerly sitting at a long table enjoying a meal. "More nectar your grace?"

His blue-gray eyes studied her as he swallowed, "You have been gone a while."

"Only to visit some of the other queens. My pets bore me."

A cruel smile formed on his tiny lips. "Perhaps it's time for another one to take their place on this pitiful star. I will request one from the shadow stars. It will be a pleasure to tame one."

Creeping over to the table she poured the pale-yellow liquid into his glass. "I was told this is the best nectar within the stars. Your father's favorite vintage, I believe."

Eagerly Griffith snatched the glass. "It's about time you did something to please me." Then he drank every drop from the glass. "Pity there isn't more." He slammed the glass down shattering it on the table.

Starlis watched as a maid hurried over to clean up the broken pieces apologizing for the glass being inadequate.

Rolling his eyes Griffith pushed away from the table. "I am going for a walk. Do not follow me."

Lowering her gaze Starlis mumbled, "Of course your grace." Then she moved to the side allowing him to pass freely.

It wasn't until a guard rushed in that Starlis began to worry. "What is it?" She forced herself to snap out.

"He... The royal... The Azia his son... he just...."

Blubbering fool. What was so horrid that the man couldn't string together a few words to form a coherent thought. Then she heard it. Jumping up from her seat she gasped, "He just what?"

The guard steadied himself preparing to be killed just for delivering the news. "He jumped into the Void."

By the gods, what did she just do? No, she had done nothing wrong. She only gave the boy some nectar. What she had left would be tested by the Azia. Looking unconcerned she turned back to her crystal throne. It wasn't until she fussily took a seat that she even tried to speak. "Please inform the Azia that his son pulled such a distasteful act. I'm sure he will want a full account of what happened here today."

The guard paled until his once golden skin was the color of ash. He nodded only once as he turned to leave.

Starlis didn't need to wait long for the arrival of Azia. Actually, had to wait for a far less time than she would have ever thought. As he came to the double doors he used a gust of wind to blow them open not caring if they shattered or not. Unfazed by his temper she slowly stood, "Azia."

His eyes blazed with anger, "What did you give to my boy!"

Holding the small jar up she showed him the liquid that still resided. "Only nectar my lord. Would you like to test it?"

With long strides, he approached her snatching the jar from her hands. With nothing more than his thumb, he broke open the cap. Slowly he sniffed the contents. Sweet and spicy. Taking a single drop, it rolled on his tongue. Golden honey. Nothing about the beverage said it was tainted. And every spell that he cast all came back only that it was nectar.

Throwing the jar across the room Azia hissed as the glass shattered as it crashed against the solid crystal wall, "What did you do to make him jump?"

"I do not know what you are implying my lord. We discussed my boredom with my pets, which prompted me to visit a few of other Star Cities. Which you gave me permission to do seeing he was here to oversee this Star City in my absence. Once I returned I refilled his glass." She paused seeing the hate still seething in his eyes. "I don't know what caused him but he had threatened to jump several times before. He was one for theatrics always trying things just to see if he lived."

Azia's eyes blazed with anger as his voice lowered into a deep growl, "Are you saying my son was unstable?"

"Of course, not my lord. But the offspring from two different kinds of Fey sometimes does wield unfavorable result." Or very freighting ones like those of her sister. But this was not something that she would say. Least of all to him.

Sagging in her seat Starlis closed her eyes. Challenge one complete. Now she had a day to figure out the rest. The Azia would never believe that another royal child jumped into the Void. At least not one from this star. Not now when he was receiving reports of the other royal star children being claimed as unfit and tossed into the Void by the rulers of their own Star Cities. Not when several of the adults on those stars were also being forced into the Void. All of their power now forever lost.

Getting to her feet she shuffled to the door of the throne room. Passing a maid, she held her head high and growled, "I want every wall, window, and everything that should be see through to be scrubbed. I grow tired at this filth. And make it known I require this of every resident as well."

She hurried past making her way to the inner sanctum. Just outside the only solid door of her little star, she spotted a guard. The way he was trying to avoid her wasn't uncommon. "You, come here."

"My queen?" His voice as soft as a whisper. Too much fear from speculation about what she would require from him.

"Stand guard here. I do not wish to be disturbed."

Relief too apparent in his eyes as he nodded.

Once inside she sighed. How would she ever get through all of these scrolls before Avyanna returned? How to find the law that her sister hinted about among all these stacks of rolled parchment. This was hopeless. Reaching for one that looked aged she sagged against the wall. This was hopeless she was never going to find whatever she needed to.

She was never going to get through all of these scrolls. Never going to find the answer.

No, she had to find … what… her eyes scanned an ancient scroll. The trial of the royals. "What do I have here?" And why hadn't I heard about this before? She wondered.

Her eyes read through the text. Carefully word for word. How did Primitiva know about this text? No better yet… would Azia allow this to happen?

Yes… an amazing smile formed on her lips. He would have to. This law… this trial was set by the Silent Ones themselves. Licking her lips, she stopped herself from laughing. Either her darling niece was going to come face to face with her mother or… may the gods take mercy on her… she would come face to face with the Silent Ones. Either way, this was the answer that she had been looking for.

Going to her private room she felt as light as a feather. Filled with more joy than she had in forever long. She needed to look like the queen of Lunaista. She needed to be the Fey her sister thought that she could be. She needed to be cruel and cunning. She needed to sound like a royal Fey not some spineless house Fey.

Drawing a bath, she soaked away all her doubts. All of her fears. Washed away the dull grime that has built up in her hair for far too long. Scrubbed her skin until she could see the tiny specks of gold once again shining just beneath her skin.

With the last drop of water leaving her bath she let her old self leave with it. Gone was the girl who saw only the best. Gone was the Queen who allowed herself to be ruled over. Gone was the fail ruler of Lunaista. Today she would greet her niece as she should have all those years ago.

Today she would be the queen and absolute ruler of this star. She answered to know one. Today she would take her little city back.

Pulling a silver dress from its hanger she narrowed her eyes.

Her mother had never dressed to intimidate. No, she had done so during her Culling. She understood that now. As she also understood the cruelty that she forced upon her pets. She did so to save the others … to save the citizens.

Well, she was not her mother. And she would not permit harm to any who she ruled over. That to stopped today. That stopped as soon as Avyanna left for the trials.

Her dress was shimmering silver covering her chest leaving her flat belly exposed. Two strands of material attached the top to her skirt at the sides. The skirt cut short in the front then ended at her feet in the back. Stepping in front of her mirrored glass Starlis smiled. Her gold hair like a waterfall of sunlit gold cascading down her back. Her crown silver and shining. She was ready.

The sound of breathing from her door had her facing away from her mirror to her husband. "Why do you look at me that way?"

Slowly he pushed off the door. He had never spoke since the trials. Didn't even remember his name after all of this time. Still, he could not help but to smile. "I have never seen you look lovelier."

She turned back to the mirror, "I'm not trying to look lovely. I am trying to look like a queen."

Coming up behind her, he kissed her neck and whispered, "Then you have succeeded." His lips hovered over her collarbone savoring this single moment with her. "Avyanna will arrive shortly."

Keeping his arm around her, she turned, "You have never come to me like this."

"You made it clear the night we were joined you already had an heir. And taking a mate was for appearances. With Avyanna ascending soon I thought a single moment …" He let the rest trail off no longer able to keep her gaze.

Placing her hand on his handsome chiseled face she sighed, "I want you to do something and not ask questions."

"You command is absolute my queen."

Swallowing hard she made her choice. "Find all those on this star with royal blood. I am banishing you all to the Void."

Horror fell on his face, as did the fear. "Am I not worthy to feed the catacombs?"

"You and all those with royal blood are more than worthy. That is why you must feed the Void. I cannot explain further but I will not allow another moment of pain to come to you. Now go. You must be gone the moment Avyanna comes to the palace."

He blinked away his doubts. "You will no longer have a guard left in the palace."

"I know. One will not be needed. Now go."

The palace was eerily quiet as she watched her niece draw closer. Gone were the guards. Gone were most of the men who dwelled beneath the castle. More than half of the population was gone or soon would be. Their bodies floating with the Void.

Hopefully, Primitiva could carry them back to her star. No, her sister would carry them. She had to. The warriors had to survive.

Her eyes closed as she counted the footfalls until the door blew open and shattered to the ground. Then her niece's thunderous voice. "How dare you summon me back to this pitiful star."

"SILENCE!" The cold in her own voice shook her.

Avyanna crossed her thin tan arms. "So, you decided to be the queen? Hmp. What good it will do you. Azia will let me ascend any day."

Slowly Starlis got to her feet then slowly drew closer to her niece. "You will ascend when I allow it, Niece."

"You forget who Azia favors, Aunt."

Starlis narrowed her eyes into narrow slits. She would not play this game with Ayanna. Nor would she play it any longer with Azia. Holding her head high she kept her voice level as she hissed, "Azia does not have the authority to dictate laws here. I am invoking ancient text and you will abide by it."

"Oooh, so scared." Avyanna turned back toward the entrance way, her raven black hair swirling around her as she did, "Don't forget who has the power here."

With a flick of her wrist, Starlis called forth the ancient staff of Lunaista. "I am inciting the trial of the chosen. As written by the first Fey." The butt of the staff tapped three times on the crystal floor. Fine mist filled the room dissolving into both of their skins. "As of this moment, you cannot ascend until you meet the challenge. Do so and the moment my crown touches your head you will be destroyed. Nothing of you will remain. Not even the mist that you were born from."

Scared perhaps for the first time in her life Avyanna fell to the floor. Azia will not be, please. You cannot do this. You can't."

"I already have." She drew closer to her niece then glared down at her. "I wanted so much for you. But if I must destroy you I will. The tribute coach will take you now to the tomb of the Silent Ones. And as you leave this star perhaps for the final time take a look out of the window and at the bodies of those who I removed from the grasp of the Azia. Their fate will be yours."

The Fallen

CHAPTER 27:

PRIMITIVA

With the both her sister and Magmas heading away from the tomb, Primitiva turned to take in more of the beauty. More of the splendor of this wondrous cavern. Sitting in the tall sweet grass she let her fingers feel the blades. Not course like the green stalk that grew on her star but feathers, soft and flowing. Each one unique. Each one different from its neighbor. Some, one solid color others a mixture of those around it.

"The fairies that tend the grass will get mad if you sit in one spot too long."

Magnar. "I have never felt anything so soft that smelled so sweet."

"Then I insist that you take some of the seeds with you. Perhaps you can grow it on your star. Something to remember this place by."

Seeds? "Of course. Thank you." Slowly she got to her feet. "I told the other royal Fey I would remain here for one light cycle. I think I should have asked if I could before I offered them."

"There are rules. If you can obey them then you may stay." He paused then let out a loud sigh. "Look. I was born here. So, this is my home. But make no mistake I am only a caretaker here. Come I will show you what I can. Perhaps it will help you decide what you can help with."

Puzzled she followed him down a long corridor. He paused once and pointed to another cavern, "That one is off limits unless you wish to become food for the Silent Ones."

"They are alive?!?" She gasped. Her knowledge of Fey already expanding once today. The thought of the once fear race of Fey still alive… she could not fathom it.

"Alive? Dead? I'm not sure. They lay in slumber but are not to be wakened. My parents. They …" He paused trying to find words to explain everything. "They each came from different Star Cities. Forgive me but I do not know what ones. They found each other here. After a time, I do not know if it was out of boredom or they were drawn to each other. But they created me. Sometime later. Not long ago they started auguring. Little things like who was more gifted. Who had a greater wingspan? Nonsense. Anyways… they woke one of the Silent Ones. I tried to warn them.

Anyways by the time they listened it was too late.

He. I think it was a he. I always thought of it as a he. Anyways he ate them. Tore them apart. He said nothing. Not a sound. The look that he gave me … I took it as permission to stay. I cleaned up the blood of my parents and have been tending to this tomb ever since."

"Your parents were both creators?"

"They were. Nothing they tried stopped him. I think he did something so their powers didn't work."

Wonderful. Just wonderful. Didn't she have enough to deal with without adding some ancient race that killed everyone and everything? No that wasn't fair. If they were left alone they were harmless. She just had to make sure no one ever disturbed them. "Is that what you wished to show me?"

Slowly Magnar shook his head, "No the library is this way. It is filled with lots of useful information about Fey that can create. It has notes on how our abilities work. Training guides. Spells and incantation that no to her Fey can possibly do. And there are scores of scrolls on the Silent Ones."

That would be most helpful if she had time to go through everything. "Can I take the scrolls with me?"

Magnar nodded, "This is why I am telling you about them. You may take what you wish. All but one. It is attached to the Silent Ones. As long as it remains here then they can slumber."

"Very well then with your permission, I would like to entomb it so no one will ever be able to find it."

Shyly Magnar smiled, "I was hoping you would say that. I know the incantation but it takes two creators to perform it."

Primitiva stood back admiring the work of Magnar and herself. The scroll was now encased in the heart of the star. Traps that would destroy any that approved the area all carefully hidden. Even knowing where they were she could not approach the scroll without setting off a trap.

"I think that should do it. Any who pass the mouth of the cavern will become food for the Silent Ones. Expect for you of course."

"Your daughter approaches? Yes?"

Prim didn't respond. Instead, she looked far beyond the chamber, "She should be coming soon."

Magnar took her hand. "I will meet her and complete her trial. You need to gather the others now. Once she leaves I will join you on your star. Perhaps together we can find a solution to what is coming."

"How do I know that I can trust you?"

Looking deep into her eyes he offered her his solution. "You bind those that live under your rule. Do you not?"

"I do."

"Then please bind me to you. I will not be able to betray you and you will gain access to my powers."

Shesha flew around the dark star until he was sure the tribute carriage had landed. "Are you well my queen?"

She turned her hand over feeling the power of Magnar and knowing he was the answer to the problem but he needed time to grow into the power. Many more years then it would be before the coming war would begin. "Yes. We must gather the others."

"Do you not wish to see your offspring?"

Primitiva sat back on his back and thought hard about her choice. "No. Now is not the time to see her. Soon but not now."

With nothing more than a hard pump of his wings, he found the speed required the navigate between the Star Cities. Soon floating bodies came into view. "There is more this time."

"Many times, more. If I am correct it is not just the children that they sent but half of the warriors as well."

"This is good. Yes?"

Standing now between two of his long-spiked scales she thought. "It will make the star appear weak. There is no honor attacking a weaker opponent. And by sending me their warriors it will give them time to learn skills that they haven't needed before now."

Saying nothing else she called forth her mist as she had before. Last time there had been a mix of lower skilled Fey and a few royal. This time. They all had at least some royal blood. Even if they were not considered part of the royal family. Castoffs. The extra children who had been sold to other Star Cities.

So not all had become slaves but were given post as guards. That was fortunate for her since she wouldn't have to completely train them.

Patting her friend, her yelled, "Go deeper. I have those that were here."

After moving three times Shesha called back, "They grow heavy."

"Then we will take them to our home and return. I think …" She paused then nodded to herself. "I have always promised you that you would not be the only one of your kind. I should have thought of this sooner."

"You are wise my queen."

CHAPTER 28:

Avyanna

"I will make her pay for this. Treating me… *ME*… Like some common child. How dare she." Avyanna stormed back to the tribute carriage that she brought back to this worthless star. "You. Messenger."

The young man lowered his eyes not wanting to be on the receiving side of her rage.

"Take me to Azia at once. I will see who has more power. My worthless aunt or the great Azia."

He bobbled his head and hurried open the door for her. The fact that he was tired after bringing her here didn't matter. The promise that he could rest once he had taken her home nothing more than a fool's dream. No, all that mattered was taking her back to Pallas. And hoping to rest on his arrival. A hope he didn't think would come true.

Landing within the golden gates of Pallas Avyanna barely let the carriage land before she threw open the doors and jumped out. Her fury a living thing right now. And Azia would fix it. He had to.

Storming up to the palace she didn't take notice of the guards who were dressed in battle regalia. Didn't notice the wary looks on the faces of the former Star City rulers. Didn't notice the tribute carriages being made into war transports.

Paid no attention to anything but her own rage. Her own feelings. At least until she saw Azia leaning over a large map and gazing into each of the Star Cities. Now she used caution. "My lord?"

"I did not call for you Avyanna." His dismissive tone should have been a reason to leave. It wasn't.

Taking a small step into the room she noticed the tension weighing in the air. A violent storm brewing. "There is a matter I wish to discuss with you. If you permit."

His eyes glanced up from his map. "I need the distraction. So out with it."

"Starlis thinks she has the power to enact the ancient trials of accession."

"Does she now?" Azia scratched his chin with his long boney fingers. "I am surprised she even had the backbone to bring it up."

"My lord. Tell me she is being ridicules."

Slowly he came to her. "On the contrary, I think she is finally acting like a queen. Pity that I might lose my favorite but that is the gamble to the trials."

She mouth hung open. "I actually have to…"

"Of course, my sweet. It is usually frowned upon. And in fact, most choose not to enact it because the survival rate is dismal. But if you succeed then you can help me with my little problem I seem to be having. If not. Ah well, I have nothing but time."

"You do not think I will survive?" Her voice came out as a scared squeak instead of the demand that she had wanted.

"Darling you are not made of flesh and blood. You were created from the mist. One day I would like to know how that was even possible but not today. Today you will go to the tomb of the Silent Ones. Perhaps you will succeed where so many others have not. Now leave me. I have much bigger worries to ponder."

She huddled in the carriage to scared to speak. Azia had always treated her as a powerful Fey. A true Fey. If he didn't think she would survive, how could she? No, she had to survive. She had to prove her worth not just to Starlis but to Azia. She had to.

Opening the door, she hissed, "Well it took you long enough to get me here. I would have you whipped if there was any here to hold the tack."

His eye didn't move from her feet.

"You will wait here until my return."

A bobbled nod then he stood aside allowing her to pass. Hoping beyond all hope she would never return.

Now just a handful of steps from the carriage images rushed her mind. So vague she could just make them out within her own vision. Tall structures reaching into the Void. Each a color that she had no name to. So pale and still vibrant. Flowers growing within her footfalls.

A group of children playing some kind of game. Their hands clasped in a circle something forming between them.

Women in long flowing dresses laughing with one another. Men flying above them weaving in and out of the buildings. Younger boys following them.

What was she seeing? Surely this dead rock didn't have a population like this.

Then just before her eyes an explosion. Buildings collapsing. People running. A child stuck under a large stone. An army descending on this place like locus drowning out the sky. The warriors trying to hold them off. Mothers trying to save their children.

No use. The army was devouring the citizens. Their blood spraying everywhere. All colors. From the royal Fey down to the lowest of the Feyen kind. They all died.

The army descended without a word. She could see their faces now. Their mouth, when closed, looked stitched together. The Silent Ones. They came and attacked never saying a word. Never giving a chance for survival.

Consuming thousands of lives in a single breath.

Slowly the vision changed Gone were the buildings Only dust remained of the great Star City. The Silent Ones growing desperate. Turning on each other. Devouring each other.

Only a dozen or so left.

In the sky. Fey. Not just any Fey creators. Their dark solid wings carrying them through the Void. Several dozens of them. They attacked not with weapons but … it had to be a spell…

The Silent Ones retreated. Digging themselves underground. The creators leeched the life from the star turning it dark. Creating an entrance of golden stairs deep into the ground. There the images stopped.

So much of that power was still contained here. If she could harvest the power from a silent one then not even Azia could stand in her way.

Greed consumed her. Slowly a malicious smile formed on her face. If she did have that power then she could rule all of the Fey. Not just those who lived on that pitiful star that she was born to. Oh no, she could rule Pallas. And the Fey would bend to her will.

Following the golden stairs down, she stopped and marvels at the cavern. Fey. Tiny, little Fey lived here. For the most part, they ignored her. She used that to her advantage. Her hands grasping one from the air.

It didn't seem frightened. Looking around her, she could see why.

No more did they look like benign weak Fey. The kind that she could swat away with nothing more than a thought. No… they were armed with tiny weapons and their wings were now those of a creator.

A deep voice spoke from behind her. The words seeping into her very marrow. "We have been expecting you Avyanna." The voice paused then added, "You would do well letting her go."

She spun toward the voice. Just a male. Nothing about him to take notice of. "And why should I?"

He crossed his arms then shrugged as he leaned lazily on the archway of the cavern tunnel, "The last person to snatch one became dinner for them. "

She narrowed her radiant violet eyes into tiny slits, "I could kill them all if I so pleased."

Pushing away from the stone wall he slowly approached, "Can you? Are you sure? You don't look like a creator. In fact, you don't even smell like one." He leaned near her neck and sniffed, "In fact, I think you are nothing more than a creation. Though your creator gave you more liberties than you deserve."

Avyanna stumbled back losing grip on her captive. "I am a Fey. A powerful Fey. You will yield to me." Somehow, she no longer believed that herself.

In one quick movement, he grabbed her arm in one hand and reached into her chest with the other. A quick shove and he pushed her away, shoving her to the ground. Leaving her heart pumping in his hand. Blue mist covering his hand and dripping to the ground.

She tried to scream. Tried to cry. Could do nothing as he held her heart. He could control her or exchange hearts with her. She would live for as long as he did. Her life would be forced to be whatever he wanted. She would be little more than a slave to him.

No longer would she be the powerful Fey she had always dreamed of being.

"Now. I think I will hold onto this for the moment." He sunk her heart into his own chest. His eyes closing as he understood her abilities. Understood, all that she had been told. Understood, all that she had been raised to believe. "Come Avyanna. We have much to discuss." He turned from her not seeing if she would follow him. Knowing she could not disobey his command.

She followed him wordlessly into another cavern. This one looking like a small home that she would find on a star belonging to a dark Fey. What will you do to me?" She could speak now but only what he allowed her to. Words that she found to be annoying. Words that made her sound weak and feeble.

"Did you know all creators are seer's?"

She shook her head to keep from speaking. Not giving him the satisfaction of hearing his own questions said by her voice.

"Pity. I will educate you shortly. However, I was given this by the one who created you." A thin tube of royal blue blood appeared in his hand. As well as some instrument. Forcing her head to the side he exposed her neck, then slowly injected the blood into her. "There that should be enough."

A single tear rolled down her face. Not from pain from what he had done but the pain that lanced her chest from the memories of the pain that she had inflicted on others. "Why do I feel like this?"

"It is called remorse. As a creation, you were lacking in the emotion. The blood of your creator is now weaving itself into your very cells. With it, every emotion that a Fey should feel so shall you. However, she is wise and has added that you will feel the emotions of those you harm. Their pain, hurt, and sadness will now be felt by you. Haunting you. It is a suitable punishment I think."

Her chest heaved heavily as the tears streamed down her face. Too many emotions battering her. Her voice broke into a sob, "That is impossible. The one who created me is dead."

"Sadly no, Avyanna. She only left so you may live." He took a deep breath and broke his illusion spell. Gone was the man who was older replaced by a youth several decades younger than she was. The same midnight black hair and pointed ear. His eyes nothing more than black and blue fire constantly kissing the red orb that was his pupil. His face too young to determine if he would have his father's chiseled jaw or his mother's narrow face and high cheek bone. Temporarily he broke the spell that her mother had created just for her. Allowing her to calm herself he began to speak as though he had this conversation every day. "I am Magnar. From this moment you are forever bound to me as my mate. Though it will be many light cycles before we live together as such."

A moment and a cruel thought came to her, "If I am to be your mate I should carry your heart."

Taking a seat at his small table he crossed his arms, "I do not give you my heart Avyanna. That is something you must earn. However, the moment I allow you to leave this place your life will be mine to control. You may see and hear everything but your actions will be of my creation. Try to fight me and you will only harm yourself. The physical pain will be much worse than the emotional one that you are currently trying to deal with. Trust me for I will not lie."

No. No. No. He could not do this. He couldn't. Somehow, she knew not only would he cause her pain he would take perverse joy in doing so. "Why not just kill me. Surely you have the power to do so."

"I do but for the moment you are worth more to me alive. And under my control." Getting to his feet once more he towered over her. His fingers holding her jaw. Slowly he forced her lips apart with her tongue. When he pulled away he smiled. "See my dear I can do anything I wish to you and you are now powerless to stop me."

"I shall see you dead." She spat out.

"Hardly." Magnar took a deep breath. "I will walk you back to your carriage. You will return to your Star City.

No more will you follow the will of Azia. His laws, his way is no longer yours to follow. You will stand against him."

"No... I…"

"Avyanna. You don't have a choice. Once you leave this place you will be mine. I only tell you this now so you understand. Perhaps one day you will grow fond of me. Perhaps not. But you never rule anything without me. No creation shall."

Following Magnar out of the cavern it became too apparent no matter how she much she tried, she was powerless to do anything. She could not speak unless he willed it. Could only walk in the direction he allowed. Even her wings would not flutter without his consent. She was less than a slave.

She had come here a great and powerful Fey. And she was leaving here not even worthy to be a messenger.

Her body jerked to a stop and she felt the heat of temper rising off of her master. The only thing she had control over was her eyes. There was nothing except the messenger that should cause an alarm… Nothing…

… Then she watched his measured steps. Watched and he offered his hand to help the messenger to his feet. Watched in horror as the bindings that kept the messenger bound to the carriage melted away.

"Come here Avyanna."

Her body once again in motion at the sound of his voice. *What now?* She willed herself to say but no words came out.

"This is Quacey. The first son born to Queen Oriana of The Star City Aurora and King Mehry of The Star City Fauna. He should be revered not treated like …" Magnar narrowed his eyes searching both of their thought for the right word. "… Slave. No more will he be regarded as such. You can take yourself back to your Star City. Your wings shall carry you. Quacey will accompany me."

When she made no move to leave his voice took on a dark growl, "Go now Avyanna."

With that, her wings lifted her without her command and took her deep within the great Void. And hopefully to her death.

CHAPTER 29:

MAGNAR

For a long breathless moment, Magnar stood watching Avyanna flying beyond his desolate star. Watching until he was sure his spell would hold her. Stood silently staring into the darkness of the Void for far longer than what he needed. His temper too volatile to be sure that even speaking he wouldn't destroy the Fey that was watching him with fear resonating within his eyes.

Kicking a stone that had once been part of the great city he turned not caring if it landed a mere foot away or drifted endlessly within the Void. His voice although young still held the hint of embers that burned deep inside him, "Come you can rest within my home until you have your strength back."

Taking a short quivering breath Quincy asked with a soft tenor voice that he had rarely been allowed to use, "What are you going to do with me?"

Narrowing his black and blue fire lit eyes Magnar smiled but not enough to show his teeth. Not his true smile but he hoped would look friendly enough. "In short, I'm going to take you to a place that I know is safe. Now you can either choose to eat and rest before we depart or we can leave post haste."

Food. Just the thought of it made his dry mouth moisten. Ah, and the thought of resting but for a moment… how he longed for a breath for himself. "A meal would be much welcomed. Thank you."

Looking at the tribute carriage He nearly melted the finally molded gold and crystal to the ground. Narrowing his eyes, he looked far beyond the simple contraption. Looked far beyond this time and space. He wouldn't tell this Fey what he had seen but he could tell him something else. "I think we will take the carriage with us. Prim may like to see one up close."

"Prim?" Quincy pursed his lips together. That was not a common name for a Fey.

"Hmm. Primitiva, mother to Avyanna. And the only other living creator other than myself." *Or at the very least the only one he knew about.* "She will house you until it is time for you to come home and live among your people."

Stepping back as though he had been pushed Quincy balked at the thought at returning to his birthplace. Balked at the thought of returning anywhere that housed those who lived for cruelty. "My people? I was cast aside many years ago and forced into a slavery that is worse than death." Then in a deathly low voice, he snarled, "I have no people."

A slow reluctant smile touched Magnar's moist pale lips. A true smile this time. Understanding the man's resentment and all that he must have been told in order to remain a slave. "Has it never occurred to you that all those who are deemed messengers and are forced into this slavery as you call it, is because your abilities are too great to be controlled by the rulers of Pallas? That you are the ones that not only are gifted enough to travel the void but are descendants of the warriors that defeated the Silent Ones?"

Quincy stumbled back too stunned for words. Too scared to trust the boy was saying the truth. Too scared not to. "That cannot be."

"Oh, but it is. Come I will show you." *And together we will create a true army.*

Entering the hidden cavern Quincy gasped, "What is this…? How…." The waterfall, changing from a misty violet to sea foam green. Bending into the next vibrant color before him then changing colors before his eyes. From a misty purple to a sea foam green than a vibrant yellow. Tiny creatures flying about weaving in between the flowers that had been extinct for more years than any could remember. "This is some trick. Not even Pallas has this rare beauty."

Holding Quincy's shoulder Magnar smiled, "Sadly, this is no trick. This is my home. Alas, what you see was created long before Pallas was the star that it is now. And long before the Star City declined into the shadows of what they now are."

"How? Why?"

"This is the tomb of the Silent Ones. They stay in slumber deep within the catacombs. One day they may wake and seek vengeance. If they do the Fey … the Star Cities will be nothing but a memory." He paused giving Quincy time to understand what he was saying. "It is this that we all must be prepared for."

A moment of choice. A moment to define who he wanted to be. "What can I do?"

"First we eat. Then we will go see Prim." *And we prepare to defend not only the Star Cities from each other but ensure they can defeat the locus that were named the Silent Ones.*

The Star was far bigger than he could have imagined. Hovering just beyond the outermost rims, he could feel the pull of the gravity. So much stronger than the pull of Pallas. So much stronger. And the image was so many times better than anything that could be found on any star even that of Pallas. Deep blue covering the majority of the star. Vibrant greens and browns laying way to a shape within the blue. Tiny specks of the greens and blues dotted every so often with white.

"What is this place?"

He could hear not fear but awe held within Quincy's voice. Awe that he too felt. So far from the nearest star yet he could see so many from here. A great vantage point for when the war began. So many ways to defend this star. He could see them all now. But that could wait. Right now, he had a question to answer. "This is the great Star City that belongs to the Creator Primitiva."

"Does it have a name? I- I mean no disrespect I only wish to understand."

Magnar shook his head, "If it does or not, Prim hasn't yet told me. Come, she is waiting. Someone will guide us to her once we break the atmosphere."

It wasn't Prim, but a long silver creature that was many times larger than either of them combined. Larger than the tribute coach that they were pulling behind them. It seemed prudent to speak to the creature. He just hoped it understood words. "We seek the creator Primitiva."

Pumping his massive wings so to hover, he gave a sibilant smile. His long narrow tongue just barely flicking past his large pointed teeth. "I am Shesha. I will not eat you." He paused before leaning his gigantic head closer to the two Fey. "At least not yet."

That was not comforting. "Thank you. We will follow you."

Too quickly, Shesha bolted up further in the sky before he turned, nearly hitting his own tail. Suddenly he grabbed the golden box that the two had brought with them, jerking them from pulling it to the ones that were pulled. Too quickly, he rolled over picking up speed and disorientating both Fey. Insuring neither would be able to see where they were heading.

Magnar stumbled as his feet found the ground. The ropes that bound him to the carriage falling to the ground. It didn't matter how. All that mattered was standing still and filling his lungs with the air.

"I see my darling found you."

Her voice was serene and airy. Almost filled with amusement. Turning to fast and nearly falling as he did, Magnar snapped, "This is not what was agreed to."

Too quickly Prim was on him her thin narrow fingers gripping his throat. Her long red tinted nails prickling his skin, "I agreed to nothing except keeping the fallen children safe."

Clawing at his fingers he struggled, "He is a fallen child."

She didn't look at the other Fey not really concerned. "I do not care about the boy. I care about the box you have brought."

"It will be needed."

At once, her hand let go dropping him to the ground. Her feet turning into a long scaly tale that propelled her to the carriage. A breath more and she once again had feet completely hidden under her long glittering dress. He eyes narrowed at the Fey for a brief moment. "Very well I will house this contraption… somewhere." She didn't turn as she growled, "Donovan."

Magnar hadn't seen him standing in the shadows. Really hadn't had time to see anything other than the enraged Creator that had been standing before him. Seeing this Fey now… he could not be sure that his abilities would save him. Could not be sure he had made the best choice in allies.

Stepping out of the shadow he adjusted his black robe covering most of his large muscles but did nothing to hide his size. Did nothing to hide the raw power that laid far behind his dark soulless eyes. "My queen?"

He breathed in a sigh of relief since his voice sounded much kinder than his expression said it would. Still, he could not hide the quiver of fear. A sideways glance to Quincy and he knew the boy felt that same fear. It didn't matter if both were dark Fey. But clearly, Quincy didn't have the level of darkness and rage that this Fey carried. Just being near this man he could feel the life bleeding out of him. See the colors around him being leached out of the flowers. Out of the grass. If Prim noticed or not she didn't seem at all concerned.

"Take this carriage someplace for safe keeping. I will build a tomb for it shortly."

A small gesture of his hand and carriage was engulfed in a cloud of black smoky mist. When it faded the carriage was no longer resting in what he could not see was an inner courtyard. Tall pillars reaching up to the sky. Each made of a different dark stone. Each carved with intricate designs inlaid with either gold or silver.

Carefully he got back to his feet. "Perhaps we should go inside to speak properly?"

Primitiva narrowed her now radiant violate eyes. "We have time to prepare. The defenses you think of will take both of our skills. But a proper trap should also be created. Come Magnar, you showed me your home. It is the time I show you mine." She turned to head into a door then paused, "This is my home. If you think of betraying me I will destroy you."

And that would be the only warning he would ever receive from this creator. The only warning that she could read thoughts as well as foresee the war that was looming. However, it raised the question of why she hadn't read his thoughts while on his star.

The only answer he could come up with was something there had blocked that ability. Or perhaps she had been hiding that ability. Either possibility worried him. Far more if their enemies found out about it.

The Fallen

CHAPTER 30:

Avyanna

Avyanna landed on the platform for the tribute coaches. She was hot and dripping with sweat. Her mind racing but she was powerless to do anything that came to her mind. She was nothing more than a puppet. Her eyes roamed the streets. Saw into each of the clear glass buildings.

Nothing that happened there concerned her. Males being whipped by their mates. *Their masters.* Children huddled together fighting over scraps of food. She knew many of them would never survive. Nor should they. The weak would feed the lower catacombs never reaching the tribute boxes destined for the other Star Cities. But she wasn't looking at these things for herself, she was showing Magnar. All that she saw he too would see.

The only difference is where she found everything acceptable he did not. Even millions of miles away she could feel his disdain. His anger and his awe. Why would he see the awe in such a boring star? IF he wanted action he should have sent her one of the dark stars. At least there she had things that entertained her.

Her body jerked to a stop as she reached the first step that would take her into the Crystal Palace. He wanted her to do something. To say something. But… her eyes scanned everything. A single guard was approaching. She knew this Fey. He was good for a quick tumble in a bed but nothing she would find palatable to be seen with.

He bowed his head averting his eyes from her as he spoke, "Lady Avyanna?"

She had caused him great pain the last time she had summoned him to her bed. He still held the visible scars and pain. Her hand reached to his face. Too softly her finger trailed his jaw line. Her finger caressing his dry lips. What she longed to do was hear him scream but that wasn't going to happen. Not while Magnar controlled her.

Instead, a soft white light surrounded him. Veins of mist licking at his skin. He moaned softly but not with pain. It sounded more like a sound of relief. The sound of his pain being taken away. She didn't know how but she knew Magnar was doing this. She knew she was not created to heal worthless beings. She was destined for greatness, not this menial task.

She wasn't.

"So Avyanna you did pass the trial."

Starlis. Her aunt. She didn't see her but she would know that shrill pathetic voice anywhere. *Of course, I survived. Now step aside and give me my crown.* Slowly her head bowed as she said the words that were not her own, "Yes aunt. Thank you for allowing me to partake in the challenge. It showed me how unready I am to rule. Please teach me what my mother wished for me to learn."

No. No. No. That's not what I wanted to say. This cannot be happening. It can't. The glee in her aunt's eyes told her plain enough that not only was it happening but she had known before she had sent her there.

Starlis crossed her arms and smiled. Not a friendly soft smile but an I'm-laughing-at-you smirk. "I see you met your mother."

Do you think I would be standing here if I met her? She would be dead and I on my way to Pallas. On my way to bring an army to destroy you. "No, my queen. But I met the man who holds my heart."

Linking her arm with Avyanna she continued to smile as she gently pulled her into the palace. "How delightful. And did he have any messages for me?" Not that she knew of who could possible hold her heart but she could bet Primitiva did.

Snapping back her eyes focused on something far away as words tumbled from her lips. The voice not hers but that of the demon that stole her heart. "Declare your star free from the influence of Pallas. Cite the reason that Pallas has become corrupt and the traditions of the Fey have been called into question. Prepare your people for war. Destroy any who come that do not follow Magmas." The words paused for a moment as she felt that information was being exchanged between the demon and someone else. She could almost understand what that information was but was helpless to do anything about it. "You must break the link between Pallas and your star."

Starlis stumbled back a step gaping and trying to form words. After she let herself acknowledge the fear she nodded in agreement before quickly darting inside of her most private room. A room only the ruling royal Fey could enter. A room that would block all from being able to see or hear inside.

I will not allow you to do this. I will fight you. I will destroy you. Avyanna screamed inside of her own mind. Resentment bubbling up along with her rage. Both being snuffed out will little more than a thought of amusement.

It was then the voice of the demon filled her mind. His voice washing over her. Her body craving the touch of the one who owned that voice. *You will change your mind. However, I have many for you to destroy when the time is right. Providing you live that long.*

She was the heir to Lunaista she had to survive. She would survive. *You may control this body but you will never have me.*

You are nothing more than a puppet. Now behave or I will take away the liberties that I have given you.

A breath more and she knew he was once again gone. Her mind at least was hers even if her body no longer was.

CHAPTER 31:

STARLIS

Slamming the heavy wooden door behind her, Starlis sagged against it trying to catch her breath. How could she break the link with Pallas? It couldn't be done without destroying her star. Her home. It was lunacy to even consider doing so.

Forcing herself to take a step to the single round table that was in the room she gripped the cold edges. Whoever was controlling Avyanna was going to destroy her star. Unless…

Prim had slipped a cold black stone in her hand before she had left. She had only said if you should have need of me. Calling it to her now she sat it on the table. Her heart pounding in her chest. Was Azia using someone to control Avyanna? Someone that he knew that would destroy this star?

It was a possibility. But she had the means to find out the truth.

Steadying her breath, she sat in her high back chair. A minute or two passed before she reached out for the cold stone. Another long minute before she summoned the courage to call out to it. "Prim?"

The solid black cleared into a fine gray mist. Another brief moment and she could see her sister's angelic face. "I am need of your counsel."

Prim blinked then nodded to someone who was beyond the vision held within the stone. "You are worried about breaking the link."

Well, that answered one question. Her sister was controlling Avyanna. However, it rose more doubt. "It cannot be done."

"Actually, it can." Prim's eyes closed as she continued to speak, "Deep within the ancient catacombs is the house of scrolls. Call them to you now."

The house of scrolls? It was mostly useless ramblings. And something her sister should never have known about. But that was not a conversation she was willing to have. At least not when they had tens of thousands of miles between them. Closing her own eyes, she concentrated on the room deep in the center of the star. Deep within the ruins of the first castle. Rolled parchments made of flesh. Books written in blood. All of it having the feel of un-drained power. More power than the gate of Pallas.

Her eyes opened as the room filled with things that had once been hidden. "What am I looking for?"

"For the answer. It is there Queen of Lunaista. It is not for me to tell you. This is an answer you alone must find. However," A cruel smiled formed on Primitiva's face, "… those who live in your star you must now bind to you."

Starlis shook her head, "Bind? I do not know how."

"It is quite simple dear sister. Cut your hand and bleed into a barrel of nectar. Have each of your subjects' drink from it. Have them swear their loyalty to you. Have them say they give you all that they are to use, however, you need. You will understand then."

"I will do that once I find the answer here."

"When you do. Share it with our allies." The gray mist once again filled the stone until it was again nothing more than a solid polished rock.

Pressing herself back in her chair, she glanced up at the ceiling and screamed in frustration. "Just once can you not speak in riddles?" Shaking her head, she signed to herself. *"Fine. I will do what you have already done and once we meet again I shall scold you."*

Not that her sister would hear what she was saying but it made her feel better. After many light cycles of having these imaginary conversations with her sister… the thought of actually have one come to light was more than enough to lift her heart.

With every scroll that she unrolled, and every book that she opened she knew two things; one her sister had stolen some of the power that these artifacts held. If she knew it or not, she not at least some of the power of the ancient ones. That though alone was terrifying. And would have petrified her if she too now held at least some of that power.

The second thing that she knew was how the Star Cities now were ruled was not how the great ancestors had willed it. If the knowledge that was held within these dried pieces of flesh could be trusted… then there was enough to point out how to accomplish their vision.

Unrolling the last scroll, she found what she needed. The spell that would disconnect her star… or any star… from the pull of Pallas. It would disconnect any Fey from the power from any Star City except their own. It was risky but it would take away the power from Pallas. Azia would know within hours what she had done. He would attack within a day.

Another scroll. Another answer.

It would be dishonorable to attack her or those bound to her for enacting the laws of accession. Those who attacked any star who had enacted those laws would be an act against all Fey. Or at least until the other Star Cities chose sides. And that would take many light cycles. It had to take at least one thousand light cycles according to those counted on the first Star City who enacted the terms.

It was a risk but once she sent messengers to the others that she knew… Then it would be understood. Azia would spend a lot of time trying to convince them to side with him. He could not force them. Could not order them. He could only try to persuade them or risk tainting the powers that flowed through Pallas.

And that above all else, she knew he would not risk. Not when for every corrupt Fey one foot of the star would change into a horrifying result. If a whole star became corrupt then the citizens of Pallas would begin to change. If what she was reading was true then it was a possibility they would become the creatures known only as the Silent Ones.

That was too great a risk even for him.

Stepping out onto her balcony she took a deep breath. She was not wearing her long golden robes of her royal house. Today she was dressed in long forgotten battle regalia. Yellow-orange metal that fit her form and moved like a second skin. Today she not only a queen but a Fey that would be feared.

A Fey that needed to be feared.

A thousand Light cycles ago, she had stood on this balcony looking down at those who were of age to enter the trials. Back then there had been fear and worry. Longing. And hope. There had been children watching with awe and anticipating the ball and fine dinners of the royal house.

Today it was different. Darker. The weight of their fears weighing heavily on her.

The woman all dressed in long sheer dresses only moderately veiling anything stood directly in front of her. Their heads high as they all faced the palace.

The adult men stood to the right of the circle. The guards were off to the sides all dressed in white and sunburst yellow. Their kilts hiding their male hood but showing the carved muscles in their legs. Their wings held tightly to their backs. And arrogant smirks darkening their faces. The rest of the males stood looking at their bare feet. Most no longer allowed to wear their wings. Those who did… looked too unwell.

The children stood to the left of the females. So many young faces dirt smeared and much too thin. Until today only the strong received food. The weak were tossed into the Void if they were lucky. Today that ended. Today was the real start to her rule. A rule that should have begun a thousand light cycles ago.

Turning to see behind her. Not into the room but beyond that. Onto the street well out of view of the others. It was the last of the citizens of her Star. The forsaken and disgraced. Forced to live on the dark side of the star where nothing grew. Where food was scarce and children rarely saw adulthood. Citizens who could have great abilities but were forbidden to use them.

Out of everyone, it would be these Fey who would be helped the most. Well them and the children.

Using the same spell, she had used when she ascended the throne she spoke clearly and decisively, "My citizens of Lunaista, please raise a glass of nectar in celebration as today we begin a new era in our history."

She knew what they were thinking. They were all choosing to believe either she was with child and Avyanna would never ascend or that she was now ascending well before her time. Still, they raised their glasses.

As the last drop of spelled nectar drained from the last glass she commanded, "My people you will now take an oath to me. You will give yourself mind, body, and ability to me to use as I see fit. No more shall we be independent but of one people. My people."

Nearly in unison, they all raised their glasses and chimed in, "I give to you my, mind, my body and my ability to use as you see fit."

Rays of light encapsulated her. From the lightest of white to the darkest of blue. Power. Abilities that she had only dreamed of. All of them living within her tiny star. Dark Fey. Fey of light and life. Fey who could if trained would bring back the dead and fallen. Others she had no name for their abilities but they were all hers. She could feel all of those powers now flowing through her, adding to her own.

This is what Azia wanted. What Avyanna craved. Power that was freely given. Power like Pallas has not known for more light cycles then not. She understood now and it frightened her.

"I am declaring by the laws of the ancient ones that this Star will no longer follow the laws of Pallas. For far too long we have strayed from the will of our ancestors." Calling in the staff of Lunaista she flew up as high as she dared seeing now that every eye was now focused on her. Rising the staff of clear golden crystal, she channeled as much of the raw untrained power as she could. As much as she dared. "I release this star from the pull of Pallas. I evoke the guidance of my ancestors to create this star in their memory. "A stream of light shot out of her staff encapsulating the star itself before fading.

As she landed once more she could feel the difference. Already the light of Pallas was fading from her star replaced by the power of her people. By her catacombs.

"As of this moment, no Fey who lives on this star will be harmed. Your blood is no longer required. There are no disgraced Fey. You are all one people. And you will all learn how to defend our home. Guards train them well for this is your army."

CHAPTER 32:

AZIA

Sipping on a glass of his favorite sweet nectar and enjoying a moment of silence as he planned his next move Azia lounged lazily in his private sitting room. Avyanna hadn't returned to him so either she had died or she had turned against him. Either was a possibility. Closing his eyes to let his mind wander only to snap up from his seat not a moment later.

Power was leaching away from his star. Leeching away from the catacombs of Pallas. He could feel it just as he could feel something else making his skin prickle. Something that couldn't as of yet name. "Guards!!!!" He yelled has he fastened his long red robes around him narrow body.

The door to the adjoining room crashed open as his personal guards stumbled in too terrified to delay even for a moment. "My Lord?"

"Which Star City dares to defy my will?" He hissed out now recognizing the warning. Understanding what was the only possible reason for the power to be leaving the great star.

A seer ran in before the guards could dare try to deny it. Her long tangled black hair cascading down her bare back. "Lunaista has invoked the trial of the ancestors. They are no longer yours to control." She paused looking at something that only she could see. "All those who thrive on her star are now bound to her. Even in death, they would not follow you."

Damn her. Damn Starlis. He should have killed here long before now. So, she wanted a war. He was going to give it to her. Wouldn't be much of one when he had thousands of Star Cities behind him and none behind her. "Get my carriage and summon the fighters. We will destroy her now."

"No."

Azia spun toward the seer and grabbed her throat. "You dare defy me?"

"The laws and spells are enacted. If you start a war before the shield of truce and you will taint this place. You will corrupt all that has been build. And you will create more of the Silent Ones." She gasped out, "You will destroy all of the Fey. Pallas included."

Tossing her to the side he paced as she fell to the cream stone floor, "Bah. It's an old tale told to scare children. Fey do not become Silent Ones. There has never been such a race." *And if there had been they had long been exterminated.*

The seer gasped for breath as she looked up at him determination in her voice, "No, Azia it is not. There is truth in those words. If you do not believe me then I cannot stop you, but I would rather die in the void then become a Silent one."

"Then go to the Void. And take any with you who feel the same. I will snuff this problem out before it takes hold."

Magmas ascended the stair of Pallas. Gone were the sentries blocking entrance into the palace. Hidden away were the maids to afraid now of the darkness that was overtaking the lush flowers in the courtyard. Prim's plan was working. This would buy her the time that she needed. And he would do his part to buy Prim as much time as he could.

Buy her time that they all needed if they were to survive as a race.

Knocking on the throne room door he waited for it to open. "In your worthless fool." So Azia was already pressed into growling. Well, he would just have to see how much more that he push him. How much more until Azia would do something reckless. How much more until more of the Star Cities saw him as a weak ruler worthy of only death.

Standing within the doorway he watched as Azia pace the confines of his throne room. Watched as he heard Azia muttering to himself. Finally dipped his head in a bow, "You wished to see me, Lord Azia?"

Turning sharply to the voice, Azia snapped knowing nothing within the Star Cities escaped this Fey. Not even things that no one should have known about except him. "What do you know about the laws of succession?"

He knew plenty about the laws. Much then he was willing to say. Acting unconcerned he began to speak in a voice that sounded bored and unconcerned. A tone that he had taken with very few Fey. A tone that would surely annoy the Ruler of Pallas. "Once the spell is enacted you have 1000 light cycles to convince other Star Cities to rally behind you. She, in turn, has the same time to do the same. Since there are currently one thousand Star Cities only one can decide per light cycle. If you threaten, harm, or do anything to force the Star Cities to align themselves with you, you, in turn, will corrupt Pallas. Likewise, for her Star to I suppose."

"Bah. I will find a way around this spell or law and then you will stand beside me as I tear her limb from limb."

Not likely. Not when he had already sided with her. Or more importantly sided with Primitiva. Stepping over the buffet table unconcerned with Azia, he filled a glass of sweet nectar before issuing a warning. "You should read the laws of Pallas, *my lord.* I doubt you will persuade any Star City to side with you when all you offer is pain."

Read the laws of Pallas? Who did the boy think he was to tell him, The Great Azia on what he should or shouldn't be doing? Frustrated he slammed yet another useless book on his now filled large white stone table. This was useless. There had to be a Fey somewhere within Pallas who knew how to find relevant information. There had to be.

Aggravated and beyond fed up he growled toward the door, "Guard!!!"

The Dark crystal door slid open to a young tall guard that had just been sent here from his home star not more than a few days ago. "My lord?"

He hated this guard on sight for no better reason then he was a youth. "Bring be a Fey that is versed in word craft."

The young man slid further into the library and smiled relieved to be at service for something more than standing and looking fierce. "If it pleases you I could help you."

"You? You're nothing more than a guard. And a youth at that."

A wicked smile bloomed on the boy's thin face, "True, however, my mother is the queen of Athenaeum. I assure you I am well versed in mundane word craft." He paused before saying something that got him killed or worse.

"Athenaeum?" Azia scratched his chin trying to place where that star was located." Ah, the little library that pretends to be a Star City. Very well amuse me. Use your craft and find me the laws of succession."

If this was any other royal Fey he would have never have helped. He would never consider helping anyone who disregarded his home in such an offhand manner. Yet he wanted to live. With a raised eyebrow he let thin wires attach to each of the book held within this room. Slowly his eyes closed as his heart slowly beat. In a matter of mere minutes, he had found three books that referenced the laws that the Azia was seeking. Another minute and found the book that would be most helpful.

Oh, not to Azia. But to whoever had enacted the laws. Or in this case the trial of Pallas. Since that was in a sense what this was. However, he didn't need to tell Azia that. He was only required to tell him about the laws and the consequences to sliding around the laws. In a deep breath, he slowly began...

"The laws of succession are really simple. One Star City wishes to leave the collective of the Star Cities.

They have one thousand Light cycles to either provide their solitary star a way to live without the constant give and take of power from Pallas or risk extinction. However, during this time they are free to ask others to join their new collective. You in turn as the ruler of Pallas have the same amount of time dictated by the star cycle of that star, to convince the other cities why leaving would not be a good idea.

In addition, all collection of tribute from all other Star Cities will cease until the thousand light cycles have passed. And of those needing to be hurried to the catacombs will only feed their home star."

So, nothing that Magmas hadn't already told him. Well mostly, the fool hadn't bothered to tell him about receiving any more tributes. "And If I break this honorary tradition?"

"Since there are strong incantations evoked there are consequences that can be dire to whoever goes against them. I believe the first Fey created this to ensure all Star Cities are free to be governed how they see fit." There was more. Much more but he was not going to help Azia. Oh, no he was going to help whoever had evoked this trial. Calculating the risked he lowered his head, "If you would allow I could go back to Athenaeum. I may be able to find something there."

Azia narrowed his eyes into tiny slits. "Go. Return only if you find something useful. I have no need for dead weight living within My Star."

Turning he smiled. Azia was such a terrible ruler. He couldn't even see what was placed before him. Couldn't see the war that was now brewing. Would never see the knife that was pointed at his throat until it was much too late to do anything about it. Oh well, that wasn't his problem. At now that there was an out.

The Fallen

PART 3

THE GREAT WAR

"War is at our door steps. I can feel it like a shadow darkening our land or the blood that flows through my veins. Prim has done all that she can to prepare us. To prepare those who will fight to save what is left of the Fey race. I pray that it will be enough. I pray that I will once again see my home. My precious Star City. I pray that I can take my family there to bathe in its rich lava pools. Yet I doubt it shall ever be."

- Private journal of Magmas II, the fallen prince.

CHAPTER 33:

GWYDION

The first sign of trouble had been the sudden disappearance of Bradwr. Not just the boy hiding somewhere and causing his own brand of trouble. But truly gone. Nothing whispered in the wind, not a single person neither living nor dead knowing where he had disappeared to.

No, wherever he was, it was wrong. Deathly wrong.

Gwydion slammed his hands down on the low wall of the balcony not caring if he had the strength to break it or not. Wasn't fazed by the stone cracking and falling onto the dirt street below. "Damn him. I swear he better not be doing something stupid."

Thin narrowed hands came from behind him lightly setting on his waist.

He need not turn to know who was now behind him. Closing his dark eyes, he choked back his anger and hoped his beloved would understand should he not turn to face her, "Terhi, you should be resting." His voice barely controlling the rage that he was now feeling.

"Your child is not yet due and already you insist on me resting. I cannot help but wonder how you will react once he has arrived."

Slowly he turned to her. Her midnight black hair framing her angelic face veiling just the top of her swelled belly. That same belly keeping him from holding her the way that he needed. The way that he wanted. Kissing the crown of her head, he softly spoke. "I need you to do something and not debate this with me."

Gradually she glanced up at him. In temper, he was his father's son but in looks… his mother could not be prouder. Caressing his thin narrow face… the face that in shape was common to the Fey yet where they were plainly handsome he was breathtakingly handsome. His short coal black hair neatly combed back. His high cheekbones drawing attention to his eyes. The color so deep green they nearly appeared to be little more than two soulless black orbs. Eyes that even when he was sleeping with dark rage still held a rare beauty that even the sea could not compete with. Softly her thumbs ran over his moist pale rose lips. To her, he was the air that she depended on to breath.

Drawing back just enough to rarely understand that rage in his eyes. Narrowing her own sea green eyes, she really looked into those dark eyes understanding what it was that she was seeing. In a light airy voice, she softly said, "You are not your brother's keeper"

She was right, he knew that but that didn't matter neither did the knot that now grew in his stomach. "No, I'm not. But I am king and I cannot trust he will not do something to provoke the Star Cities from attacking."

"My sweet it has been many years since the Fey have begun to flee here… I doubt anyone wishes to attack. Not when the queen could destroy all of them with nothing by a thought."

His eyes closed hoping to never have this conversation with her… with anyone… but she needed to know what he knew. If for no other reason than to make sure she did what he needed without much delay. "I have spoken to the queen. War is coming. It could yet be days away or even years. But it is coming and my brother will be the spark."

Terhi took an alarmed breath and swallowed hard, "If the queen knows this why has she not dealt with the problem?" *Or Nicco.* Not that she had the right to ask. Least not yet.

"Because he has now vanished. She has every available warrior looking for him. She, herself has already covered more land than I ever thought possible. Wherever he is, he is not here… Not on our little star."

"You need me somewhere that is safe." Not a question but confirmation.

"As my queen, I need you to take all of the children to the nearest castle. Do so quickly and extremely quietly. There is no reason to think anyone would know how to look for you but I do not wish to take chances. Not now. Not when everything we hold dear is held in the balance."

She patted his chest reassuringly, "We will go now. I know Castle Night is closer but from a defense standpoint The Fire castle is safer."

He turned back to look out at his people. Looked out at the children playing unaware of the danger that they all could be in. "Do what you think is best. Stay in mist form for as long as you can."

She said nothing as she shifted then melted into the air around him. She would not tell him goodbye. Would not say all the things a wife should tell a husband. No, those things could all be said once whatever this was had been settled. That he understood.

He was still looking out over his little city of Eostre when a hand touched his shoulder. There was strength in that touch as well as love and understanding. "Kibitzer?"

"Come with me." The voice too deep… too cold to be Kibitzer his senior member of his counsel.

And that was the second sign of trouble. His grandfather…the first Eostre. The first and the most dangerous. He didn't honor ties such as family. Ties of those he should trust because they say they serve him. No, his grandfather only had one tie and that was the goddess. He had killed at least two of his own children. And more than a dozen of his grandchildren. The reason for any of the deaths had never been told. Least not to him.

Following this man now… his nerves danced beneath his skin.

"Relax grandson I have not come to destroy you."

He had rarely heard his grandfather's voice. The last time he didn't have that air of authority but a kindness that he now wished to hear. "Did you or someone else find Bradwr?"

Nicco stopped short and hissed, "He is on Pallas with several others who support him. Should he return his life is forfeit."

No, his life was forfeit the moment the queen had seen his defection. He only wished she had killed him before he had fled. "It is a shame he was not taken care of before this."

Pressing his hand to a stone wall panel Nicco gave a hard push revealing a hidden staircase, "Come we shall speak in here. There are too many that I cannot trust lurking about."

For just a moment his heart stopped beating. For just that moment his lungs refused to work. His grandfather was a famed hunter. His instincts never faulty. Even so, if there were those who were not trustworthy why were they talking instead of ripping them apart? But that question could wait as his eyes took in what he saw before him. A room made of bone, deep beneath his home… his castle. A room that was hindering his ability to shift into mist… hindering his ability to do anything but speak. "Grandfather?"

"Each of the castles has a room such as this. Do not be alarmed only the first know how to access them."

Wonderful. Just wonderful. "Why are we here?"

Nicco turned away from his grandson and bowed his head. Weighting what he needed to say versus what the goddess had told him to do. After a long moment of arguing with himself, he finally said. "I need your word what I am about to say will never leave this room."

His father had sworn that oath once, then broke it. Not long after he had watched his father's body was torn apart not by his grandfather but by the dragon. The pet of the queen. Something that should not have been possible yet had happen just the same. Taking a deep breath, he cautiously said, "You have my word."

"Prim has seen what will happen. Or at least most of what will happen. What is to come cannot be stopped."

"I-"

Raising his hand, Nicco stopped Gwydion from speaking. "War is coming. But is not just going to be us against the Star Cities. There is too much at stake. The

Fey that have fled and now live here … some are not happy with the way Prim rules. They want more… what I cannot say. Others are proud and will defend Prim and this star with their lives."

"You're talking civil war."

"No, I'm talking those you see as friends may, in fact, be your enemy. Neighbors who have known nothing but peace may now wish to see each other's blood run in the streets."

"Can the goddess not prevent this? Surely she has the power to do so."

"Long ago she promised those who lived where she ruled would have the power to decide their own fate. Even if that choice meant their death. Despite knowing what will happen she sees no reason to take that choice from her people."

Gwydion closed his eyes, "What can I do?"

"The Eostre are yours to rule as you see fit. And I am making that clear right now…" Nicco turned, placing his hands on his grandson's shoulders, "I am not giving this order. I am telling you as the once ruler of the Eostre what I would do."

A choice or some kind of test. Do as his grandfather would or risk defection of his people. People who could destroy everyone. "I understand. And I appreciate your console. "

"Look at your people. Look in the depths of their minds. Those who wish to side with the Star Cities… those who are not loyal to you or the goddess. Kill them. Destroy them completely so not even their bones remain. They do not yet know only an Eostre can kill another Eostre. Not even a Draken can kill our kind."

This he knew as did every king that would rule over the Eostre. Squaring his shoulders and preparing for needed to be done he asked, "Out of all those I know rule over how many do you think will die?"

"Whatever you do it is not up to me. My queen has talked me into keeping as many safe as I can."

"Grandfather, please … I need to know."

"I do not know. Out of all of the cities, it could be but a handful or several scores. But know this the reason for their deaths need to be made public. Any secrets now could tip the war into the enemy's hands."

"Very well. It will be done. I will also have the warriors made ready."

"And the children?"

"Terhi has already taken all of them to the fire castle."

At that Nicco smiled. He knew his grandson was born a leader. Was prouder still to know this grandson trusted the goddess and her will but also know enough to send those who were too young to fight someplace safe. "I know this is hard on you. Trust yourself. Trust the goddess."

"Does she know how many will die?"

"What I can say is this… This is only the prelude to war. What happens now will liberate the Star Cities. But this comes at a great price. Prim will fight when it is time. But not before. Her powers although great are not yet fully developed. For her to fight too soon would destroy every living thing… both those within the Star Cities and those here. It is a price she will not pay."

"And the war she worries about?"

Nicco turned away from his grandson and rubbed his thumb across his forehead, "It will be beyond our time."

A hint of panic now. All that he had known would be destroyed. His grandfather… one of the first… "You will die in this war."

"It is a possibility… Still, I will fight. As we all shall."

Gwydion swallowed hard trying to keep his breath steady, "I have work to do. We may not win this not in the truest form but I will make sure our enemies work for their kills."

With a flick of his wrist, Nicco called in a map. "This is all of the known land that our queen rules."

It all seemed surreal. Everything… this couldn't be happening. But he couldn't focus on that instead he focused on the map. "I have never heard of Manicora."

"The goddess just formed it. Those there are gifted warriors. Not much for brains but still gifted. They are now in charge of the castle defenses." Using a bone that he pried from the wall he pointed to different areas on the map. "This area around the Castle of Night is now shrouded in darkness. Most of the dark Fey and others with darker tendencies are tasked with defending it. To the north here is now brighter than the lights of Pallas. Prim hopes those who come to fight will not tolerate the light. The Draken have taken point along every place that a troll has tunneled under."

"I thought they were confined to the mines?"

"Most are. But you will always have those who would rather be eaten than work. Now to the south in the marsh… those who dwell there… be wary of them. They are no friend to the queen but as of yet have not done anything to warrant their deaths."

Looking at the map Gwydion shook his head. There is so much ground to cover and protect. "Do we have the support of those who are not warriors by trade?"

"Prim has been planning this for many years. We have all the support that we need."

"Where is Freya guarding?"

Nicco tapped part of the map. "Right here. She will straddle the line where the darkness meets the light. A great structure now borders the two. The goddess calls it a Spire. I know not what lies inside. But I suspect some great weapon. "

So much to take in. So many new things being created. Most he would like to see for himself yet he didn't think that would ever be. "And the Castle of Fire? Who defend that?"

"Prime and Shesha. According to the rules of Pallas the home of a royal Fey cannot be invaded until surrender. "

"There is no guarantee that the Star Cities will honor that rule."

"No, but I doubt the ruler of Pallas would break the only rule that has kept him alive for more than a millennium."

Turning to leave Nicco paused once more, "The pillars of the stars. Destroy them. If we win this they will no longer be needed for Prim will rule Pallas. If we don't… then at least the bastards cannot use them."

For a long time, Gwydion did nothing but think about what his grandfather had said. Something more was going on here. If Prim wanted to rule Pallas… she would already. If his brother needed to die he would already be nothing more than a memory. So, no matter what was really taking place, Prim had already known who would die and who would be left among the living.

There was the reason. Whatever it was… there was a reason. He only wished that he knew what it was.

Making his peace with knowing he may not be among the living when this was done he slipped back up the stairs and into the main corridor. A simple thought to his trusted guards and the pillars of the stars would be destroyed. The draining houses all but one would be leveled to the ground. Then one more thought… all those who were not already bound to him in the truest sense was now ordered to show themselves to him and take the oath.

He would not tell them but any who refused would be killed so nothing not even a vapor of mist would be left behind.

No whatever his brother was up to he would have no army to help him.

CHAPTER 34:

PRIMITIVA

Primitiva sat back in her overstuffed chair. The seer's stone resting within the scepter that she had made for it. The scepter itself resting across her lap.

Her hands shaking as she watched the on goings of the Star Cities. Watched as two sides from the same race tore each other apart. Both sides wanting the same thing. Both sides wanting the needless killing of their own kind to stop.

Both sides believing that their chosen ruler was in the right. Those who sided with Azia had been told that Magmas had been behind the recent decision to kill the ones who could rule. He had been unhappy that is his own offspring were too weak to rule. And he had insisted that all of the other Star Cities be made to undergo the same trials.

Those who had sided with Magmas knew the truth. Azia was killing those with enough power that they could rule all of Pallas. He was paving the way for only his bloodline to ascend after him. The only thing he hadn't counted on was his only heir throwing himself into the void.

She continued to watch as two proud cities destroyed one another. Watched as the stars lost all signs of life. Two of the dark stars have fallen one belonging to Pallas the other to those who oppose Azia. No life remained on either. The Fey who could bring back the dead already fallen. They had been the first Fey to be wiped out from all existence.

Azia saw them as a threat many years ago. Those who had remained within the Star Cities wiped out as soon as he thought something was being planned. None had a chance of survival. All truly gone except those who she had saved from the void.

A tear rolled down her face. Still so many innocent lives lost. So many more that still would be. It was almost time for her to show them her true nature. Almost time for her to show the Star Cities why she would never rule them. Almost…

… but not yet.

A soft tap on her Solaris door brought her back to the present. Wiping the tears from her face she willed her voice to stay level and calm as she said, "In."

Not her consort but one of the children she had rescued so many light cycles ago. The boy who she had raised like her own son. But he wasn't … not in the truest sense but he did respect her as his mother… as his queen. He had grown so much since his time here. Not just in age and ability but in maturity and as a leader. "Magmas?"

"Alec wasn't sure if you would like to see him or not."

Her lips pressed together into a tiny thin line. "He begs be for a child for more light cycles then not. Now that I finally agree he hides. Is this the rational of all males or just him?"

Deep red blush lit Magmas' face, "I cannot say for sure. I can only speak for myself."

She waved the thought off. "I do not really require an answer." Her hand rested on her swelled belly. "I do think it would have been wiser to create this life another way."

"You still could."

Her eyes closed for just a breath, "I could. If I become anymore uncomfortable I will. For now, I am fine."

Sliding into the room just a bit further Magmas saw the seer's stone and its scepter resting on her lap. He knew what that meant and none of it good. "Can I know what you have seen?"

Attentively she caressed the stone between her fingers Primitiva nodded. "Close the door."

Carefully he pushed the plain darkly pained painted door closed, and then came to sit at her feet. As a child he had sat like this with his brothers and other royal children. All of them learning to be strong leaders. Loyal and obedient. All of them learning what it truly meant to be Fey. They were the caretakers of the stars. It was their responsibility to keep the stars glowing bright. Be he wasn't here to hear a lesson or hear a story. He was here to find out what she saw and hoped with all that it was that they could defend against it.

"Two of the dark stars have fallen. One from both sides. The debris will come this far. I doubt it will cause more damage than a moment of inconvenience. There will be balls of fire lighting the skies tonight. It will be best if the children do not watch."

His throat closed for just a breath. The dark stars were the furthest away from Pallas. No, they were *now* the furthest away. The stars that held the Fey that could restore life had been the furthest away… until they were completely destroyed. Prim had been able to save some of them and brought them here to recover. Perhaps she could do so again. "Those who have fallen can you…"

She took his cold hands in hers offering him as much comfort as she dared. "The dragons are already keeping watch. If any bodies are found they will be brought to me. Or to the ones that needs to learn the skill." Slowly she got to her feet so that she could gaze out of her window. Watching the lava bubble up to the surface, she made a choice. So many would die in the coming days, the best she could do was save those who would need to survive to protect the ones still too young to thrive on their own. A scroll that she had wrote out just days before formed within her hand. "Magmas, I trust you to not ask questions."

Coming to her side he nodded with respect. "I only try to please."

"Take this. The names held within are to be with the children in the rooms below. I task you with keeping all those held there safe. Do not leave until you are sure the danger has passed. Or if I send word."

No need to ask if it was important. She wouldn't have mentioned it if it wasn't. He knew this. So why did his hand shake as he reached out to receive the scroll? He had no answer to that. Or at least not one that he wanted to admit to himself. Slowly but carefully he unrolled it reading several scores of names. Some were grown Fey next to each was who she thought they should be paired with. Each dangerous in their own right if the paring was accepted their children would be more then dangerous. Other names further down. Most were barely old enough to be considered youths the rest not even old enough to crawl. "I will gather them now." He paused, just a step, considering where each would be. A few would already be reading themselves for the battle they all knew was coming. To clear with this parchment if they fought, they too would die. Too clear that their lives for whatever reason would be needed after the battle rather than for any ability that they could use during the battle itself.

Before she could say anything, her stomach hardened with pain. The pain only infuriating her. A dark thought about how she would make Alec pay for causing her pain crossed her mind. Just as quickly was the solution to give him what he had asked for without the necessity for the pain. "Have Freya meet me in the room she deemed safe to have this child."

"Prim…" Worry filled his voice. Never had she ever looked unwell. And certainly, never had she looked in pain.

"It seems that this child wants to be born today. But not this moment. I have time. Tell Alec I will call for him once this child if free from my body. To come before would be too dangerous as I do find him amusing most of the time."

Not a moment after she held her son in her arms Alec crept into the room unsure if he would ever be welcome in her sight again. "My I enter?"

Primitiva studied him for a long moment before glancing back down at their son. "As your son is here I doubt I could keep you from him."

Alec smiled taking the little bundle from her arms. "I think he wanted to see me before I left."

He was leaving. Why? She hadn't told him to. No but he would regardless. War was brewing and he had to stay in command. "You are joining your brothers in the glacier village? To protect what is left of the human race." Not really a question but clarifying to herself

"I am. None there have any skill in fighting. Actually, none there have even an ounce of Fey blood in their veins. It is too dangerous for them to remain in their village. Most refuse to leave."

Her eyes closed sleepily. A vision coming to her as she did. Two choices. If Alec stayed with her both he and their son would die a most horrible death. She would not be able to protect both and save her people. If he left their son would survive. The chances of her ever-seeing Alec again… questionable. "Listen to me. The first sign of trouble take those who you can and flee. Fly as fast as you can to the castle of Night. **Do not** stay and fight."

He kissed her head and forced a smile. "My sweet you worry much for no reason. The Fey king has little use for those who do not have Fey blood. Going there is just precaution."

She grabbed his arm tightly reminding him of who he was speaking to. Reminding him she was not just his lover but his queen. "Alexander, this is not up for debate.

Any sign of trouble I want you at the castle of Night. Take Nicco with you. I want that castle locked down." *And I want you safe. Please understand what I cannot bring myself to tell you. Please understand that I cannot bear the thought of losing you. Please.* Her eyes locked with his as she hoped he understood all that she could not bring herself to say. Hoping he understood for the sake of all that she had created she could not tell him the words that burned in her throat. Words that she knew had been there since the night that they had met.

Alec looked into her eyes. Glowing orbs of red fire, Lightning flashing between the flames. Souls of the dead crashing into the fire like waves. This was an order from his queen not a request from the woman who held his heart. Giving her back their son he nodded. "I will go to the castle now. Nicco can join me once I arrive."

"Agreed."

Once the door was once again closed behind him she sat back against her headboard made of intricate gold lace. Both relief and longing washed over her. She would not change what would come. She couldn't not without crossing a line she had long ago decided that she never would… yet she hoped by making her love stay in a place that should be safe that would survive the coming attack.

Something in the back of her mind told her otherwise. No matter what would happen even she did not have the power to change it.

Freya crept into the room hearing quite sobs from inside. Her heart ached as her queen held her newborn baby to her chest, her tears raining down like liquid gold. "My queen?"

Primitiva wiped away her tears as she studied the woman before her. Not one of her first but close enough. Because she was a daughter to Mary, and related to Alec by blood she was a trained warrior skilled in all manners of weapons. Her speed alone deadly as was her rare ability to go undetected even by those who were of Eostre blood. But it was her exceptional beauty that men usually fell for long before they saw the threat. She was a trained assassin and the captain of her elite guards. The ones who in life had been out cast but in death had no equal. "Freya, come I need of your assistance."

Softly stepping so her feet made no sound she gingerly took a seat on the edge of the queen's large bed. "As always my queen I am yours to command."

Holding her son close to her she breathed in his fresh clean smell. "Azia will stop at nothing to find my son. The child of my blood. He needs to be hidden. He needs to be protected at all cost."

She closed her eyes for just a moment. Just enough time to think. "I can take him to your under kingdom. You and I are the only ones who have access. Those that dwell there will keep him safe."

Primitiva squared her shoulders. She had already thought of that. If Azia killed Alec he too would gain entrance to her under kingdom. It was too much of a risk. "No, he will be kept in plain sight. Azia is clever but tends to overlook the obvious. This will be his undoing." Vines of purple and white mist encapsulated her baby. Not a sound did he make as he was lifted from her arms and placed on the floor. Her heart broke, but she had to keep him alive. His life to precious to let harm come to him, one day he would rule Pallas. She had seen this. He would rule, as it should have been for the start. At his side would be the ones who knew what would need to be done. A deep breath then the mist was no longer translucent at it covered him completely. "I'm sorry my little one. One day I hope you will know my love."

When the mist subsided, an overstuffed chair made of course deep purple fabric and snow-white trim stood where the baby had once lain. Her voice cracked with effort to speak as she said, "His name is Ari. Please take him to Caste of Night. He will require nothing for food. Nor make a sound. He may eat any that foolishly sit in his embrace. As this day he will only be known as a fury. A creature made sole purpose to eat unwelcome guest. I will make others to put in the other castles as well."

Freya stood stunned for more than a few heartbeats before regaining her composure. "I will take him myself. And I pray when this is over he can be the child that he was meant to be."

So, did she. With all of her heart she hoped to be reunited with her darling baby while he was still but hours old. Her eyes closed once more as she weaved her final incantation around him. "He will. For every light cycle that passes he will age but one day."

CHAPTER 35:

BRADWR

Bradwr sat alone in the large room his body stretched out over some large ornate pillows sipping something called nectar. The low table was nothing like he had ever seen before. Polished white stone with mist like veins of gray and black. The room made from something different. Course walls of cream rock. Crystal lighting… that he knew because several of the castles has lights hanging such as these.

He wanted this. Craved this. Soon he would rule this place. No longer second to anyone. He would rule the Eostre, enslave all those who are not of his race. Use them to create the world to his liking. Kill any who would dare stand in his way. Then…

… Ah then… he would come back here and finish off the Fey of the Star Cities.

But first he would need the help of the feared Azia, in order to rid himself of the weak queen. The self-proclaimed goddess Primitiva.

The door slid open with the sound of stone rubbing against stone. Heavy foot falls. Three sets. One lighter than the rest. Still he didn't move just took another sip of this drink and waited until one of them made a move.

"You requested an audience but you show no respect."

Unfazed he glanced over his bare shoulder. Unlike his brother he preferred only to cloth himself from his waist down. Preferred cloth that moved with his body like a second skin. Now he saw the wisdom in his choice of clothing.

Both men… guards… were dressed nearly the same but they were clad in some kind of skirt each fold made from another spear shaped cut of metal some kind of fabric beneath that. The Azia on the other hand …

He should laugh. Feared? He was nothing more than a bag of bones. His skin hanging loose from his body. Why start a war he would be dead soon enough? He should leave this place, and would if he didn't need the help of the warriors that lived here.

"I did not seek an audience. I came to offer an alliance."

Azia glanced down at him. Anger and intrigue lighting his eyes. "And why should I make an alliance with you? You are not Fey. Your abilities too weak to be of interest to any true Fey." Azia bent over coming nearly nose to nose with Bradwr. "You are insignificant."

Too quickly he turned to mist. His anger to volatile to be contained. The guards tried to defend their king. The mist over coming both in the same breath. Nothing but their armor and weapons remained. Not even a single drop of blood.

Reforming at his seat Bradwr smiled cleaning his front row of teeth with a sliver of bone. "Your guards are quite tasty. Not enough meat to make a decent meal but good enough for a light snack."

Azia stumbled back trying to flee from this demon. Tried and was stopped but the demon himself stand right before him. A heartbeat more and he was just behind him his hand clamping down on his shoulder. Whispering in his ear Bradwr laughed cold and viciously, "Come now Azia surely you are not trying to flee."

"What are you?" Azia gasped fear now too apparent in his wrinkled face.

"My kind are called Eostre." He leaned close enough to Azia neck to feel the tiny hairs standing on end, "If I wanted you dead you would be." Pulling back once more he hissed, "Now do we discuss an alliance or should I finish you off?"

Azia swallowed hard. Never had he feared for his life. Never had any dared to touch him. This boy was not to be taken lightly. "Yes, I see the wisdom in an alliance."

"Good. I should hate to think I only came here for a snack."

Watching this fiend, Azia carefully took his place across from it. "Will you tell me how it is that you survived the voice to arrive here?"

"It is no secret that any from our … what you call star… can travel throughout the void. I find it rather boring if you ask me. The air to thin remain in mist form. But it doable."

Obviously. "I see." Azia reached for the canter of nectar finding it almost empty. "I see our beverage is to your liking."

Placing his elbows on the table Bradwr leaned in and smiled this time not hiding the sharpness of his dove white teeth. Nor hiding his poisoned fangs that he could retract at will. "In truth I do not need meat to survive. None of my kind does. We just find it appealing." He leaned back no longer taking a threatening posture. "Now should you like to hear my terms?"

Seeing no choice Azia nodded slightly. "I trust the terms will be mutually beneficial."

"Of course." *At least until I kill you.*

"Then I look forward to hearing them."

Cleaning under his nails Bradwr looked uninterested as he spoke. His words no more important than any after dinner conversation. "It is no secret that only one of my kind can kill one another. However, it is not widely known if the king is killed all those who are bound to him will die as well."

"What are you proposing?"

"My brother is king. Now I could go back to my home but I suspect Primitiva would destroy me the moment that I do. She has eyes everywhere."

"Smart on her part." Azia mumbled. To someone who didn't understand the Fey this would be been seen as a weakness that she didn't trust her people to defend her. To him he saw this as power and told a great deal about her defenses.

"Yes, but there is a way to kill him without ever leaving your home. Providing you agree to my terms."

Do I have a choice? Not that he would ever say that. "And what are your terms?"

"They are really quite simple. In exchange for my help you will see that none of your kind ever comes back to my home. They are a filth that I will see eliminated from its borders."

Filth? If he knew he would survive an altercation with this spawn he would have put him in his place. Instead he too calmly said, "I think that could be arranged providing you agree that your kind will remain on your own star."

"As it will take time to see to all of the changes. I will agree." *For now*.

"What are the rest of your terms?"

"You see that Primitiva is completely destroyed. She is a threat to all that I hold dear."

"I think that can be arranged."

"Now as far as incentive for you…" He paused and let a brutal smile form before saying, "…She is currently with child. I know for a fact she will do anything to protect that child. And it's father."

"What are suggesting?"

"There is something else that she protects. A race that is nearly extinct now. They live south of her greatest castle. Well south west. In any case I think if you do a two-prong attack one near her private gardens. That will draw out many of her lesser warriors. The main body would be near the castles."

"The second prong would…"

"My brother is hidden within the city of the glaciers. I will give you what you need to destroy him. I will then take control of his army destroying what is left of her forces. You will have an easy time dispersing of the Fey who side with her."

Azia scratched his chin carefully considering this plan. He had nothing to lose. Fighting those who sided with the creator within his own Star Cities was proving futile. More Star Cities were rallying behind her every day. The only way to stop this was to destroy her… completely. It would be a shame not to have her powers to feed the stars but it was much better this way. "Then we are in agreement."

"As it would seem." Getting to his feet Bradwr turned away from the table. "We will need to create a device to act as the weapon that we need. And you need to choose which of your warriors you will sacrifice in the name of peace."

"Oh, I think I know exactly which ones would do well as a sacrifice."

CHAPTER 36:

MAGMAS II

Magmas slipped down to the lower rooms hidden under the belly of the castle. All those who were on Primitiva's list would be arriving shortly if they hadn't already. Magnar would be the only one who wouldn't be here. He was already somewhere among the Star Cities. Which one exactly no one knew for sure. But that didn't matter. He was well trained and didn't much care what was honorable or not. No, the only thing he cared for was his own survival.

Prim could scold him later. Or whenever she found out about his foolishness. Unless she agreed with him about his methods. With those two he could never be sure who would have the last word and who would wish they had better foresight.

Voices carried thought the halls bringing him back to the present. Children laughing even though they were still out of sight. Adults making up stories to keep the little ones happy, some even singing. Guards fluttering in and out of the shadows.

None of which helped him. Somewhere deep within these halls laid the archives. The true number of lives Prim had created. What each could do. Their abilities. Their power. There may be something written there… something over looked…. something that could be used to end this without the loss of life that he could see mounting every day.

Of course, he wouldn't know what to do with that information. Flint on the other hand would. Searching these rooms. Theses corridors would take hours. Asking a shadow on the other hand…

One fluttered near his foot. In and out of his own shadow. Now was his chance. "My good shadow would you know where my brother Flint may be?" No way to know for sure if the shadow understood him. No way to know if it would listen to the question.

Then the shadow stopped fluttering. Stopped moving. The sense that information was being passed between the other shadows hung in the air. A moment more and his brother fell through the ceiling. Through another shadow that he had failed to notice until now.

"Ouch. That really hurt. Not to mention you're not allowed to do that." It was then Flint looked around at where he was. Recognizing the corridor near the entrance to the underbelly. A breath more until he acknowledged his own brother who was doing his best not to say anything. "Damn creatures I should ask Prim to remind them that they are not allowed to transport people." He paused then thought about it before sighing, "I doubt they would listen anyways. However, would you mind telling me why a shadow brought me here?" Getting to his feet he looked right at the shadow that he had fell through, "And some warning would nice if you insist on not listening to the one who created you."

Rubbing his neck in an attempt to look sympatric Magmas meekly said, "I didn't know shadows could transport a person."

He rubbed his backside and grumbled, "Yes well it is frown upon." Taking a deep breath Flint asked, "Why did you ask a shadow to find me?"

Now that he was standing here perhaps he hadn't thought about this completely through, "I was hoping you could help me in the archives."

Narrowing his eyes Flint growled. "I was *in* the archives. As was Karnack. We were going over some things that would make for good defenses. What did you want to see there? I recall you having less interest in parchment the Apollo." He just hoped his voice was enough to tell his brother that he had interrupted important work to bring him here just to go back to the archives.

"I was hoping to find something there that Prim hasn't already thought of. I know she wants father to rule Pallas. But there must be a way to do that without killing more than half of the Fey in the process."

"My dear brother. The Fey are not dying just simple living somewhere else until it is time for them to retake their place among the stars. However, the rocks they live on are being destroyed." Flint paused, "Prim didn't discuss this with you? Did she?"

Magmas turned then let out several dark curses before once again looking at his brother and snapping, "No, she did not discuss it with me."

Rolling his amber colored eyes Flint laughed, "She has been busy. Come we will *walk* to the archives then I will try to explain everything the best that I can." He paused, "You should know something else. Those who are protected here are also protected in case those they are bound to somehow die."

Oh, he didn't like the sound of that. "Meaning?"

"As an example, if Nicco or his grandson die in battle… and I'm using them since it is the least likely to happen… then those who are here and are blood bound to them will continue to live. Terhi just arrived with every child born in any of the Eostre villages. As well as several score of the Eostre warriors. For all tense and purposes, she is queen of the Eostre. Those here are now bound to her. The binding not complete but enough to ensure the line of ascension will transfer to her unborn child."

"Why do I get the feeling that whatever is going to happen is going to press Primitiva into a path that she does not wish to walk?"

"Magmas, do not ask questions you are not yet ready to hear the answers to. But yes. Whatever is about to happen will press her beyond her normal control."

By the gods that did not sound good at all.

He knew the archives was a large room… but this? They were already three stories beneath the most lower floor of the castle, and this room scaled down six more. "Is this the main archive?"

Flint frowned, "This is just some of the work from the past three thousand years. Everything else is stored in the new Spire."

"What Spire?" For all he knew there was no place called the Spire. And he knew every place that held a name. At least those that had been created before yesterday.

"Oh, Prim just made it a short time ago. Provisions, maps, weapons, and the rest of the archives are being stored there. Along with some creations that only Prim can control." Flint paused before adding "I didn't ask what the creations are or what they may look like. So, I assume they will terrify just about everyone."

That did not sound good at all. In fact, it sounded worse than the possibility of Prim losing control. "Do I dare ask if they will be confined to the Spire or if you know what they might be able to do beside scare the Fey?

"Do? I dare not think of an answer but there is a Dracaena. Her upper body is that of a beautiful woman. Each will see her as their vision of a women that they desire. The lower part is purely that of a dragon. Prim made her after reading some text about something called Echidna. Of course, she put her own touches to the creature. Such as being able to breathe liquid fire. And lusting for the taste for hot blood. Only the ones who are no longer alive can be near her safely. For the moment she is confined to the Spire as a defense for all of the parchment."

"How wonderful."

"Yes, and her skin, is not able to be damaged. Not by Fey nor by weapons. Not even an Eostre can harm her. Nicco has already tried. However, she one the other hand was able to hurt him... while he was in mist form. He was not pleased with the discovery."

No, I don't suppose he would be. Narrowing his eyes something in the back of his mind turned. Something about a story Prim read to them long ago. Something about a horse that was given as a gift. The gift in fact brought destruction to a city. He couldn't remember all of it but the principle might work. "Perhaps we can send her as a gift to Pallas. She can eat any that dwell there and we can be done with this war."

Flint balked at the idea, "The rules of engagement still apply. That would be dishonorable."

He could choke on all the thing that would be dishonorable. How many of those same things did Azia do on a daily basis? How many children did he kill because their parents sided against him? How many children did he kill just because the needed their power? Yet the things that Azia had required his citizens to do had forced more Fey to rally behind their father. "Fine. If we can't do anything to Pallas what can we do?"

Karnack flew up from one of the lower levels to where they were standing. "I think I found something."

"I didn't know you had wings?"

He narrowed his eyes at Magmas, "I didn't until last night. The goddess decided I needed them. The gods only know why."

Magmas lowered his eyes to keep from laughing. Not his fault if he did. Not when Karnack looked barely old enough to be a youth but sounded like a grumpy old Fey. "What did you find?"

"You are bothersome and trouble." Then to Flint, "Have someone take this to the goddess. It tells of a witch who spelled all of her subjects. Making them invisible for a short time. Then when the enemy passed their gates the spell faded. The army was surrounded and destroyed."

"Interesting. Thank you, I will have a shadow take it to her now."

The Fallen

CHAPTER 37:

PRIMITIVA

Primitiva sat on her gold and magma throne. Her Castle of Fire was quite almost too quiet. Gone were the children running through the halls laughing. Gone were the heated augments of her first. Each now protecting those that only they could. Alec should be safe in the Castle of Night. Should be, didn't mean that he would. If one person told Azia who he was... what he was to her... his life would be forfeit. His power no matter how limited would be absorbed by the filth that called himself Azia.

Her fingers curled around the armrest. Too tempting to destroy him here and now. Destroy him as he entered the outer most layer of her star. It would solve nothing. No, she had to play this out. She had to show the Fey that it he alone that was killing their children. He was the one hording all of the power for the Star Cities for himself. Moreover, it was he alone that had started this war.

Lava bubbled out her window. The sound echoing throughout the halls. Another bubble or was that an explosion coming from the Star Cities. She could know for sure.

Another thought. Ari. Her Ari. The only child she had ever given birth to. The child that she had waited so long to give Alec. It hurt her heart to know she may never see him grow. Never see him ever be the Fey that he was meant to be. He would grow and learn all that he needed. He would one day be released from his present form. She had seen that. As she had seen that, she would not be the one to release him.

Would Alec know what she had done to insure the life of their child? She did not know. She couldn't. There was much still clouded in mystery for her to know what the full outcome would be.

A pain lanced her heart from the thought of losing him. The thought of losing both Alec and Ari.

She would not shed the tears that burned her throat. She couldn't. Azia and his army were on their way to her star. Not by way of coach that would have been expected. No what was worrisome was each flying here on their own accord. Each navigating the void in hopes of being the one to destroy her.

Something had changed. Something horrible. Something she could almost point her finger at.

If she had to bet, it was because of Bradwr. He had aligned himself with Azia. He wasn't worthy of being an Eostre. He wasn't loyal to *anyone* but himself.

Her anger grew not at him but herself. She should have killed him many light cycles ago. Alas, it was too late to rectify that now. He was bringing the enemy to her door. And with them he was bringing deaths to countless others.

With her eyes trained on the large double doors of smooth black stone she calmed herself for what would come through that door. Resigned to be the powerful queen that her people needed. Resigned herself to act with the honor that Azia had long ago forgotten. A breath then two… Someone was coming. Too fast to be a page or even a messenger. Whoever it was, they were strong. Their natural powers were that of …

The doors blew open with a crash. Magmas not the boy who she had raised but his father… stood in the doorway panting. His golden red wings covered in many shades of blood. Testament of those he had faced in order to come here. His fire red robes that marked him as a royal Fey little more than rags hanging from his body revealing his metal armor that had been made for him. From where she hadn't a clue. The smell of smoke clinging to him. Flames danced wildly in his eyes.

Slowly she rose from her seat. On the star of the Silent Ones, they had been equal. Here, she was Queen. Here he would yield to her or be destroyed. Her temper already too close to snapping to tolerate any disobedience from anyone. Even an ally. "Magmas, why have you come?"

Taking a breath, he took a knee a sign if surrender to her "The bastard Azia is on his way here. One of your people sought him out and gave him the means to travel throughout the void without the need of carriage. Those who would side themselves to you are now trapped within their own Star Cities." Magmas took a shaky breath. "None of those who had been holding the void survived his attack. This will be the last star to see war. I'm sorry Prim, I have failed you."

"Oh, stand Magmas you oaf. I have known for some time the war would come here. I had hoped to buy more time but … It matters little now." She turned watching the lava creep up the sides of the castle soon it would spill over the mountain taking all in its wake. Her people knew this day was coming and had prepared for it. All of the homes that would be destroyed were already empty.

Her people already carefully hidden within plain sight. Others posed for open attack while, others… Well she didn't have play with all of rules of Pallas.

"You knew?" Slowly Magmas got to his feet tossing aside his tattered robe. "You have prepared for this?"

"I have. Even since Bradwr left this star to seek Azia out I have made changes."

His eyes watched lava slowly rise past the window. "You seek to destroy this castle?"

She turned sharply following his gaze, "Oh, the lava will expel from the top of the mountain. We are safe within these walls. As there is also another way out should I need it."

Catching his breath, he nodded, "Those you had patrolling the outer ring of the star have fallen. It is their blood I wear now."

"Oh, they are of little consequence."

"Prim?" Worry filled his voice. Fear that he had sided wrong.

"They were already dead Magmas. Most for more than a century. Their remains will be collected and returned to my other kingdom, there they will either pull themselves together or choose to remain … dead does not sound right. I have yet figured out a word to describe them."

"They were… why would you send them..."

"Magmas, I do not send anyone anywhere they are free to decide for themselves. Now come. I was expecting a report from a messenger seeing you have more information then he would… you will join me with meeting with my generals. There is much to discuss."

A few steps and she was at the door her fire red hair braided down her back. Looking ahead she said, "Come. We shall join my generals in my war room. I will show you what I know for certain. Then you will tell me what you know. Together we will figure out a means to an end." She just hoped with that end she didn't need to destroy everything that she had created. Hoped when she unleashed her power that she wouldn't wake the Silent Ones.

With Magmas trailing behind her, Primitiva stopped hallway down a long corridor. The out wall made of white stone the inner side made from crystallized lava. "Do you find my castle interesting, Magmas?"

"It's unique." He hesitated, "But from a defense stand point is it safe?"

"I assure you that out of all of my castles only one is safer. But that one is too close to where I wish to draw Azia near."

"Prim, Azia is smart he won't go into the open unless he must."

"I know. It is why I will give him little choice. Come my generals are waiting."

Magmas stumbled back a step seeing what she called generals. Their races he had no names for. One nearly as tall as the room itself muscles the size of boulders.

Eyes of black coal. And the spikes that protruded from his body. He could almost feel the poison that each carried. The rest of the chosen warriors… each looked more frightening then the next. Each he had no doubt would tear apart a Fey with nothing more than a moment of inconvenience.

"Generals, this is Lord Magmas he has been leading our efforts within the Star Cities." Prim paused as she glanced at him, "We no time for proper introductions. Now shall we get to work?"

The one who was the tallest nodded, his hand over his heart swearing allegiance to his queen. "The pillars have all been destroyed."

Carefully she took a seat at the head of her large rectangular table. As she did the rest of her generals took their seats along the sides. "Good. Then Nicco was successful speaking to Gwydion. What else?"

The one that had the feel of a dark Fey stood up from the table and called in a map. Slowly he unrolled it, "Here…" He pointed to a spot on the map near what was labeled marshland covered a wisp of mist representing her dark veil; "… what is now farmland. We have declared the bones of the fallen enemy to be taken… With no disrespect, those who are loyal to you my queen do not wish to live for all eternity with the enemy."

Prim nodded in agreement, "If this is the will of my people I will allow it. The bones as they free themselves of skin and tissue will be made into structures. I leave the details for those structures up to the builders. I see no reason to restrict their creative ideas." She paused for but a moment. "Are all of my castles placed on alert?"

"Yes, my queen. Several of your dragons are attached to each. Shesha is now roosting near here as the lava has now become too unstable for him to land within his tower."

"And they are all watching the skies?" Another question she didn't need to hear the answer to but Magmas however did.

"They are. None shall attack until the enemy has fallen. As requested Castle Golden Light has been vacated. The town's people have all taken shelter deep below. The entrance sealed up for the moment." The Dark Fey paused, "Is there a reason that castle has been more or less emptied?"

Slowly Prim locked eyes not with her general but with Magmas. Licking her blood red lips, she smiled. Not her friendly smile that most welcomed but a smile that chilled those that were in the room. "General Daegal as I understand why you are asking that, I will answer but it will not be repeated beyond this room."

With a tip of his head General Daegal retook his seat. "Of course, my queen."

Setting back, she steepled her fingers together. "I have conceded both Castle Golden Sun and The Castle of Glass."

Magmas stood up trying to find the markers for both of the castles. "Prim?"

With a flick of her hand tiny castles appeared on the map. "The Castel of Golden Sun will be used by Azia for the moment. As it is most like the Castle of Pallas. It is imperative that we push the enemy to a place that we can control. And away from heavily populated areas."

Shaking his head Magmas said, "The rules of Pallas are clear…"

"This is not Pallas not is it a Star City. As I will concede to some of the rules of war I will not bother with those that *only* apply to a Star City."

A tense deep breath and Magmas slowly let it out. "I apologies, nothing like what you have created and are now defending has ever been …"

"Actually, Magmas there is evidence that once all of the Star Cities were at one-time part of one collective entity. But that is for a discussion at a later time. Right now, we need to keep or focus on defeating Azia."

"It will not be as easy as that. Whatever Azia has backing him his fighters are now stronger than any Fey that I know. Nothing we have seems to penetrate their skin."

Prim nodded once, "I will assume Bradwr has given Azia a sample of his blood. If he did then it may act like a temporary shield for the enemy. However, the brat wouldn't know that it would only shield those from weapons from the Star Cities. Those that my people carry… And I mean that to include those who have fallen and have decided that they will fight for this star… They now have weapons to break that shield. Once the shield is broken…" the rest trailed off with her shrug.

"My queen?"

"Azia will attack the most populated cities first leaving the villages for last. He does not know that any place he chooses to attack is only filled with trained warriors. As it stands today we out number his forced by nearly ten to one. Once his attacks fail in this area…" She pointed to a place that now sparkled with light, "Those who are hidden below Castle Golden Sun will attack. I have given them a device to watch each battle as it unfolds."

Still looking at the map Magmas shook his head in disagreement, "Azia will stay, and fight."

"No Magmas he won't. Azia is not a strong as the Star Cities think he is. His natural abilities are not even a tenth of what they should be for being born to Pallas. His son on the other hand if he had been leading this attack then things would have been different."

Magmas narrowed his eyes, "He leaped into the void some time ago." Almost remembering the day, he heard the news. And like then figured out Prim had collected him from the void.

"He did and was raised by me. He is truly gifted and nothing like his father. One day he will be a good leader. As it stands he is posed to lead the resistance near the City of Night. He has also asked to be the one to accept his father's surrender seeing there is no honor in attacking *my* star."

General Daegal stood up, "My queen if we are done here I would like to join the major."

"Of course."

It wasn't until they were alone Prim got to her feet. "Magmas you have been quite for much too long."

"I'm looking at your map. There is a lot of ground to cover between each city. So many places for Azia to attack that wouldn't fit with your defense plan."

"Azia is arrogant more so then any Fey and he seeks revenge which makes him stupid. In every city in every village there are only warriors. Those who can't fight… those with no ability to do so or children who are much too young to see the gore of war are all protected deep with the nearest castles. "

"It is possible that Azia or his forces will find them or destroy the castles themselves."

"My darling, only a creator with greater power then I can destroy the lower sanctums of the castles. True the visible structures can be destroyed but nothing can touch the lower buildings. Nor can anything penetrate the rooms without being let in."

"You sound sure in your ability."

"I have tested every ability of every Fey that has fallen against my defenses. I have also tested the ability of all of those that I have created and their people. In addition, I have granted more power to a select few including gifting them the blood of an Eostre. None have been able to withstand my defenses. In fact, the only reason they lived at all is because I so willed it."

Magmas wiped his mouth hiding the fear that had chosen the wrong side. The fear that the creature that sat before him could and would destroy all of the Fey. "You could stop this before another drop of blood is shed."

Prim sat back her eyes focused on something far beyond this room. Far beyond this time. "No. If I unleash my power… all of my power… I will unleash a greater threat then Azia. I alone cannot defeat that threat. Least not yet. The one who will be needed to help me won't be born for more years then I can see. But I know her name. And only her name not what she will look like."

Leaning forward Magmas stayed silent for a long moment understanding the threat that she worried about.

Worried if the Silent Once may still wake because of this war. Choose not to speak of them but instead asked "And her name?"

"Nisha. The daughter of the night. The conqueror of the Silent Ones."

CHAPTER 38:

AZIA

Azia smiled as he took a deep breath of the sweet-smelling air. It was different from any Star City. More than that, it was a worthy conquest. His deep soulless eyes scanned the area. Not a soul in sight. Just Objects that he had no name for. Deep browns with green sprouting from its appendages. A sea of green dotting the ground. Buildings made of some kind of pale cream stone. More stone this one white and round creating a wide path. Nothing here he could name but everything soon would be his to rule.

Slowly Bradwr formed beside him glaring at the empty city. "There should be thousands of people filling these streets. Or their bodies littering the ground." He turned slowly desperately trying to find a single soul. Trying to find anything of flesh and blood. There was nothing. Not even some vermin scurrying to its home. "Something isn't right."

A cruel smile formed on Azia's face. "It is custom for a ruler of a Star City to house the attacking Fey in a safe and luxurious home. In most cases opposites of where they are housed. It gives both sides the advantage of watching the battle." He paused watching his slaves … his army… falling to the ground. Each taking a knee waiting for his intrusion. "Come I would like to see this place before I decide if it is worthy to house me. Even for a short time."

Bradwr narrowed his eyes and hissed, "You underestimate Primitiva and those who follow her."

"I underestimate *no one*. She is nothing that I have not killed before. Her kind has been bred to feed the catacombs. To feed Pallas and nothing more. Now come I would like to get this little pissing match done with and collect her powers for my own. "*Then I will destroy the star that had created such a fowled creature. With its destruction I will destroy the one I had thought to possess. The creature known as Avyanna.*

It wasn't a house but a palace made of sparkling white stone. It's highest tower reaching more than a dozen stories. Windows facing wherever a battle could be fought. "Marvelous. Perhaps you should have come to me sooner."

Still looking for any sign of life Bradwr hissed. "I do not like this. She conceded an entire city. For what purpose? Mark my words if you trust what is before you then you are a fool."

"Why should I trust her when I have you to distrust everything for me?"

"She has destroyed the pillars and I cannot find any of my kinsmen who side with me."

At this Azia turned. This boy had promised an army. Had promised a weapon that could destroy his brother and those that were bound to him. And yet he had yet to produce anything other than meaningless words. In a deep growl he spat out, "Explain."

"When I left several scores of my people had pulled away and hidden themselves. Nothing could have destroyed them. And none could have been found by any but me. There is no one stronger then myself among my people." Slowly he changed back into his mist form trying to find any of his army. Trying to find anything to point to where they might be. What he found was chilling. Changing back be stumbled back a step. "They're gone."

Azia's narrowed into tiny slits. "So, you have no army."

"They were destroyed. Not even a sliver of bone remains. I do not know how this is possible. It shouldn't be possible." His brother should not have had that kind of power. And their grandfather was too old and feeble to kill anything larger than a mouse. This should not have been possible. It shouldn't have been. *He* was the most gifted Eostre… *He was…* Gasping for a breath he gathered himself, "But you have an army. The trolls will fight for you as well as all who live in marsh. We should attack all of the outer cities at one time. Divide her army; make them attack the smaller villages while we attack her most prized places."

For a long moment Azia considered what is ally was suggesting. Using his army of what was called trolls and others would spare the Fey army, but would draw out the creature Primitiva. "It sounds reasonable. Show me what you are thinking."

Closing his eyes Bradwr nodded, "There is a room near here with a suitable table and enough chairs for your leaders. I should be able to find a large map."

"Fine. We will meet in one hour. There is a pet that I would like to play with for a time."

Waiting for Azia to disappear down the stone path and back to where the Fey were still waiting Bradwr hissed to himself. "Filthy beast. As soon as this is over I will dine on his flesh..." Greed lit his young face as he imagined ruling not only his people but all of the known races.

The room was long, pale cream stones with gold wisp formed the high walls. Soft red fabric covered the floor. A long rectangle table made from the brown object outside filled the room. Chairs formed from crystal lined either side of the table. More than thirty if he counted. An adequate amount for those who would lead the Fey into battle. A large golden throne at the head of the table. Blood red fabric for the seat.

No other Star City had dared to leave him such luxuries. None dared to presume he wouldn't have brought his own belongings to show his power. None had dared to suggest he couldn't feed his army by leaving troves of food in the stores.

She was infuriating. Worse yet his army were taking notice.

Insolent creature. Who did she think she was? How dare she undermined him by leaving houses filled willed with furnishings for his army. How dare she presume he need her cache of food. He had half the mind to burn this city to the ground.

And would just as soon as she was captured. Just as soon as he could peel away her flesh just to hear her shrill screams.

The door behind him opened as Bradwr slipped in carrying a rolled parchment. "Are your trolls ready to attack." Not a question but an order. He wanted to be done here before the creature could turn his army against him.

"They are. Your leaders are waiting outside." Bradwr paused, "Should I retrieve them?"

A wave of his hand and he took a seat on the cursed throne. Might as well look like he had brought the furniture. Not likely anyone would dare question him. Not when he would make their death painful and public if they did. "Show them in and let us end this."

As the last royal Fey gingerly took their seat Bradwr unroll the parchment letting it cover the entire length of the table. Names had been carefully scribed onto the map already. A moment later several colored stones appeared. Turning to face Azia, Bradwr asked, "What color would like to represent your army?"

His fingers curled into a fist as he hissed. "The clear ones you fool."

Bradwr narrowed his eyes. For a tense moment he didn't move. Didn't dare to. His rage at being spoken to in that tone was almost enough to forgo this alliance and devour everyone in this room. If not for needing their help in seizing control of the Eostre crown he wouldn't even bother with them. In a low hiss he responded, "Watch it old man I'm not one of your pets that you can speak to like that."

Quickly Azia got to his feet his hands slamming down on the table showing just a small bit of temper. "You will show me respect, boy."

A slow smile reveling several rows of sharp teeth bloomed on Bradwr's face. "As long as we are allies in this I won't kill you. I make no promises for those who follow you."

He had no way to kill this creation no way to defeat Primitiva on her own territory without his help. And no way to rule what would be left should this boy turn against him. "We will call a truce for the sake of defeating the fowled creature."

With a nod Bradwr set up clear crystal stones around the Castle of Golden Sun. "This is where we are." Clusters of black stones and a hand full of silver stones covered the names of the other castles. One gold stone was placed at the Castle of Fire. "The gold stone is Primitiva. Her warriors are represented by the black stones. The silver are winged serpents. They are fierce fighters if in the sky little more than a small nuisance when on the ground. They are slow and too large to move very quickly. They are easily killed from behind.

Now the other villages should be attacked first. We need to cut off the food supply for the castles. It will draw out the warriors so I recommend the trolls and those of the marsh attack first. They are many in numbers and some are skilled fighters. After the war is won they can be easily dealt with. One of your Fey may be able to penetrate the city of Glass. Once inside they should whisper honeyed lies to turn the people against Primitiva. It will crush her to know the people she tries to protect would rather fight for you then live by her rule."

One of royal Fey, A female with short brown hair and silver colored skin raised her hand to be noticed. "My lord, are we understanding after this battle is won those who help are to be killed?"

It wasn't Azia but Bradwr that answered. His tone bored and irritated that he had to explain anything let alone answer mindless questions. Questions that he saw as beneath him. "Trolls are fonder to start with. They fight because they have no reason not to. Either way they will die. The people of the Marsh however have no alliance to anyone. Make no mistake if you do not destroy them as soon as the war is over there will be nothing to stop them from destroying your kind." Not that it was true. The people of the Marsh all had some ability for most it was so minor it wasn't even considered an ability.

He paused waiting for anyone else to ask stupid questions. "Now here…" he tapped a placed called the castle of Glass. "This should be where your troops are in greater strength as well as here… Primitiva's private meadows. She will stop at nothing to defend both."

Getting to his feet once more Azia stared at the map. "How many does she have within her ranks?"

"Not more than twice your number. And none have my blood to keep them safe."

"Very well, we will do this your way." *For now.* Azia paused before greed lit his face. "You said the creature has a child."

"Her consort would know where the child is. The Castle of Night would be the most reasonable place for him to hide within. "Bradwr paused considering what he might be able to do providing he could find someone to help him. "I may have away to draw him out. If I succeed you can hold him as random. Or at least pretend that is what you are going to do. After all, out of all of her elites he is her favorite."

Azia waved his hand and smiled, "Very well bring him to me. He will die the moment the creature shows herself to me." His smile grew more sinister as he said, "She will watch as I destroy him so completely his blood won't even have time to fall to the ground."

The Fallen

CHAPTER 39:

GWYDION

Creeping in the Castle of Fire, Gwydion slowly took his solid form then fussily adjusted his dark suit. A moment longer to fix the cuffs and attach the golden cuff links his wife had designed for him. Then he was ready to report to his queen… to report to the goddess Primitiva. Under normal circumstances, he considered her a friend. Someone that in many ways had been part of his family. However, today he wasn't here to see his friend or speak to a member of his family. Today he was here to report to his queen. Today just being here made his nerves dance beneath his skin in a way it had never before.

Bringing his hand to knock on the blood red door it opened just before he could connect with the wood. Peering around the opening he smiled, a smile that quickly faded. Seeing her dressed not in formal attire had calmed him but the fact she was clad in her comfy black robe puzzled him. Noticing that she was seated in a far corner sipping something that was steaming from one of favorite dark crystal goblets only made his nerves dance once more. Nothing about this made any sense. Then again, nothing had made much sense at all for more years then not.

Suspiciously he asked, "May I enter?"

The moment her eyes met his, he truly saw her. Not his queen but his friend who had simply chose this room in an attempt to find a moment of peace. A moment longer and he understood something else. She was a woman filled with immense worry and grief. His eyes slowly narrowed as he took in more of her appearance in an attempt to make sense of what he was seeing… what his heart was telling him to understand.

She looked ragged. Her fiery red hair that was always neat now poked out uncontrolled. Her eyes filled with grief even though very little blood had been spilled. But she smiled at him anyways. Her smile wobbled as she softly scolded, "You are no longer a child, and there is no need for you to act as such."

Carefully he pushed the door the rest of the way open and slid into the room. Her war room if he remembered correctly. His eyes softened as he realized what it was that he was seeing. As he understood why despite the late hour she was here alone instead of surrounded by those who would try to give her comfort. "This war weighs heavy on you."

Taking a sip from her goblet her eyes narrowed as she reconsidered her choice to sit here passively. The goblet crumbling in her hand as her rage built inside her. "I should have killed your brother long ago, but like a fool I thought he would change."

Stepping up to her he took her hands in his, "It is not a fool's dream to hope for the best."

A soft smile touched her lips as she shook her head once. "I do not like this melancholy that has fallen over me. Come we will discuss what you have to tell me." Carefully she got to her feet and padded over to her long table and retook her seat at the head of the table.

Following Gwydion took a seat to her right. Licking his lips, he carefully chose his words. Carefully he chose what he needed to tell his queen verses the scores of words he wanted to tell his friend. "The Eostre that sought to side with Bradwr are either blood bound to me or completely destroyed. Also, all of the star pillars are no more but I did allow for one draining house to remain. It is in my home village." He just hoped that he had made a wise choice in letting that one draining house remain.

"Couldn't bear to destroy your gardens."

The amusement in her eyes was a welcome surprise. Placing his hand over his heart he smiled, "My gardens? Oh no I would have destroyed them in a moment. My darling wife's beloved gardens on the other hand… Oh no, I may be king but I have no reason to hear *that* lecture if I need not to."

"Very well I will permit this *one* draining house to remain. I would never do anything to distress Terhi." She paused and squared her shoulders. Regaining her posture as the queen and no longer his friends she took a deep breath then asked, "Now, are my castles secure?"

With a nod he began to tell her what she needed to for him to confirm. "They are. I have confirmed that Azia has fortified himself within the castle that you have so thoughtfully abandoned."

Mock horror filled her angelic voice and she laughed out, "Oh dear did I leave to many stores of food for his army?"

A cruel smile formed on his lips. "Many are whispering why they are attacking a Fey who not only thinks of her people but those of the attacking army."

"Good. Then I will hope more of them decide to fight for what is right instead of fighting for Azia."

Looking at the map on the table he tapped the edge, "May I?"

"Please, what have you learned?"

Considering the map, he shook his head at how little detail had been marked out. Shook his head knowing that the none of the troll mines had been marked not by a pin nor by any other indication. Yet this was something he couldn't do right now. "Bradwr is planning on using the troll mines as cover to movement Azia's troops. The trolls have sided with them."

Prim nervously picked her lip as she considered how the trolls may be used. Finally came to the conclusion that they were of little consequence. "Someone must have promised they would no longer be food. It's quite preposterous if you think about it. No matter what side wins there will be those who like the taste of troll. Which is why they are bred on farms than allowed to work in the mines if not sent for slaughter."

Gwydion grimaced at never wishing to know the breading habits of trolls. And truly wishing that Prim hadn't told him now. "In any case. The people of the marsh lands are also sided with the enemy. However, as it stands Bradwr thinks they are only outnumbered two to one." Meaning he had been in the castle listening to most of what had been said. Not an order that he had been given but his own instinct to do so.

Leaning forward Primitiva smiled as she nearly laughed. Not a laugh of joy but one at the expense of Bradwr's foolishness. "It is good he has never known the Fey who Azia tossed into the void have lived here."

"It is, but I wonder what would happen when they find out."

For a long moment Prim didn't speak. After everything that she had planned for she hadn't really thought about what Azia would do… Hadn't even really thought about how Bradwr would play into what would decide this outcome. No, that wasn't true. She had given it a brief thought but hadn't truly explored it. Now it may be too late. Not something she could say. Least not to him. "The Fey… Azia's army will come face to face with those they thought long dead. Children who had been taken from them. Loved ones. Royal Fey who should have ruled most of the Star Cities. Fey that will return home after this." Sitting back in her chair she asked with a Cheshire cat's grin on her face., "Now, what else?"

"They are to attack the villages and farms first. I have already spoken to Freya about this. As such troops will be waiting for them. Enough to deal with the serpents and trolls but still more than enough to defend to castles."

"Good."

Gwydion shook off the uneasy feeling that he was beginning to have. Shook off the feeling that she… his queen… was using them al as pawns…

No… No, that wasn't fair to her. For at least three millennia one had been protecting everyone on this star. Never killing… never harming those who didn't do harm to her people first.

This was not the fault of the Goddess this war that they were about to face was solely the fault of Azia.

Maybe not solely his, since Bradwr now had a hand in this. Regardless, this was not the fault of the Goddess. "The dragon army will continue to guard the skies." A deep breath then he lowered his voice, "All of the Fey… those who fight for Azia… Have been given blood of my people. They think it will protect them."

"Aye, I know of this. Fear not it has already been handled."

Pushing his chair back he began to stand yet he waited for permission to do so. "Good. Now with your permission I would like to be with our troops at the Castle of Glass."

"There is a reason?"

"The Castle of Glass and your meadows will be attacked by Azia and his Fey."

"Then I will allow you to defend those who live there." A brief paused then she tilted her head, "Bradwr does not try to attack the cities within the woods. I find this rather peculiar even for him."

"I don't. He thinks when Azia wins that he will rule my kingdom." Gwydion paused and narrowed his eyes making sure he didn't step out of bounds but still wanted his say, "One way, or another I want to be the one who kills that traitor."

Taking his hand Prim offered him everything that she could. But she could not allow him to kill Bradwr. This was something that she as queen and ruler of this star had to do. She had to or risk showing a sign of weakness to the other Star Cities. To the other Royal Fey. "No. For his hand in this I will be the one destroying him." Prim turned from him making a decision. Choosing to tell him exactly what he would be walking into. "The Castle of Glass is empty. Expect for the lower sanctums. My elite forces are down there waiting for just the right time to attack. When they see an opening … they already have the order to do as they see fit. Any Fey… any citizen who sides with Azia is to be killed. Only Azia and Bradwr are to survive."

Ah, now he understood the whispers. He understood the statement that one of the shadows had spoken about a Trojan castle. She hadn't abandoned anything she had simply left a gift that glittered and shined. Left something to appear that she was following the rules of Pallas. A twitch of his lips and he asked, "Will Azia surrender?"

"Once he has no other choice, he may. It is possible I will need to kill him before he sees surrender as an option. As of now I do not know."

Squaring his broad shoulders Gwydion squeezed his eyes shut knowing… understanding… what would happen if she … the Goddess… had to kill Azia. Understood that if she did most if not all of those who were near him… in the same city or surrounding area… could and would also be destroyed. Knowing he too may not survive. Somehow, he had to make sure that didn't happen. Somehow, he had to do what he could to save as many as possible.

The knot of unease twisted in his stomach as the reality of knowing that there may not be much he could do to stop what was coming. Swallowing hard he whispered, "I will do what I can to force his surrender."

It was all he could say without letting her hear the fear that was in his voice. All he would say before evaporating into the air around them.

CHAPTER 40:

ALEC AND NICCO

Alec stared out the tower window gazing out into the desolate empty city. He could hear explosions in the distance. See the streaks or white fire running across the skies well beneath the veil of darkness. Knew the army would gather many miles from here. The Castle of Golden Light would house the enemy. He could take his army and crush them before they had the chance to recover from falling. He could slip into the castle and slit the so-called king's throat without a second thought.

If he wasn't bound to Prim, he would. TO protect her and their kingdom he would do what needed to be. Being one of her First, he couldn't. He couldn't betray her by going off on his own. And he wouldn't do something to put her in danger. And he would never do anything to put his son in harm's way.

"Still sulking that our queen won't let you lead the troops into battle?"

If he had to be stuck in this place why couldn't he be stuck here with someone he could tolerate? More than that why did Prim send Nicco to watch him. "Am I or am I not the one who is in control of the army? And who trained the majority of them?"

Turning to mist Nicco dissipated to reform not an arm's length away from Alec. Stuffing his hands into his pockets he shrugged, "This has nothing to do with ability. This has everything to do with making sure you're not near the final battle incase Prim needs to unleash her true power."

"She wouldn't need to if we killed the bastards before they had time to adjust."

Hard to argue when he had brought up the same point. "Prim wants the bastards as you put it to think she is playing by the laws of Pallas. Or at least most of them. She wants his army to turn against him and from what I'm hearing they just might."

That sounded promising.

"However,"

That on the other hand didn't. In fact, whenever Nicco had ever said *that* things always went from bad to worse to somewhere between a living nightmare and something that no one had ever been able to name. "I don't want to hear the words however. Not from you."

Nicco smiled showing more than one row of his sharp pointed teeth. "I think we need to keep an eye on Prim's allies. Something smells off with the King of Osiris."

Closing his bright golden sun-kissed eyes Alec counted to ten before trying to ask for any answers. "The last time you said they we were sent to the under kingdom for a second time. Prim was not happy."

"But I had been right. And what she wasn't thrilled with was the fact that we… meaning you and I… couldn't come up with a suitable punishment in case I was right."

The gore rose in throat at reliving that conversation. And like then he reached the same conclusion. "Eating your son… your heir was not the best answer."

Nicco narrowed his eyes into tiny slits, "No, eating him wasn't a suitable solution for *you*. For my people it was more honor then he deserved." He took a deep breath before slowly releasing it. "I'm glad Shesha found his flesh appetizing even if I would have preferred to handle that mess myself."

They could debate this for next century and never reach a compromise. In fact, they have been debating this for more than that and they still ended up hissing and snarling at one another. "Fine, I can understand why you wanted to destroy someone who you had help bring life to."

"You understand nothing."

That low growl was a warning. The feral red eyes that was that was now left of the first Eostre was far more than a warning. "Actually, I do. He was your son and it dishonored not only you but your people that he would do something to undermine our Queen."

A burst of power and Nicco had Alec pinned to the floor gasping for breath. His teeth bared not in anger but in pain. "Damn you. I didn't want to be the one to destroy him because of his transgression. I needed to be the one to end him so not to kill the other of my people who had been forced to bind themselves with him."

Shit. Why hadn't Nicco had said that when he had first suspected his son was up to no good? Why hadn't he told Prim … told anyone… The reason for Nicco was simple He was the First king of the Eostre it was his responsibility to protect his people. "You could have told me." Pushing against the black polished stone floor as hard as he could Nicco hissed, "I shouldn't have needed to."

Giving Nicco a moment to collect himself and step far enough away that neither felt like a threat to the other Alec quietly said as he nodded in agreement, "Your right you should have needed to."

"I don't want your pity."

"Agreeing with you isn't pity. It's understanding. Now if you would what do you know about the King of Osiris?"

Turning sharply toward the captain of the queen's guards Nicco growled, "When this war is over we should not be near one another." Heading for the door he paused, "He is hiding something. My operatives have not found out what... yet."

Watching the tall red door slam shut Alec winced. If he had known any of this years ago he would have convinced Prim to let Nicco handle it. Of course, that would have needed for Nicco to say more than it was his problem to deal with. In any case he wouldn't be able to fix this until he had some much-needed time with Prim that didn't involve this war or her snarling about being with child.

He scrubbed his hands over his face trying to clear his thoughts. Nothing about any of this made sense. Magmas the king had been an ally since his children had been rescued. Then again if he put aside everything that he knew he could make a very compelling case for Magmas using Prim to rid the Fey of Azia just to take control of Pallas.

But if he wanted to rule Pallas why go through the trouble of enlisting Prim? It didn't make sense unless …

Darting to the door he used every ounce of strength he had to make his voice echo thought the halls of the Castle. "Nicco!!!!"

Not a breath later Nicco stood before him looking ready for a fight, "This better be damn important."

"Listen to me. Set our differences aside. Go to Prim and stay with her. I think your right."

An arrogant smile curled the corners of his mouth as Nicco spoke, "I'm usually right so what am I right about today?"

"I think Magmas isn't making a play for Pallas. I think he wants to use this war to force Prim into binding with him. She had said long ago she had come here so not to be forced into marrying him."

Turning quickly Nicco hissed, "The only way she would marry him is if you and your son were dead. And I mean far beyond her ability to save you."

Looking around at the castle he did a quick mental check of the castle's defenses. "I'll go to the lower levels. Not to the sacrum but close enough. A shadow can move me to someplace else if it needs to."

"So, play cat and mouse."

"Until Prim has a better idea."

Or a moment Nicco thought then listened to a whisper, "Freya is on her way here. She will stay with you along with my grandson. As soon as I inform Prim of what we suspect …"

"Go. The longer you're here the closer Magmas is to getting his prize."

The Fallen

CHAPTER 41:

AZIA AND BRADWR

Fussily adjusting in a high back chair Azia mumbled yet again, "These chairs as you call them are useless."

Bradwr rolled his eyes half tempted to change to mist just so he wouldn't have to deal with this whiny sack of bones. "Ornate pillows are rarely used. The abomination Primitiva calls them uncivilized."

Azia leaned forward in his seat. "She has no right to speak of what is uncivilized. Once this little war is over her powers will be mine and she will watch as all that she created burns under my rule."

Not if I kill you once she is destroyed. Not that he would dare say that to his prey. Lest not just before he was ready to devour whatever meat was left on his brittle bones. Glancing at the bright golden door he narrowed his eyes. "One of your Fey is approaching. She seems in hurry."

"You did not tell me you can see through walls."

Imbecile. Of course, he could see through walls. What did this so-called king think he was? Just some ordinary creature with no real value? Bah. He would be glad when he could be rid of him. "Each of my brethren has different abilities."

Scratching his chin Azia gave a devious grin. "I see. When you rule over them I look forward to seeing what they can all do."

He wanted to tear Azia to shreds. Wanted to do vile things to him before he finally killed him. But he could wait. He had to if the Fey would to follow him and destroy the over glorified queen. Luckily, he didn't need to say anything as the woman ... the Fey warrior burst in the parlor where they had been waiting until all of the fallen were rested.

She bowed low revealing her ample breast despite being covered in some kind of metal mesh that he assumed served at armor. Not something he would call pretty but still worthy to bare his children. Whatever her ability was he could feel it's strength and it was intoxicating. "The trolls and others are in place, my lord. We await your orders."

Leaning lazily back in his own high back chair he smiled. "Good. Then let us begin. Have them attack every city and castle simultaneously."

"You forget your place Bradwr. This is my army not yours. We will do this as my laws dictate."

Before Azia could dare think of moving he appeared just behind him. His arm wrapped around his wrinkled throat. A long-curved knife pressed against his thin pale skin. "No Azia, it is you who forgets who gave you the means to travel here. Now, order your army to do as I say or die this minute."

Azia laughed not in fear but in as if this was all some joke. "You would dare kill me? My boy, who would kill this abomination if you do?"

"I would find another way even if that meant destroying your entire army to do so."

With a wave of his hand Azia conceded, "Do as he says." *For now*, was left handing in the air.

"As you wish my lord. The attacks will begin at dawn."

Pushing Azia back into his seat, Bradwr growled, "No, they will begin in one hour. Every minute your army is resting is another minute the damned creature Primitiva has to create something to destroy you." He turned and glared at the Fey king, "Unless you still don't believe me."

"Do it. If my army is not ready then I will kill them myself."

Pulling his long red robes, closed Azia took a deep breath counting the minutes until the battle would begin. The minutes until the creature bowed down before her master. He could see it now her surrendering at his feet. Her hands bound in irons as he ripped her heart from her chest.

Oh, how he would relish in the moment. But first his army had to draw her out of her hole.

"Do you think you can manage watching this skirmish without me or should I hold your hand as you watch blood being spilt?"

Damn this fouled creature. If he didn't need his knowledge he would have destroyed him long before now. After all, there had to be a Fey within his ranks that was up for the task. "Have something better to do, boy?"

Bradwr shrugged unconcerned, "No really. Just a pet project I want to see too. I may find it entreating."

"Oh?"

"You too I suppose. That is if you think turning Primitiva's pets against her as a form of entertainment?"

No that would be entertaining. Far more than just enslaving them once she was vanquished. "Go. Notify me when it is done." He paused calling in a spelled stone, "in the mean time I will watch as her followers are torn apart limb by limb."

He couldn't just walk into the City of Glass nor could he just appear in the middle of the streets. However, if he made himself look bruised disheveled he might get close enough to whisper honeyed lies and half-truths. Yes, that might just work.

Thankfully his mother had the ability to shape-shift as well as see past solid objects. Both abilities he had inherited and added to those that every Eostre was born with. Now to choose his look. He couldn't be seen in normal form. Prim would have centimes looking for him. However, …

…His brother?"

That gave him an idea.

A moment to dissipate into fine mist anther to mirror his brother's rather boring look. Another moment to rip finely made cloth and make a few well-placed cuts in varicose places. Allowed black mist like blood to freely drip for several seconds covering a good portion of the cloth before sealing them… oh yes this was going to work extremely well.

Stumbling into the city he allowed himself to fall into the waiting arms of a guard. Not someone he knew but it didn't matter. The look of extreme worry filled the man's chubby face as he gasped out, "Gwydion? What? Who did this?"

Oh, this was fun. "Fey. Thousands of them…" He gasped trying to not to laugh about the sound worried the man. He could smell his fear. "They… they said they served Prim. C-can't tell"

"Damn it. I was afraid of this. Did Prim say what to do?"

"The humans should declare this city off limits to all. It's only way to keep them safe." He faded into mist before he would allow himself to say anything else. After all it would damn hard for Prim's warriors to defend people who didn't want to be defended.

Staying in mist form he watched as the few Fey warriors scattered from the city. Watched as the weak humans nervously came out of their dwellings. Then laughed to himself as they angrily cursed the warriors for leaving them defenseless. Once he was sure not another warrior was left he retook his true shape and strode into the village.

For several seconds the crowds continued to yell at one another already taking sides. Some choosing to believe Prim had called her guards to deal with a threat. Others saying, she had abandoned them. Then one of the men saw him nudging another. Soon he had more than a thousand eyes trained on him. All now reeking in fear.

"My. My. My. Has your beloved queen finally shown her true colors and left you to die?"

"W-what do you want?"

It was a young female. Nothing special except she had the balls to speak to him. "Oh, I have a proposition for you. "

The girl raised her head defiantly as she was hushed but her mother. "Why should we trust you? You have never cared for our people."

"True. But I can offer you at a chance to rule over your own people and not answer to any Fey. And perhaps we could make an area were no Fey will ever enter again."

Several of the men nodded in agreement. "And what would you have us do?"

"Nothing much. But give this city and Its Castle to the Fey King Azia. And of course, defend this village from those who would see you dead."

The battle was just beginning from what he could tell. Hideous creatures tall and bulky. Most some kind of pale green while others was the color of muck. All of them covered in a slim that he could only assume was their skin decaying. It didn't matter. They looked fierce in their numbers as they tumbled out of the mines.

Some kind of lizard looking creature mixed within their ranks. Gills protruding from their necks and ooze spiting from their mouths. The ooze melting the flesh of several of the creature's guards.

Such a glorious sight to watch.

But that was just the first wave. It was clearly going to take more to defeat those within the cities. Much more to draw out the creature. And much, much more in order to defeat her.

"Has the battle started?"

Oh, good the boy was back. "Exactly as you planned. These trolls are nasty looking beast. As well as those you have not names."

Bradwr shrugged, "They are pest. Once this is over you should use them only for food. Now, we have much to discuss."

"Very well, Speak."

"Do you not wish to do so inside?"

"No. I find that farce of a castle cluster phobic. Now Speak."

"When you are ready Another castle has been made ready for you." He paused looking at the castle. "You have Fey within the castle?"

"No. I do not have Fey within the Castle. You have them spread out all over this land."

It was then several Fey surrounded them. He could take a few but Azia would be killed before the final assault. And he could not let that happen. Not yet. He wouldn't be able to carry him far but he could get him out of the city. Perhaps to Primitiva's meadows but not further. Not by himself.

Grabbing the robe of the Fey king he tugged once then let his mist engulf him before fleeing to the relative safety of the meadows.

"What was that?" Azia growled angrily the very instant they were both back in true form.

Panting it was several long minutes before Bradwr was able to speak, "That was Prim. She must have had them weighting until you were alone before she sent them to attack."

"That is not allowed."

"You are not in a Star City. You are in world of her making. The rules you live by do not apply here." Bradwr narrowed his eyes then fell back laughing in a field of soft flowers. "You are a damn fool. You honestly believe that the laws of Pallas apply here? That Prim would follow any law that she didn't need to? You just walked right into her trap."

Azia reached down trying to grab Bradwr. His hand gasping at nothing but mist. When the boy reappeared more than an arm reach away he hissed,

"You knew. You damn fool. You knew my army would be defeated buy her yet you brought them here."

"No Azia it is you who is the fool. Call your army here. There is no place within these fields for her elite to hide. In fact, they would be leery about even desecrating a single blade of grass."

Slowly Azia turned taking into short grass. Not green but each blade a different color... a different shade, a different hue. All of it blending together like some masterpiece. Some kind of intricate art work. Trees with soft husk bordered the area in a full circle. A fountain of gold spilling out mist rather than water. Low bushes sprouting divine fruit dotted the area. The more he saw the more he realized what he was seeing.

"This is her private spot. A place she comes to be alone."

Now Bradwr smiled. "It is. And I found out something else."

Greed lit his ancient eyes, "What prey tell did you find out?"

"Prim was with child before you came here. That child seems to be no more. It was not hard to make the humans believe that she killed the child so she could watch this war unfold rather than be a mother to it."

"They will turn on her for that."

"Yes, they will. Apparently, it is a sin to kill a child. But that is not all…" With Azia raising his eyebrow in question, Bradwr continued, "I know how to get Prim to meet you head on. But first your army must be engaged here."

CHAPTER 42:

PRIMITIVA

Exhaling slowly Prim sat back in her throne tears running steadily down her cheek. It had begun. The war that was needed to rid the ++Fey of Azia. Still the loss of life wore on her. Many she could bring back but they would never be the same. The life that they once had... the memories of who they were ... would all be gone. Everyone around them would remember them and expect them to be who they had always been. But the truth was they would never again be that person.

The blood that would fill their veins would no longer be the life blood of their ancestors but that which she gave. The exception was those of per Fey blood. The Fallen as many now called them. They could be reborn... recreated... and still be whole. But her creations... those who were descendants of them... it would never be.

It was kinder to let them go. Still it did not help the ache that she now felt stabbing her heart.

Her eyes closed as she tried to regain some composure. Tears would have no use today. No use until Azia was no longer in power. Then she could allow her tears to fall. Allow herself to mourn the loss of so many lives.

She heard the heavy stone door drag on the floor. Heard the shuffle of boots, too many to be only one person. Too quickly her eyes were open pinning each of those who dared bother her when she so deep in thought. For more than a breath she held, each of the heavily armed men not recognizing any of them. A moment more and she knew they were they to protect her not harm her.

Still it begged to question who had sent them. Getting to her feet she glared at the one closest to her. A dark Fey. Not someone to disregard lightly. "State your business."

Her voice was much colder then she would have liked but right now what she was picking up from these men was troubling. Still it did produce a noticeable wince from the man.

Slowly he took a deep breath, "Word was sent. We are to keep you here until the Azia has been dealt with."

No there were here to kill her, just not yet. No, they needed her alive until Azia and his army was slaughtered. But who had sent them? That was something she couldn't seem to find. Or they simple didn't know the Fey who was now pulling the strings. It didn't matter. They would die the very moment they moved against her.

Retaking her seat, she made sure she had the look of a queen. Made sure her gaze couldn't be matched by anyone in this room. The very calmly smiled. It must have worried the men because the scent of fear now filled the room. "This is My Star City and No one has the authority to give orders as to my whereabouts."

"We have orders…"

"I don't give a damn about your orders." Her voice boomed throughout the room rattling the windows. Nearly breaking them and allowing the lava to flow inside. "This is my castle and I give the orders." His voice quieted to a soft whisper, "Do I make myself clear?"

The dark Fey squared his shoulder but didn't back down, "You may rule this rather large star but you do not rule the true Fey. You will yield."

Yield? She was the goddess Primitiva she did not yield to no one. With nothing more than a flick of her finger all of the guards were thrown against the far wall before crumbling to the ground. The sound of bones snapping echoed through the halls. Several of the men screamed an arms and legs broke from unseen forces. More screamed as their wings crumbled as easily as parchment.

Stepping over to them she kneeled to the leader. Kneeled in front of the dark Fey. Her smile now cruel and vicious, "Now, do you really think I will yield?"

"I will see you dead." He gasped out.

A quick motion and his neck snapped before she stood. "Pity, he had such great potential." Glancing over to rest of the broken weeping men she hissed, "Anyone else have something to say?"

A dark mist flew into the room before forming. Nicco glanced around at the males before dismissing them completely, "My queen, I need a moment if you would allow." Asking was a courtesy since he could see something treacherous in her eyes. Something that he was sure that he didn't want to see unleashed.

"Follow me Nicco. And have someone collect these pathetic excuses for Fey. I would execute them but that is a fate too good for them."

Oh yes something had pissed her off. But that was something that he and the rest of her first could deal with once the war was over. Or he could deal with after she was somewhere not in this room. "One of my people has heard something. And Alec thinks he understands the meaning." He glanced over at the Fey that now lay silently on the floor trying not to look like they wanted to scream out in pain. He flashed them a glimpse of his teeth taking his tongue to each of deadly pints before returning to his conversation, "It involve the Fey Kling Magmas."

Prim turned sharply to him her fury almost too hot for her to control. Something outside this room was pressing on her and wasn't the battles she had already seen. It was something more. Something that she would need to deal with. Something that she could not name. Lest not yet. "What about Magmas?"

"Alec and I agree he may be using you to rid the Fey of Azia in order to rule Pallas for himself."

A quick mental thought then she shook her head regaining some of her normal control. "Oh. Of course, he will rule Pallas. I have decided this many seasons ago. The Fey are in agreement. He will rule the Star Cities and I will rule here and rebuild what is being lost." She turned hearing a loud screech. A scream. A sound she had never heard before. Yet Nicco didn't seem to hear it.

What was it?

A footman ran down the hall coming straight toward her. One of the few of lizard like people who choose to live under her rule rather than live in the marsh. Stills she didn't know his name. "What now?"

"One of your chained creations broke loose. She has found traitors within the castle."

Ah. Her banshee. Well a modified version of it. She could hear the screams as a warning she was attacking something. But none others would unless they sought harm to her… it's master. "Very well. She may do as she sees fit. Have their bones taken to the designated sight for the unworthy." Then to Nicco, "Come with me. We will speak in a more private place."

Storming into her private sanctuary Prim slammed the heavy wood door behind her knowing Nicco would follow. Knowing he would wait until her temper simmered down enough to be approach with whatever he needed to say. Slowly black mist started to pool together then just inside the door Nicco materialized his head bowed slightly. Taking a deep breath, she held it before creating a soft overstuffed chair. Her long dragon like wings vanishing as she sat down. "Now tell me what you wanted to say but couldn't in front of the soon to be rotted flesh."

"I understand there are things you haven't been able to tell your counsel however neither Alec nor myself trust Magmas. With the Fey now openly attacking you He may try to do something to remove you once you defeat Azia."

For several long moments she sat there debating what she should say versus what Nicco expected her to tell him. Realized he only expected her thanks and nothing more. He wouldn't argue with her about what he thought should be done. Wouldn't waste his time nor his words when he could just as easily take care the perceived threat and seek forgiveness later. Finally, she closed her eyes choosing not to look at him as she spoke. "Magmas is no treat. He needs me alive for as long as it is possible in order to hold the Star Cities and insure that the changes that need to be made can. Also, Magnar is to rule Osiris once this war is over. It was a condition that Magnar sat. Avyanna will join him on Osiris. Starlis will rule my home star, as she should have all this time. If I am injured at any point Magnar will destroy Magmas and rule over Pallas.

However, that does not mean he would not try to make me his bride. He knows well enough I have the power to rule the whole of Pallas and the Star Cities and still be able to rule here."

Nicco nodded. "You could have told your counsel. We worry about you…" Suddenly he paused and looked out the corner of her eyes listening to something that only he could hear.

"Nicco? What do you hear?"

"That Fey have changed their plans. Ones that you have saved are now attacking our people. The Castle of Glass has fallen to Azia." Again, he paused trying to make sense of the information that he was receiving. So many voices all speaking at once. Images flashing deep within his mind. "Your meadows are destroyed. I – I think they are organizing to attack all of the castles not just the cities."

Taking a deep breath Prim squared her shoulders. "Then it is time for Azia to meet the Queen who he had left alone."

M.L.Ruscsak

CHAPTER 43:

MAGMAS

From high within the tower of the Castle of Fire Magmas leaned out of the window. The magma was nearly to the top now. Nearly ready to bubble over the crest volcano. Not long now and this castle would be completely closed off from the outside world. With it Primitiva would be powerless to do anything.

A cruel smile formed on his lips. Now was his time. Azia would be destroyed before he knew what hit him. But that would solve nothing. Prim would be needed in order to hold Pallas. And she would never agree to anything until her consort was beyond even her grasp.

If she ever found out about this it was possible she would destroy him. No, she would be too lost in her own grief to look for that possible deceit. After all she just lost her child so she just needed just a little push. Just a small shove in the right direction. And he was just the Royal Fey to give her that shove.

Spreading his shoot covered wings he dove from the window. His body just making it out of the volcano just as it was engulfed by the boiling magma. He had made it out just in time. Now to set his final plan into motion.

Flying high above the clouds he could see the battles happing on the ground. Or at least the explosions of power as they collided with one another. He could hear the screams of pain as another Fey or one of Prim's creations cried out. Could almost hear the bones snapping under power of stronger Fey.

Then there were the battles being raged in the sky. Not high enough to reach the clouds but close enough for him to see the long swords dripping with blood. Close enough to feel the powers of strong Fey as they attacked only to be snatched out of the sky by a large winged serpent. A creation that Prim called her dragons.

It didn't matter. He was safe as long as he flew high enough to be mistaken as a messenger. Safe as long as he didn't enter a battle. After all who would ever think that the very King that had brought the war to Azia would actually be flying about alone?

No. He was safer than any of Prim's creations. At least for the moment.

Seeing a tall black stone structure reaching up nearly into the clouds Magmas grinned. He had found the Castle of Night. If Prim was a better seer she would have never told him about the castle. Would have never told him the only way in that would be left unguarded. Well, she had been distracted after losing her child. And what a wonderful distraction that had been.

Landing gently on the lone balcony he paused listening for any signs of trouble. Nothing. Not even a sign that the war was drawing close.

Sliding into the tower room he raced to the door and signed. The hall leading down was too narrow to fly down. Or even glide. He would have to do this the hard way and run down the endless stairs. No wonder this way was left unguarded. Any who used it would be exhausted by time they reached the bottom and would become easy prey for whom ever was waiting.

By time he reached the bottom he was huffing and puffing nearly unable to catch his breath. His head buzzing with effort to remain standing. If he didn't need Prim to believe that Azia killed her little consort, then he would have blown the stone to bits. Still might, once she was bound to him.

After taking a few deep breaths, he took his first full step into the main castle. Wondrous midnight black walls with gold flacks dancing within the stone. Stars. That is what the gold reminded him of. The star cities that he watched in the nights of Osiris. Perhaps he wouldn't destroy this castle after all. Just the blighted tower that held no reason of being.

"Magmas?"

The cautious voice forced him to focus on the task at hand. Then he saw not the one consort, but something Prim called her elite. Long cocoa brown hair and delicious pointed ears. And a face that was exotic yet beautiful all the same. If she wasn't a creation he would force her to bear his children. "It is important that I speak to Alec."

The woman narrowed her eyes. "The queen sent you?"

"My dear, do you think I would be here otherwise?"

Pulling a long narrow blade from her sheath, she smiled as she cleaned under her long red tinted nails, "Well darling, as captain of the queen's elite guards I can tell you that she did not send you. So, that begs to question, why are you here? And why should I not kill you?"

Damn. The little pest knew something. Worse yet he couldn't be sure that he was powerful enough to defeat her. "I have a message for Alec… unless he is no longer in charge of the queen's army?"

She nodded once, "Very well I will take you to him." Turning she called over her shoulder, "you might as well know my name. It's Freya. If you betray my queen it will be the last name you ever say."

Huge heavy door opened just before they reached them. Cages filled with what he could only assume were some kind of animals. Or perhaps some kind of weapons. In any case, they were disturbing to look at. From the ones that had heads of some kind of gilled creature with a body belonging to a large cat with pieces of flesh removed so that he could see the muscles and bones.

Other creations each more disturbing than the rest. And each looking at him like he was their next meal.

Freya letting out a sharp whistle took his eyes off of the caged creations and back to her.

"Freya? What are you doing here?"

It wasn't until he spoke that he saw him. The little consort. Standing between two of the cages with something bloody dripping in his hands. "We need to speak. Privately?"

Alec narrowed his eyes. "Freya, please see that the queen's pets are fed. Magmas, please follow me. There is a parlor not far from here. You will come to say what you need to, then you can leave." Alec paused narrowing his eyes as he added, "Just because my queen trust you does not by any means, mean that her first or I trust you."

Smart man. Too bad he would be dead very shortly.

The room that Alec took him to was nothing like he had seen before. Soft plush furniture dark in coloring just waiting for someone to come and curl upon it. Tables finely trimmed in gold outlining the smooth polished stone tops. Their legs made in some kind of blown crystal. Not an elaborately made room but something that was meant to feel cozy and welcoming.

And would have been if he hadn't seen the chair blink.

Wonderful even the furniture was her ears. So, he would need to make this more than just believable. This would have to be honey dipped lies and partial truths. Well at least Azia had given him something to work with.

"You don't like me fine. But Prim made it very clear that her little human village was to remain safe."

Going over to a long table in the back of the room Alec poured himself a drink. Of what Magmas couldn't be sure. "There are several trained warriors there to protect them."

"You fool. They sent the Fey away unwilling to trust them. You… you on the other hand they would trust." Magmas paused, "Unless you think one of your trusted guards could talk some sense into them.'

For a long time, Alec sipped his drink appearing not to care about the village at all. Slowly he went over to the window gazing out at the city. Gazing at the gardens of man eating flora. Finally, he turned. "Fine. We will go see the village. I wanted to check the defenses at the castle before Azia was forced there."

Before… why would Prim want Azia forced to a castle… to a city that she wanted protected? Unless she was going to sacrifice the village. No. That didn't fit the image of Prim the queen. Or the image of Primitiva the proclaimed goddess. No, she had something planned to make her appear as some great protector.

Yes, that had to be it. Prim the Fey would need that gratification of being the great and noble guardian of those who were not of Fey blood. It would make the other Star Cities think twice about coming here and starting another fight.

Skimming along the tree tops it took longer than it should have to find Azia. In fact, if he hadn't thought to look in one of the few places that hadn't yet been touched by this war then he would have never have found him at all.

Magmas came in fast landing but a few feet away from the Fey Lord. If he wanted to, he could have killed him right then and there. But that would do nothing for his plans. So instead he kneeled before him leaving Alec to lay at his feet still struggling to escape. "My lord, please forgive my apparent transgression but I could find out anything useful if I didn't alien myself with the creature Primitiva."

Out of the corner of his eyes he could see Azia scratch his thin narrow chin with his fingers that were nearly nothing but bone now. "IS that what you have doing, Magmas? Seeing to my best interest?" Azia paused and moved Alec with his foot just a hair but the groan that the creation made hinted of pain that was being inflicted. "And what is this I wonder?"

"The consort to the creation." A cruel smile twitched on his lips. "I had an idea on how to draw her out of hiding and end this but it would involve me pretending to be in her service for a moment longer. To make this believable."

CHAPTER 44:

THE GODDESS PRIMITIVA

Three thousand years ago, I came to this land in hopes that I would never again see any from my home. I had hoped to create a world where there would never be a reason for needless bloodshed. A world where my actions would never be seen as less then noble.

I see now that it was nothing but a fool's dream. For only a fool would keep all of her power to herself and never seek to change those who ruled unjustly.

Yes, it was a fool's dream. Yet I am no fool.

I was born for a reason, and that reason was for greatness. This world that I have created is proof to that. One day, all who ever knew me will understand that. Sadly, that day is not today.

No today, I am forced down a much darker path. Today I am to be the goddess Primitiva and all those who witness my power will truly see me as not the kind protector of this land. But as the weapon that has been kept sheath for far too long.

Today, my greatness will come at a great price and with much bloodshed. For now, this will be my legacy.

Setting her pen to the side of her writing desk Prim gazed at her words. Only a heartbeat and they would be dry. Another and she rolled the parchment up and sealed it with a black blot of wax. Her eyes closed as she held out her hand to Nicco. "Please take this to Karnack. It is to be placed with useless scrolls. One day it will be read. And one day what happens here will matter."

Nicco took the scroll and swallowed hard, "What are you to do?"

Shaking she slowly stood from her writing desk. "What I should have done all along. I am going to destroy the threat to my people."

"I will join you…"

Not looking at him but rather keeping her eyes tightly closed she put every ounce of authority that she could muster into her voice, "No, Nicco. This is my final order to you as the queen. From this moment I can only be the goddess. Do you understand me?"

He had been her trusted advisor for more centuries then not. Of her first he alone knew the true depth of her powers. Powers that had always terrified him. Not because of what those powers or abilities were, but rather what it would mean should she need to use them. "Of course, goddess. I am yours to command in any way that you see fit."

Tuning slightly to him she swallowed hard making her choice. "I want you to go to the endless sea. Take your wives and live with Princess Sedna and her people. As long as I draw breath, so shall will you. Your brothers should find a place among their people hiding in plain sight. The day will come when their strengths and talents will be needed, but not today. I will do what I can to protect those who belong to me but I cannot make any promise that I will succeed."

Breathing deeply Nicco quietly asked, "You are preparing for the finial war?"

"I am preparing for the day when the queen of darkness will take her place among the great Fey... now please..."

Before she could say another word an Eostre warrior materialized before her. "Goddess, my lord … "fear lit his hunter gold eyes as he looked at both of them, "I have just received some grave news."

Nicco nodded for the man to continue before taking his place beside his queen.

"King Magmas took Lord Alec out of the Castle of Night. It appears he told Alec of the problem, that has arisen with in the village of Glass. I have not yet found out how the Fey King would have known before any of us."

Prim shook her head and looked at Nicco who looked just as puzzled, "Problem? What problem and why wasn't I told about it?"

Hearing not only concern but anger in the Goddesses voice the warrior changed to mist form for only a breath before once again standing before her, "The village has ordered that all of your warriors are to leave their village. They have all decided to join with the Azia."

That was more than a little problem but one that she could correct easily enough. Closing her eyes, she spoke correcting this messenger as to the other problem so that the rest of her warriors would not make the same mistake, "Not *the* Azia, just Azia. It is his name not title."

Soothingly Nicco rubbed her back, "It is not of importance of it is his name or title. But what is however is why the human village has sided with him."

Opened her eyes Prim straightened her back, "No Nicco it is not. Least not yet. They have no power to harm any of the warriors nor have any weapons that could sway this battle in his favor. They are of little consequence at this time." Her eyes then locked on the messenger. By his heavy armor she understood this was no mere messenger this was one of the off spring of both the blood of an Eostre and of a dark Fey. A highbred of both true Fey blood and that of a creation. One of few that would breed life into the blood lines that would be needed in the true war. This was a man who would be more then dangerous in the coming years.

But this too she could not worry about. Not now.

Alec was the only thing that mattered. The only one of her first that she had not been able to see a clear line to his destiny. The only one she could not be certain would live in the coming moments. "Tell me about my consort and what else you know."

"It is not clear if Lord Magmas is truly working with Azia or if he is working for himself. Either way… Alec is now in the hands of Azia as his prisoner. They are now at the Castle of Glass." He paused no longer able to watch the anger and pain dance within the goddess' eyes. "Those near the castle can hear lord Alec's screams. None have been able to penetrate the castle." Once again, his eyes opened, "I am sorry my queen. I know not what can be done to save him."

Rage built inside her hot and violent. Death would come to any who had harmed her beloved.

… Beloved. A word she had never used to describe Alec before. A word she now wished he had heard her say to him. A single word that she now hoped he had felt even if she had never said it.

"Nicco, see to the preparations I have already gave you. I will deal with Azia. Do not send another soul to the village nor Castle of Glass."

Nicco bowed his head slightly before dissipating into the air around her. Even if he didn't show it the pain of losing his brother even just in thought was already more than he wished to bear.

"My queen?"

Taking the few steps over to this man she let her fingers caress his face. A singe touch and she knew all that she needed to know about this man and the strength that he had yet to grow into. "You have given me all that you could. Now it is time that I give you what I can."

"I don't…" Her finger pressed against his lips preventing him from uttering another word.

"Shhhh, my little one just listen. The day will come when my daughter will bare a child of flesh and blood. When the time is right you are to become her mate. When Magnar returns you will tell him this. He will know you speak of what I have seen." Slowly Prim closed her eyes then whispered softly into his ear, "You will stay here. You have seen enough of this war."

Once her finger left his lips ne blinked unsure of what to say. Finally decided on the only words that he could find. "Thank you, goddess."

"Don't thank me my child. The path you will walk is a dangerous one but it will be rewarding. This I swear to you."

Before he could speak anther word she slipped out of the room and disappeared down the endless hallway. To where he would never know, yet he knew whatever was to come he had earned the favor of the goddess.

For years she had been flying over these valleys and rolling hills savoring in the beauty. Always finding solace in the calmness of the open terrain. Never had she imagined the bloodshed and carnage that would cover her home. Her eyes scanned the countryside hoping to find one corner that was left untouched by the hands of this war. Yet she could not.

Not in the far north where the shores met the endless sea. Not to the east where the trees were so dense that only the Eostre dared to dwell. The far south was little better with its wet marsh trapping the Fey who had foolishly dared to land in hopes of claiming that terrain for themselves. No, there was not a single crevice that was left untouched.

Too many explosions shook the ground sending shockwaves through the air. Her gorgeous fur covered trees now ablaze with unnatural fire. The flames would probably be seen within the Star Cities. The fires would be a beacon to those who still had not arrived. Beacons that their flawed King was winning this war.

Her anger grew as she saw firsthand the cost of the war. She had to do something. She had to…

"No!" She screamed in rage. Her meadows. Her sacred place that calmed and soothed her. Azia's army was destroying it. Her Army would never step foot there, understanding this as a sacred place. As her place.

No more. No more would she allow her home to be destroyed by these carrion eaters. No more would she allow them to assume that she was weak and their chosen king would win this war.

Her rage boiled over threatening to spill out over and consuming her people. That she would not allow to happen. Instead she focused her rage, her anger on a single target.

Her meadows and those who would destroy her home. Those who would harm her people.

Hovering high above them she called upon all of her dark power. Called the power of those of her Under Kingdom. Called upon the powers of those who had bound themselves to her.

Dark mist covered her. Streaks of white and yellow swirled within the black. A single bolt of power plowed down on the Fey before they had time to react. The few that had felt the power drawing near had tried to escape, tried to flee before the power consumed them. Their screams forever imprinted in the now blood-soaked ground. A layer of fine black dust... sand now covered what once was soft grass and white sand.

She could find another place to find solace. The land too contaminated now by the blood of the enemy. Too contaminated by her own rage.

Still, it felt good to rid the realm of these Fey. Felt right to let her power run without censor.

A grim smile formed on her blood red lips. Azia wanted to meet her and all of her dark unrelenting power... well he was going to see why her people called her the goddess. He would see firsthand why creators were gods.

Hovering over the City of Glass she saw everything. The people holding what meager weapons waving them at her. Holding them in a way to say they were against her and wanted to see her blood run freely within the streets.

Later she would deal with them. Later she would find out what she had done for them to turn on her so. But not now.

No. Right now she had something more important to do.

Using her power, she let her voice to be carried over the land. She knew it would be heard in every corner of her land just as clear as if she had spoken the words to each of the cities individually. "Azia, show yourself you coward."

The castle was still a way off but she could see the high balcony clear as if she was standing a few feet away from it. Azia with his thick red robes hiding the fact that he was ill and not far away from death. Bradwr standing behind him clenching Alec by his wings almost tearing them from his back. And her Alec barely conscious from the pain they had already inflicted on him. His golden blood dripping from several cuts that were visible.

She could see his armor had been melted away from his body. Could see the blisters that the heat had caused. Could see his sun kissed hair had been pulled in clumps from his scalp.

They had done a great harm to her consort, now she would pay them back in kind.

Flying closer to the castle she paused seeing the nearer she drew the more pain Bradwr was causing her consort. Her Alec. From this distance she would never be able to free him.

Slowly Azia smiled as she glanced over his shoulder at his prisoner. Then he began to clap as he started to speak. "Have to finally decided to succumb to your destiny, creature?"

Her voice took on a dark tone that even surprised her as she growled, "Let him go, Azia."

As Azia narrowed his soulless eyes he smiled as he assumed that he had the upper hand. "Or you'll what?

Destroy me? Try and he dies by your hand. No, my dear, you will surrender to me."

Alec blinked once then looked up at her. A single tear ran down his dirt covered face. He didn't' need to speak for her to know the truth. The only thing keeping him alive was Bradwr's hand that she could see now was not holding his wing but rather was plunged deep within his chest. A single squeeze and he would be killed. Unless Bradwr used his poisoned nails to rake across his heart.

Both were a possibility. And neither would he survive from.

There was nothing that she could do to save him. At least nothing until he was beyond their grasp. Then… oh then she could do something. She could give him a second life.

She had the power to do it. And was going to use every ounce of that power to save as many of her people as she could.

Knowing this she let a smile form on her face as she laughed coldly. "You think killing him will make me submit to you. *You*? Do you not know who I am, Azia? Do you not yet realize *what* I am?" She bent over laughing as she still hovered in the air. Her laugh ringing out over the land.

Angrily Azia hissed, "What is this? Boy…"

A slow cruel smile formed on the lips of Bradwr. Without saying anything or giving any hint of a warning, he turned to a dark mist swallowing his prey. When it rescinded he used a single small sliver of bone to clean his sharp pointed teeth. "Pity you have no use for your former consort. He made such a pitiful snack. Although he was had a rather delightful taste."

He devoured Alec in a single heartbeat, and there was nothing she could have done to stop him. Nothing she could do nothing to bring him back.

She wasn't laughing any more however Azia was. The malicious bastard who thrived on the pain of others. How had he become so twisted, so corrupted to condone what Bradwr had just done? Didn't the fool realize that the boy would do the same to anyone? It didn't matter if he did or not. All that mattered was that she knew the truth of what Bradwr was capable of doing.

Blinking everything felt surreal. The pain that was now lancing her heart should have been a killing blow yet it numbed her. The smirk on Azia's face, a matching one on Bradwr's young face should have sent her into a murderous rage. But for the moment she just blinked letting the realizing that nothing that she did now would bring her Alec back to her. Nothing that she did would give Ari back his father.

It wasn't until she felt the tear run down her cheek that she had even realized that she had been screaming. She hadn't realized that she had been reaching out her hand preventing Bradwr from becoming solid once more. It wasn't until that moment when time once again mattered. It wasn't until that single tear had dropped from her chin she felt the unbearable pain from losing the only person that she had ever really loved hit her with its full force. The only person who she had ever wished to see at the dawn of every morning. And the last person who had ever wished to see before she allowed her eyes to close.

He was gone now. Her reason for being was gone to her.

Rage started to flicker deep within her. Rage so dark even those who thrived on pain and suffering would find the depth of that ire shocking.

Catching her breath, she saw the look of amusement on Azia's face. Saw him nod to someone. Just before a she could find the person that he was signaling, a cluster of arrows whizzed in the air. Several bolts whizzed past her head creating a whistling sound. Not just simple primitive weapons that the humans still used but ones that had been spelled. Some even had been dipped in poisons that were common within the star cities.

Shouts of anger from well below her. Slowly her eyes focused on what was drawing her attention.

The humans. Those without any Fey blood. All of them actively trying to fight not just her but also the Fey who had come to her aid. Several were in the low rooftops vigorously trying to shoot their primitive weapons at her. Their betrayal was the very last straw… the last reason for her to remain bound to her own rules.

The last of her grief turned to dark brutal rage. Why had her people turned on her? What had she done to deserve this? No, it wasn't what she had done but Azia had done. This was his doing.

And he would die because of it.

She was not just some Fey that Azia could control nor kill. Her rage bubbled over as she channeled the true depths of her power. She was a creator, but not just any creator, she the most powerful that had ever been born since the first Fey came into existence. More than that she was a natural born warrior. She *was* the Goddess Primitiva and there was no one greater than she.

Suddenly with her rage the normally stark gray sky tuned dark almost becoming twilight. Fire of black and purple flames surrounded both the city and castle. Lightning poured down striking several of the crystal houses melting then to the ground.

Her power ran freely now along with her rage.

Azia the corrupted Fey was laughing her. She could see in on his face. He should be cowering.

It didn't matter he would be dead soon, as would those who had turned against her.

A wisp of fine white mist surrounded her. Information being passed to her. Her castles… all of them were being attacked. The buildings themselves were showing signs of collapsing. The Castle of Night had already fell trapping all of those who had been beneath it in the under rooms. There was no word on those who had still been above defending the castle. No word from her dragon force.

This ended now. Azia had taken her love. He had destroyed her home. But worse of all he had destroyed her Ari. Her child.

Summoning all of her power… all of her will… She let a single large bolt of power plow into the city of Glass. The blast sending a shockwave back to her nearly knowing her from the sky. Rocks and debris being sent from the earth and into the sky above. The cloud of dust spreading out over the land.

It would cling to the air for hours. She had the power to settle it but she would not. No, that would be a kindness that those who died this way did not deserve.

Flying higher she looked at the destruction of her prize city. No longer did she have a city made of ice and crystal. No longer, would there be a race that she called human. No longer could this land be used for life. Nothing would ever thrive here again. Her raw power now filled this land tainting it. No, it was her rage that now tainted the land.

It gave her little gratification.

It was then something else hit her. An emotion that she had never felt before nor could she name.

Looking around at the now large crater that had been blasted deep into the earth she saw alone figure standing within it center.

Still enraged that something survived she flew down ready to grasp the figure. Ready to rip it a part with nothing more than her brute strength. Almost upon it she saw it was not a person but something that was made completely of mist.

Slowing now, she back-winged to land. It was then she saw the child that she had named. The man who was the King of the Eostre. He was no longer alive. Nor would his people be. No, they were now what was called a Shade. A race that only existed in her Under Kingdom. "Gwydion?"

He raised his hand to keep her from speaking. "I knew the risk of coming here. The death of my people is solely on my hands."

Seeing him. Standing within the crater where so many had died… she nearly broke… she…

It was then Magmas landed beside her looking triumphant. Arrogant. "We won. With Azia's death the rest of the Fey surrendered."

Too many emotions collided within her. Joy wasn't one of them, nor should it be. A quick motion and she faced the arrogant Fey king and growled, "Won? Damn you. Look around! NO BODY WON!" Primitiva screamed.

"You might be the next ruler of Pallas, but make no mistake… no one won this war."

Either not understanding or not caring Magmas shrugged unconcerned with her little outburst. "Are you or are you not a creator?"

Without thinking, her hands grabbed his throat. "You…"

"My Queen, Stop." Gently Gwydion pulled on her arm trying to get between her and the new Fey King. "Let us mourn those who cannot be brought back and help those who can. This Fey…. Is not worth your anger."

Letting go she stepped back and spat at the feet of Magmas. Spat on a man who she had thought of as an ally. "I don't know how but you are responsible for the death of my consort. His blood is on your hands."

CHAPTER 45: KING MAGMAS

Standing in the crater that had once been a grand city not just moments ago, Magmas shook his head as Primitiva began to turn to leave, "For a seer you are blind."

He saw her turn sharply back towered him. Watched as something that he could not name formed in her eyes. "Blind? Oh, no Magmas I am not blind. I see everything clearly. It is you that is blind."

A moment of shock ran through him as she too quickly drew upon him. Rage and smoke grey mist flickered in her now dark eyes. In noting more than heartbeat He flew through the air not by his own accord nor by her physical touch, but rather from her power. From her dark will. He landed backwards much too hard and much too fast in the now blood-soaked ground. Blood that he knew had been left by both her worthless pets and those of great Fey.

Now he felt a jolt of fear. Fear that she would destroy him before she heard him out. Fear that he had greatly underestimated the one person he had always wished to take for his bride. A mistake that could cost him Pallas.

Not yet moving in an effort to look passive. An effort he hoped she would see as the now Fey King yielding to a greater power then his own, he tried to plea with her, "Prim, listen to reason. You have said for yourself that this battle is meaningless. The war has but not even begun."

A bolt of lightning landed on either side of him scorching his armor. The look of rage-filled grief alarmed him. Fey don't grieve for the dead. At least not publicly. The ones that did? If their powers… their natural abilities were tied to their emotions the results were always catastrophic.

In a blink of his eyes she towered over him. No longer just a thin warrior Fey but something else. Her narrow body now blending into some kind of scaly tail that coiled around him. Her wings… it had to surly be trick for now Fey could ever have cooled Magma formed into dragon like wings.

Slowly she leaned forward her narrow nose almost touching his as she growled, "Reason? If the Star Cities didn't need you to lead them from this darkness that Azia created, I would destroy you here and now."

"Prim, listen to me please." Swallowing hard he once again pleaded.

Letting him go from her grasp she stood once again in her true form. Now towering over him, she let her tears freely fall. "Why? Did you honestly think that by taking my consort from my grasp that I would decide to rule Pallas with you? Did you think that I would bind myself to you?" An arch of uncontrolled power flowed out of her fingers exploding the ground creating smaller craters within the larger. "Damn you! Did you not think what would happen if I did? You fool. You *damn* fool. A creator cannot be blood bound or tied to any other Fey. You wouldn't have felt the depths of my power, I however would consume yours." Letting a mist of fine dark purple slip from under her long midnight blue dress, she once again grabbed his throat.

There was nothing he could do to escape this grasp. Noting he could do to escape this mist that his fingers passed through yet was choking him. Clawing at his throat he desperately gasped out, "You were meant for greatness… c-come… with me."

Tossing him aside with little more than a single thought she let her sobs turn into a low growl, "I had greatness. I had all that I dreamed of. And *you* took it from me." She paused before spreading her large dragon like wings, "No, Magmas, I will never again see the Star Cities. Nor shall I ever be bound to the laws of Pallas. Leave and take your Fey with you." Anger seeped from her as she glanced at him over her shoulder, "Don't ever return. I destroyed Azia, I would have no problem destroying you or the rest of the Fey."

She couldn't mean that. She couldn't.

Waiting until Prim had vanished from sight the shadow of a man slowly approached him. "My queen has spoken. You and the Star City Fey have seven dawns to leave. Any Fey who stay will be bound to the laws that we set."

Gulping air, he looked at the man who stood before him. He could see the mist that he was made from. Still he could see the razor-sharp teeth waiting to devour him. "You could have saved the little consort."

The mist dissipated and reformed several times around him as the man hissed out, "Damn you, you insufficient piece of flesh. The moment you gave Lord Alec to the bastards, his life ended. He was poisoned the very second the former ruler of Pallas touched him. None of my people could reach him in time. And none dared to kill you before our Queen gave the order."

Shit. This creature saw… if he did… then surly Prim knew everything. Damn it. His plans. His dreams… all of them destroyed the second the little consort had been taken out of the dark castle.

The realization set in hard and bitter. "Prim knew before she came here. Didn't she?"

"My queen knew the very moment that Lord Alec flew away. She decided then if Alec died then she would grant him a second life. However, not even the goddess has the power to grant life to those who become food."

Magmas didn't know how long he sat alone in the crater. Didn't know who of his army was left to return home. He didn't even know if his children…. His boys…. Had survived the finial on slot that Azia had ordered.

It didn't matter. As the ruler of Pallas, there were now things that needed to be done. The first would be contacting the Fey and getting them home. After that? No, he couldn't worry about anything else until he formally had the power of Pallas to help him.

Flying as high as he dared he look down not at the celebrations that he had imagined but rather needless destruction. Fires burning uncontrollably. Smoke clouding the air. Bodies littering the ground. Blood soaking into the earth feeding it. the powers of the dead wasting away on this star. So many could have benefited from those powers. Wasted. Everything he had hoped for wasted because of his single action.

Regret filled him like poison lancing his heart. Something else he would need to lock away deep inside of himself before doing what needed done.

Closing his eyes, he let his power fill the air. Let it touch all of those with Fey blood. Knew within minutes how many thousands still lived. Thousands not the millions that he had assumed would still be among the living. Not even enough Fey to populate all of the still livable Star Cities.

Staggered by the shear carnage he nearly tumbled back to the ground.

Gasping for a normal breath he allowed himself to settle not in the crater… no… not now…not now that he realized the amount of Fey that were now truly gone. No, he would never again step foot in that hallowed ground. However, the mountains that stood to the south? Yes, they would do nicely as a place that he could think. A place that he could gather his thoughts and decide on the next course of action.

Dawn was just starting to streak across the desolate sky by time he had truly figured out what he wanted to do versus what he needed to do. No longer could he think only for himself. No longer could he put his needs above those of whom he now ruled over. He had to do what he had promised all those light cycles ago.

The life of not only himself but also all of the Fey now depended on it.

Stretching out his golden red wings Magmas once again took to the sky. Once again, let his power flow across the lands. Almost made the connection with those of true Fey blood. A connection that felt as familiar to him as breathing. Yet he held back seeing someone flying toward him. From the distance he couldn't be sure whom or what was heading his way. But whoever it was, they were coming at him with speeds that he couldn't phantom.

Before he could draw another breath, he was forced to the ground. Cold white powdery stuff being forced into the air around him. A dark Fey now towering over him. Hatred ran deep in those hunter green eyes. As did the realization that this was not a true Fey but one that Prim had created. This was a Fey that even among Dark Fey that would have been considered a law unto himself.

"You are damn lucky that I cannot kill you. Least not yet."

The deep voice could have turned his bones to stone, as it was he dared not move in hopes of not provoking this creature. "I will have my people taken from your lands soon enough."

The man bared his teeth as he snarled, "I don't give a damn about the other Fey. I care about the one who killed my brother and betrayed my Queen."

A burst of dark power hit just behind him blasting away the rock to form a deep cavern. "As a Fey I acted in what I thought was best for my people. I do see now how flawed that judgment was." No what he really saw was that he wouldn't have minded sharing Prim with the little pet as long as she had been by his side.

"No King Magmas you don't but you will. As a member of the counsel to the goddess I have come to give you a message."

Magmas swallowed hard having never feeling this depth of fear before. Not once had he ever feared for his own life. Not even when Prim had turn on him. But this wasn't Prim, this was something that was bound solely to her who wouldn't hesitate nor be stopped if he were truly sent here to destroy him. "What message?"

"Your boys will never return to the Star Cities. That was their choice. Seek them out and one if not all three with destroy you. You dishonored them. That is the words they used, they have little meaning to me." The man narrowed his eyes and gave a cruel smile, "But I see they mean much to you."

A rolled piece of parchment landed at his feet. Yet he dared not reach for it. Not yet. "What else have you come to tell me?"

"Tell you? Oh no, I've come to show you what your treachery has caused."

The Fallen

CHAPTER 46:

GRIFFITH

His black onyx blade sliced cleanly through the royal Fey that had foolishly challenged him. Midnight blue blood now clung to his armor obscuring the crest of the goddess. More blood concealed his rank as one of her generals. Looking to the predawn sky, he cursed as more of the dishonored Fey fell from whatever Star City that they hailed from.

"Filthy beast. Mindless drones." He mumbled under his breath. His army could deal with reinforcements, after all, they would need time to adjust. Most would be dead long before they even reached the solid ground.

Making a quick and rash decision Griffith ascended as quickly as his midnight wings could carry him into the vast darkness of the void. The falling Fey would ignore him thinking that he was just some page or messenger. Foolish ingrates. Foolish to follow Azia to the home of a creator. Foolish in thinking that with their numbers that they would be victorious. And foolish not to realize who it was who was hovering watching several battles and already planning his next move.

Cold hands grabbed his shoulders. Only two people could grab him while in the sky without causing him to plummet to the earth below. Not thinking twice his eyes stayed on a battle near the Castle of Earth. "They could use some reinforcements. The Castle looks ready to fall."

Magnar let out a deep sign, "Let the dragons help. You're needed elsewhere."

Griffith clicked his tongue not willing to concede a single battle, "Fine let's go and show me."

Letting his fingers tighten his grip Magnar leaned closer, "Not yet."

Several dark curses slipped from his wine-red lips before he remembered whom he was speaking to. Taking a deep breath Griffith calmed himself, "Forgive me my temper is much to frayed to be doing nothing."

Slowly he let his fingers relax, "My boy you have never done "nothing". You have been a fury of motion since you first came to this land."

"I guess I could have behaved better when I first arrived." It was a murmured response but the only one that he could say that shouldn't have him being ripped apart by this creator.

Shaking his head to clear his thoughts Magnar whispered, "It is not the time to discuss the past. However," He paused then pointed to a point where he could just make out The City of Glass. "…What do you see?"

Squinting Griffith cursed, "Why is the Goddess heading to the heart of battle?"

Blue light encapsulated both of them enhancing tier sight. Suddenly everything right down to the smallest of humans could be seen. "No Prince Griffith, what do you see?"

Horror filled him. Alec the consort to the goddess held captive by Bradwr. Azia saying something grinning like a damn fool. The humans were vaulting a bray of bolts at their queen. What in the name of Darke were they thinking?

Before he could say anything a pillar of blinding white light reached into the sky colliding with a mesh like shield that Magnar was now creating. Their powers blending together seamlessly. The pillar of light now turning into flames of deep purple and midnight blue before plowing into the Castle of Glass kill everyone and everything for miles around. The blast reaching as far as the Castle of Night. Tremors would reach well past the coastal areas.

He could almost understand the fear that Creators were known for. Almost.

Worry filled his deep tenor voice, "Magnar?"

"Once the Prim as left check crater for survivors."

There was no arguing with that voice. No reason for him to question the only other living Creator. No, he would do as the man had asked knowing he would be the one to seek the goddess out.

Check the crater he said. Look for survivors. Damn Magnar and his useless orders. Didn't he know that nothing had survived? Didn't he understand that the crater was filled with the dust that had once been bones of the humans? Their homes were now less than dust.

Damn him.

Squatting down his heart ached. It hadn't been only the humans that had died here but the Fey that were loyal to Prim as well as the traitors that were fighting for Azia. The Eostre too had died here. Their bodies little more than shadows dancing at the edge of his vision.

The sound of stone shifting caught his attention. The hilt of his blade already clutched within his fingers. A quick turn and he saw the bloodied hand clawing out from under a spot where the castle had once proudly stood. Quickly he darted over hoping he wouldn't be too late to pull the survivor from the debris.

He would never be sure about how long it had taken to pull the man from the earth. Would never really be certain about the feelings that had collided within himself. But he would always carry with him what had happened after he had come face to face with the butcher of the Fey.

The Fallen

CHAPTER 47:

GWYDION

He fluttered in the shadows trying to understand what had happened. Thousands of voices filled his mind. Legions of his people now lost and confused. They were dead. No… no … not dead but not alive either. Somehow there were in between straddling the line between the two.

It only took a moment to understand that this was the will of Goddess. She needed them here. She needed them to be her eyes and ears for whatever it was that she knew would be coming in the years that followed. This would not be easy to explain to his people. As king, he should try. As a man that understood the goddess, he knew he mustn't.

The bond with his people would break under that strain. The blood bond would hold true but the respect would no longer be there. This was a price that he needed to pay in order to serve the goddess.

Movement caught his attention. A Fey too quickly trying to reach the now desolate crater. Shifting closer to a natural shadow he watched and listened as General Griffith landed. Saw that he understood that the lives that had been lost here were now the soil that he stood upon.

A sound of stones shifting. An aspirated grunt, neither the general had seemed to hear. Well, he could change that. Or at least he thought that he could.

Swirling around creating a small funnel of wind, he lifted some of the powdered soil away from a hand. It was enough to grab the attention of his friend. It was enough to find out who had survived.

Going back into the shadows he watched as the events on folded before his eyes. Watched as Griffith pulled the man from the earth. Knew the instant that they understood who each were looking at.

Well, maybe that wasn't true. Griffith knew he was looking at the man who had not only bred him into being but also had slaughter tens of thousands of Fey. Whereas Azia only knew that he was looking at an enemy. Carefully he watched ready to step in should Griffith need his assistance.

"Well, well, well. Helping your sworn enemy. How weak the crater has made you?"

Griffith narrowed his rage filled eyes. "Kindness does not make one weak. But I suspect you wouldn't understand that." He gave Azia a shove breaking whatever shield that he had placed around himself. A shove that landed the butcher on his ass.

"You…"

"I what? Broke your pathetic excuses for a shield? Dared to lay a hand on the Great Azia of Pallas? Ha." Griffith turned for but a moment as he spat on the ground. The gray dust turning red. Turning to the color of blood that had been spilled on this hallowed ground. "You dare come to my home. Slaughter my people. Destroy buildings that I helped to shape." Quickly he turned a rope of black mist flowing from his finger and around the throat of his captive.

Clawing at the mist Azia still grinned, "You don't even know the laws of your people. You fight with dishonor and disgrace."

Scratching his chin Griffith let out a robust laugh. The sound echoing through the crater. "Oh, don't I? The laws that states only royal Fey may take the life of another?" In one quick motion, his onyx blade pierced the belly of Azia. "Well father, I am a royal Fey. And one of your blood. If I am dishonored then so too are you."

Sputtering blood Azia gasped his last few words. "You… you died. Leaped into the void."

Shoving his blade up to its hilt Griffith smiled cruel and bitter, "You were always blind to what was right in front of you. Pity that now you must spend the rest of your days in the Under Kingdom waiting for your flesh to melt away from your bones. Feeling your great powers leach away into the land that you sought to destroy." Pulling his sword free he allowed for Azia to fall to the ground. "I only regret that I do not have the power to give you the death that you gave to Lord Alec."

He had seen and heard enough. Slithering out of the shadow he covered the dishonored Fey king. His mist like body poured into every cell as he dined on the power and fresh blood. When he was done he took shape and stood before his friend one last time.

"Gwydion? How?"

Gwydion bowed his head in acknowledgment. "I had followed Lord Alec in hopes of being able to save him. The was not the time for me to flee this place before the Goddess leveled it to the ground. Nor would I if given the chance."

Slowly Griffith nodded in understanding, "Your people? They are now…"

"The goddess will give us a new name. But make no mistake we are still her eyes and ears. Great information can be passed from one of us to her."

His eyes solemnly closed, "Then she knows that I did not have the power to destroy her enemy."

"No. She will know that he died this day. It will not matter if by her hands or by those of someone else."

Opening his eyes Griffith shook his head, "But…"

Offering his friend, a smile Gwydion continued, "But nothing. The death of but a single person weighs heavy on our queen. The destruction that was caused here could have been avoided yes. But would not have changed the carnage save that of but a select few. She understands this. One day she will come to terms with her single action. But today… today is not the day to place blame. Today we mourn those who even she cannot bring back."

Taking a deep breath Griffith turned, "What will become of you now?"

"I will take those who are still bound to me and we will oversee where the bodies of the fallen will be housed. It will become out solemn job to watch over them until we are once again needed in this realm."

CHAPTER 48:

PRIMITIVA

THE FALLEN QUEEN

Prim landed in what should have been the interior courtyard of the Castle of Night. There should have been grand statues and vibrantly colored plants here. Enclosing the courtyard there should have been black polished stone reaching up into the sky. Windows of stained glass should have been standing. Countless other things that had once been here should not have been destroyed.

This castle should have been safe. Her Ari should have been safe within the castle walls.

Collapsing to her knees, she let the tears fall.

This had been the castle where Alec had always felt the most at home. The place where he kept all of the creatures that she had made for him as pets. The castle that mirrored the labyrinth that was found in the Under Kingdom. This had been his home more so than hers.

Gasping for a normal breath, she tried to clear her vision from the tears. Tried to find anything that remained of his home. Only a single wall remained. It had been a part of the spiral staircase that had gone up to the high tower. Three windowless arches that had once peered into the library still stood under the stairway. Nothing else stood above the ground.

A soft warm hand barely pressed on her shoulder. Black polished shoes and dress pants. Sniffling she let herself see who had dared to disturb her. "Nicco?"

Kneeling next to his queen, he pulled her gently to his chest. "I hope you forgive me for not being in the Endless Sea."

"Everything is gone. I have failed." Too quickly she fell into his arms as she let her tears clog her throat.

For a long moment, Nicco sat quietly holding her letting her tears falls. Sat listening to everything that was still being whispered. Looking up he took a deep breath. He couldn't tell her what he had just heard. He could not tell her that her burst of power hadn't ended Azia. He would never tell her that the beast has used some kind of spell to appear to be within the Castle of Glass while he and several scores of the humans had fled into the deeper parts of the castle hoping to escape. And he would never tell her who had actually killed the disgraced king. No, he would not tell her but he would try to give her what little comfort that he could. "No, you haven't."

She pulled back just a hair, "Look around you. Those I saved from the Void turned against me to rejoin Azia. The Humans. The last of the first race that had claimed this star... they did what they could to destroy me. Countless others of those I brought into creation... they too turned against me. Why? Why Nicco? I do not understand."

Wiping her tears, he took a deep breath, "The Fey you rescued were seeking favor with Azia because they thought that he had the power to destroy you. The Humans were told that you killed your child."

Stunned by his words she blinked then shook her head in disbelief. "How could they believe that? I have never harmed a child. Never."

Nicco shook his head, "I do not know. My grandson went to find out what he could in hopes of speaking to them."

Gwydion. That was why he had been there. He was trying to help her, and she destroyed him. "I ..."

"He is a Shade now. I know. My heart aches because of it but I understand the cost of this war. This was not you're doing. My Queen, you must understand you were just the means to the destruction, not the cause."

Gradually getting to her feet, she called in her crown. A sad gray mist holding it just above the ground as she shuffled through what was left of the interior courtyard, what was left of her grand castle. In her footfall sprouted flowers of white and gray- lavender. Green grass filled in the rest of the space.

Slowly her face looked up at the sky. The lights of the star cities visible now. Pallas glowing the brightest. A single explosion lighting the sky. What it was she couldn't guess. Her mind already filled with too much.

Another tear fell from her face, "Please tend to the rest of the castles. I-…" Prim pulled herself to her full height trying to look like a queen while her heart broke. "…I wish to be alone. I will send words about what I want to be done."

Bowing his head slightly Nicco left without saying another word. In a way, he understood that this would be the last he would see his queen. Trying to convince her to stay would only add to her heartbreak. Letting her go he hoped she would one day return to lead her people.

Prim didn't know how long she had stood there gazing at the fallen castle. Didn't know if she even had the strength to carry on. But knew she had been a mother before this day. Knew she had years to tell a man that she loved with all of her being how she had truly felt. Words now that she would never be able to say.

Azia had come here to destroy her, and in a way, he had. He had turned her people against her. He had brought war to her home. But was she who had destroyed so many innocents lived. It was her alone who had, in the end, destroyed her newborn child. Destroyed so countless others who had been hiding well beneath the castle. How could she live with that guilt? How could anyone?

Maybe if she had been raised for cruelty… raised as other Royal Fey had been… she would look at today as a great victory. Shrug off the loss of life as nothing more than a causality of war. As a means to an end. But she never wanted to cause anyone pain or suffering. She had never wished to live by the rules of Pallas.

No, she had always believed that she had been meant for greatness. Trusted that her name had truly meant something.

It didn't.

Her name meant nothing more than what she was to be called. She was meant to feed the catacombs of Pallas as she mother had wanted. Or marry Magmas as her father fought tirelessly for. That had been her destiny until she had fled. Now she was no longer worthy to feed the catacombs. No longer worthy to rule the people that she had created and the ones that she had seen born into creation.

She was no longer worthy of anything except live among the dead in hopes of one day truly becoming one of them.

Letting her simple crown fall to the cold ground she called in a piece of parchment and began to write out her instruction. She knew who should rule in her steed.

Knew they had survived where so many others had not. Flint… yes, she could trust him with this. He was smart and quick to respond to matters. Yes, he would figure out what she wished for her people.

A shadow could take the parchment to him. How he would accomplish what she asked she would never know. Could never know.

The door to the Under Kingdom formed before her with nothing more than a simple thought. Before stepping through the gate, she took one last look around. Her Alec had loved this place. She couldn't bring him back but she could recreate his home.

Letting her eyes close she let vines of mist flow from her body. Let them feel the land that had once been the castle. A single burst of power and the stones reformed from the pebbles. Furnishings and tapestries from the dust. Everything that had once been inside recreated exactly as Alec had left it. Even his pets.

Satisfied she nodded. The Strong queen that would stand against the Silent Ones would need a home worthy of her. Perhaps she would build on to this castle. Perhaps she would level it to the ground. Either way, this would be for her now. Or at least for her once she was born.

Stepping through the gate Prim sniffled once more as she said good-bye her people, her home and all that she had ever created.

epilogue

Flint took a seat in had once been the scribe's workroom deep within the Castle of Water. The only room above the inner sanctums that had mostly survived and even so only a few things of this place remained. Only a couple walls of the once grand castle had withstood the final assault. As well as this room complete with scrolls and books. Some were about Prim, others about the time before she descended upon this place. Drawings of the castles… all of them… still held within a messenger's satchel that they had been stuffed into in haste. The messenger? His burnt body had been removed just moments before he had entered this space. A deep sign escaped his throat. The castles at least could be rebuilt. The memories of the fallen would be cherished. But no one who could bring back the dead ever would.

The mighty queen? So many were already asking about her. Only he knew the truth.

Primitiva was alive but broken. She had made a single request of him. Her request;rewrite history. Erase her from everything. Make it so she never existed. She was so heartbroken over the war and the epic loss of life that she was beside herself. Unable to see that as long as she lived that she could bring whoever she wished back from the Under Kingdom.

Well almost everyone. Even she did not have the power to give flesh and bones to those who no longer even had that.

Sighing to himself, he took another look around this room surveying the destruction. He could not go back in time but he could make sure no one remembered her. Once he figured out just how to do that.

Looking over at her silver crown laying bent on the table, he shook his head. That would need to be remade as well. Perhaps not so divinely. Just a simple silver circlet. Something closer to what the royal Fey in the Star cities wore. Perhaps…

A soft cough from the door pulled him from his thoughts. "Magmas?" Not his father but his brother.

Carefully Magmas took a step into the room. Broken stones shifting beneath his feet. "I thought I would find you here."

A little bundle of pink was peeking out from behind the ash red wings that his brother had cradled around him. "Kaida had the baby." Not a question but a relief that both of them had survived.

Despite his grief on how the war had ended Magmas tried to smile as he nodded. Even if that smile had to be forced. "Actually, Kaida gave birth during the assault. It is a miracle that either are alive. For some reson she had thought that she could help with the defenses until she went into labor. One of the shodows help get her back into the sactrum where she should have been to start with." Taking a breath before he did or said something that he might regret he abruptly said, "We decided to name her Alista."

Magmas paused and looked down at his little blessing. What he needed to say was going to weigh heavily on both Flint and himself. In a low solemn voice he told his brother, "Prim has opened the door to the Under Kingdom. All those who are no longer fully living are now there. Only the bodies of the humans still remain as well as those who belonged to the enamy. The goddess said burn the humans so nothing remains. She so blinded by hurt that she can't understand why they choose to fight for the Azia rather than fight for their home."

Nodding once Flint turned from his brother understanding Prim's distress. There had been no winner today. The Star Cities who had sided with Azia barely had enough citizens left to be called a city. The ones that had helped their father were little better. And here? So many places that were now no longer fit to be lived in and those that were needing massive repair. The land its self that was once was lush with vibrant colors scorched and drained of all life. The white sand of Prim's private meadows was now black with the blood of those who died there. No there was no winner. But in war there never was.

After a long moment of silence, Magmas asked, "Did you decide on how to do what Prim asked?"

Turning to the shelves lined with scrolls Flint started pulling them out looking for a map or something close to it. After nearly clearing out two shelves he finally found one that might work for what he needed. Placing it on the desk he answered softly, "I think but first we … and I mean you as well as Apollo need to decide who will rule."

"Apollo has no wish to rule but will do anything that we need to help rebuild. I think he is quite content with being underfoot but not being the center of attention."

Looking over the map Flint started to draw lines with the dirt that laid on the desk. "Fine. Then your blood lines will rule what will now be called Feyen."

"Fey-en?"

"I was looking at some of the maps before things turned bad. At the time I thought that this land was too great for just one ruler. I think Prim understood that since she had her court rule over different areas. At the same time, I was also trying to figure out the wording for the marriages or blood unions."

"Fine. We'll come back to the name in a minute. But first we should discuss the binding. I'm glad Prim found a way for Fey to be bound to their mates not just by heart but by blood. However, are we sure it can be done safely?"

"I am and it can. We just need to make sure that the wording for marriages is exact. Karnack said, just before he joined Prim in her Under Kingdom, that the words should sound meaningful. Something that might naturally be said but they also need to be precise in the wording. It would be the only way to ensure that one of the pair does not use the other's abilities or steel them all together. In the case of Royal Fey which we all now know are many more time more powerful than any other Fey…

those words need to be figured out so there is no unforeseen consequence."

Taking a deep breath Magmas stood silent for far too long before nodding his head. "I agree but I don't think I'm the one to help with word play. Kaida on the other hand may welcome the chance to do something useful." With Flint's nod of agreement, he continued, "Now, do you any idea on whom or what will rule the different areas? Or where these different countries would have their borders?"

"First we need to agree that the Mystic Woods is now off limits to everyone. And we will need to make that clear to those who will rule the other countries." With Magmas' raised eyebrow of question flint continued, "The Eostre that have survived because they had been hidden below the Castle of Fire, are beyond furious. They have openly said if anyone enters their woods the trespasser will never be seen again. And that was said in front of the surviving royal Fey at the summit for the surrender.

Besides that, Terhi is worse off emotionally then Prim. She lost her husband, her king, and the father of her unborn child. Not from battle mind you. That I think she might have accepted. But because he died because of Prim when it became clear that she had to destroy everything within both the City of Glass and its Castle just to destroy Azia." He ran his fingers through his cinder black hair, "I don't know. I think she is blaming Prim for his death. But not just her … every Fey. Both those who live here and those of the Star Cities. It makes her dangerous since we no longer have anyone or anything that can kill their kind if they chose to attack."

"That I understand. Out of all of us… they have suffered the worse. In terms of adults they only have a handful or two that still are alive. Only a few are trained warriors the others are elders. Then you have the several scores of children, youths and infants that Gwydion had ordered to be taken to safely… all of whom are now orphaned. Yes, I think for now we give them their space. However, if Terhi or her people ever need help from our family they should know we will do anything within our power to help them."

Flint nodded solemnly. After a minute of awkward silence, he turned back to his map, "Agreed. Now come look at this and what I want your opinion about the borders and what I was thinking." Pointing to a spot on the map he started talking using the dirt on the table to make lines as he did. "The land south of here… I was thinking Griffith could rule over that. He has said many times he has no wish to see the Star cities. And since he was the one who in the end killed Azia, it would be fair for him to rule something." Of course, the only reason he had killed his own father had been because even after Prim had destroyed everything Azia had been still standing. And thankfully Griffith had seen the loss of life and carnage as his father's doing. Had seen that his friends had died because of a man who had no right to be on this star.

"Are you sure you want to do that? If the war had gone the other way…"

"I'm sure. He is loyal to Prim, and it will be his wife, Enya who actually rules anything. Only his blood line that will continue to do so after her."

"Fine he can rule something." Looking at the map closely Magmas grumbled, "You do realize that the land south of Feyen is nearly four times the size?"

"I do. I also know for a fact the citizens that live the lower parts are not Fey but rather the creations that Prim has created over time. The veil that she created right before Azia came here still stands and has the unfortunate effect of draining all color from everything. However, those who dwell there seem to like it. So, I think Enya's sister can rule there rule there comfortable. Since she is a dark Fey and her abilities both natural and learned match that area. While Enya's abilities match the upper country."

"So, two kingdoms then?" Not really a question but confirmation

"Three. The land south of the mountains should belong to the serpents, trolls and other creatures that Azia had created that now are stuck here. If they come north their lives will be forfeit. Start war and they will do so with all of the other kingdoms including the Star Cities."

"I can live with that. So, what are we naming the other two?"

"For Enya who is a light-barer we will call her new home Lite. And the other should be Called Darke for her sister who is part Dark Fey and part … I don't even have a name for the Fey who bring back the dead."

"Necromancer. I heard someone say it once in passing. According to the other Fey. Other than dark Fey there is none more dangerous. With the exception of the creator. Which by the way is what Prim is?"

"Agreed."

"Now am I assuming that the Draken homeland will remain the same?"

"Yes. And this little place will be Manicora. Next to it the home of the Griffiths."

"So, one area of un-ruled lands controlled by beast. And the other ruled by those with little brains and nasty tempers."

"In time perhaps, we can tame one or two of the Griffiths but yes. The unclaimed lands should be left alone. After seeing them kill more of those who had sided with Azia then any other… I don't want to think about what they might do now that Prim is no longer here to control them."

Magmas leaned back against a wall that was still barely standing, "It seems that you have everything figured out."

"Not quite. I haven't figured out how to "erase" Prim from history."

With his daughter beginning to wake, Magmas turned to the door. Stopping briefly, he kicked a stone that had fallen when the castle had fell. "Is that truly what she wants?"

"Yes. She has created a space for herself within her Under Kingdom. Mag, she doesn't have the heart to rule anything anymore. With her abilities you know she would be forced into doing just that."

Taking a deep breath, he started to leave pausing only long enough to whisper, "You were always good at making up stories. Make up some lore or something that is so far from the truth that it could sound believable. I will make sure it is taught in every county before we declare those places their own. And Flint…"

"Magmas?"

"The Eostre need to be a myth. Everything about them. Make them so scary vicious that no one would dare seek them out."

It took nearly a year for the castles to be rebuilt. Those that were in what was now Feyen weren't as grand nor literal but they were magnificent. The castle of Fire now named for being near a river of magma not because it was made from molting ash with pools of lava.

The castle of water now made with clear gems reflected light from the sun and moon. A courtyard now made its way to the white sandy beach. Flowers leading the way to a dias that sat near the bank for the court from the Endless Sea or for when the royal Fey wished to sit by the sea and take in the cool breeze.

Only the Castle of Earth was made in Prim's vision. Or at least where the Feyen castles were concerned. Made from a mountain itself it stood tall over the land. Unless you knew what, you were looking at you would miss the windows that looked like crevisiouses in the sides. Nothing uniform. Nothing out of place. On the outside, everything was made to blend in. The inside on the other hand… Well, some things needed to remain secret.

Exhausted Flint sat down within his workroom deep within the Castle of Earth. He had a job to do and today he could finally do so. Magmas said to make a lore. So that was exactly what he would do.

Sitting at his newly made desk Flint pulled out sever sheets of parchment and began to write. And the words tumbled out of him. This story… this dialog that he knew as false but would be taught as truth.

Legend of the Fey:

A long time ago, long before time began all of the Fey lived on distant stars. Once called Star Cities. Each star a grand city each ruled by a royal Fey. Each housing Fey of only one known ability. Each being governed at the royal Fey deemed fit. Only one law had been translated to all of the star cities. That law was simple. War and conflict were forbidden. The will of the royal Fey was absolute. Punishment for disobeying the ruler was always harsh and swift.

However, this star was different. This star no matter how grand housed none with Fey blood. Not a single person had any ability to speak of. At the time they had called themselves human. Though they shared a similar look to the Fey in that that they walked upright and shared a common body style, they lacked any power other than words and what they made with their own hands, Intrigued One of the Fey took a human as his soul mate. As part of their union the Fey gave his human bride a few drops of his blood and took an oath they would share in what each had.

As this hadn't been done before he couldn't have known that his words would give his powers to his bride. Once it became clear that what had happen, those who had been the woman's family turned from her calling her a witch. Thus, becoming the first witch in the history of Fey.

Back on the star The Fey watched carefully as this union evolved creating new life and bringing into creation the first child of mixed decent. This gave other's ideas of their own.

Some saw the humans as weaker versions of themselves and sought out what they decided were stronger vessels. Though they did not speak words, the other creatures had their own language. And their own ideas of what an acceptable mate would be. Seeing this as nothing more than a game to become stronger as a whole the Fey started to take shapes of the other creatures. Wolfs would become werewolves after mating. Fish and other aquatic creatures would become the ancestors to Bunyip, Kelpie, Kraken, Morgawr, Ogopogo and many others.

Whereas others coupled with reptiles and other smaller creatures to begin the races of Amphisbaena, Cerastes, Lernaean Hydra . Those too would one day evolve into the races we have today.

However there has always been just pure Fey. Those who choose not to mate with any other then their own kind. We know them as Fairies, Elves, and pixies just name a few. From them we have a few who have coupled between them. They are more powerful than any other because their bloodlines have never been diluted. They have always been the High Borne. The ones who rule. The ones who even if they are not chosen are laws unto themselves for no one except their king or queen can handle them. Even then, not all choose to be handled but merely live under the rule of the kind or queen.

Coming to the more recent say four or five millennia ago the world now over ran with those of Fey decent started to break off into their own places. Those of serpent or reptile decent traveled south to warm climate. Those who preferred the dark or shady placed created what is now named Darke. The first residents of Darke created a veil over the land. No one has ever tried to understand it only acknowledge that it's there for the reason of the comfort of the citizens.

Other broke off creating what is now Draken, Manicora And Lite. Of course, Lite is brighter than any other country. It has always been assumed that because the veil is over Darke that the light was forced to go somewhere else. The most reasonable choice was Lite.

Sitting back Flint read his words. Not the best story that he had ever read. Really not the best story he had ever written but it was teachable. It was something each teacher could embellish as they saw fit. After all, the more versions of this story that were told the least likely anyone would ever figure out the truth. The less likely anyone would remember Prim or her rule.

He only hoped it would be acceptable to both his brother and his queen.

543

With her first book being nominated for both the 2017 Top Female Author Award and 2017 Summer Indie Book award, M.L.Ruscsak has continued her series with "The Fallen" and is currently working on the third book in the series.

Living in Richland county, Ohio she lives with her autistic daughter who is the first person to read and edit all of her works.

For more information please follow her at https://www.facebook.com/OfLiteAndDarke

or

Find excusive information about the world of Lite and Darke at www.doveanddragon.com and https://www.imdb.com/name/nm10729660

547

Think You know this story?

Prepare to see how many lies have been weaved in Secret of the Sword. Book One of the Obsidian Chronicles

The Fallen

Excerpt

Secret of the sword

3000 years ago.

They laughed the cool springs just behind them. Twin tailed fish jumping from the rainbow waters.

The castle of Lunaista off in the distance. Very few knew this pond, this meadow laid here. And those who did… well they were not fools. This was a private area for the royal house. So it was fortunate that she was the crown princess and her betrothed the crown princes of Obsidian.

"What troubles you my sweet?"

Zale's voice washed over her like the honeyed nectar that they had been drinking. He was trouble but that didn't matter. Nor did the fact that he hid himself away posing as a royal guard. "One day we won't have to hide our secret.'

He kissed her neck as his hands curved around her bare belly. "What secret? Your sister knows your whereabouts the moment your eyes open. I suspect if you asked she could tell you about our wedding right down to how many glasses of nectar we both consume before I steal you away for a more intimate evening."

She swatted his arm playfully, "If I asked her anything it wouldn't be of our wedding but how to free this star and your from Azia."

His lips hovered above her ear and softly he said, "The answer lays in the vault of Obsidian. A blade that only the king may wield."

"Zale?"

"It's a legendary weapon forged from before the plague of the silent ones." Slowly he got to his feet. His hand reached out to help her to her feet, 'Ask your sister who will wield it. Who will be the next king of Obsidian."

Starlis shook her head, "You're the crown prince…"

"I may be the crown prince. But the Sword chooses it's master. " He glanced at the palace fear in his eyes. "My father may use the sword in battle but he does not wield it. For him it's just a blade."

Starlis pulled her sister through the crystal palace. Down winding halls and corridors made of glass. Didn't stop until they came the wall that lead into the mountain.

She turned her head to glare at her sister, "Well or you going to open it?"

Primitive narrowed her eyes, "I suppose since you dragged me to this blasted cave.'

The stone shook but slid out of place revealing a hidden room. Dampness surrounded them. A single candle flickering above their heads.

With a huff Primitive crossed her arms, "We are here dear sister now mind telling me why."

It wasn't a question and she knew it. She may be the crown princess but her younger sister held more raw power then most of the fey who lived in any known star city. "I need you to tell me what my future my be."

"Very well. I assume you care more about that stowaway prince then anything else."

A smile twitched her lips. "That and… the sword of Obsidian."

That made Primitiva pause. For just a breath it appeared as she would say something. Yet she shook her head her fire red hair falling free from it's loose braid. "Come let us see what your future may bring."

M.L.Ruscsak